THE DAMASCUS THREAT

THE DAMASCUS THREAT

AN ICE THRILLER

MATT REES

CROOKED
LANE

NEW YORK

Copyright © 2016 by Matt Rees

Published in the United States by Crooked Lane Books, an imprint of The Quick Brown Fox & Company LLC.

Crooked Lane Books and its logo are trademarks of The Quick Brown Fox & Company LLC.

Library of Congress Catalog-in-Publication data available upon request.

ISBN (hardcover): 978-1-62953-775-7
ISBN (paperback): 978-1-62953-812-9
ISBN (ePub): 978-1-62953-813-6
ISBN (Kindle): 978-1-62953-814-3
ISBN (ePDF): 978-1-62953-815-0

Cover design by Craig Polizzotto
Book design by Jennifer Canzone

Printed in the United States.

www.crookedlanebooks.com

Crooked Lane Books
34 West 27th St., 10th Floor
New York, NY 10001

First Edition: August 2016

10 9 8 7 6 5 4 3 2 1

TO LISA ERBACH VANCE

"PATIENCE IS THE ART OF HOPING"
—LUC DE CLAPIERS (1746)

THANKS FOR YOUR GREAT PATIENCE AND
ART. NOW HERE'S HOPING . . .

WITH THANKS TO THE ICE AGENTS OF THE
NEW YORK CITY FIELD OFFICE

ICE will expand its counter-proliferation program, placing the strongest emphasis on the most serious threats: nuclear materials, advanced weaponry and sensitive technology.

US Immigration and Customs Enforcement (ICE) *Strategic Plan*

PROLOGUE

Underwood lost them in the dust and hustle around the tomb of the Prophet Muhammad's granddaughter. He cut his Jeep south onto the airport highway, watching in his mirror for the Mercedes, weaving between the donkey carts and the listing, overcrowded minibuses. In ten minutes, he was skidding to the curb outside the quiet terminal. A lethargic porter waved a warning finger toward the "Taxis Only" sign. Underwood pulled some balled-up bills from his cargo pants and crushed them into the porter's hand. Each breath came short and excruciating in the heat, flaying his lungs. He stumbled under an ill-painted placard that read, "The Syrian Arab Republic wishes you farewell and happy." It was as though happiness was such an alien concept in Damascus that the very word had blown the signwriter off his ladder before he could finish the sentence. Underwood knew where the guy was coming from.

In the empty departures hall, a trio of men in loose, black leather jackets wandered between the security X-ray and the tobacco kiosk. Underwood had been around the Middle East long enough to know they were *mukhabarat*, secret police. They stared at him with heavy eyelids and thick mustaches, as though they might deadpan him all the way dead.

He checked the package in the thigh pocket of his pants. It was small and light, but it felt as lethal as the Glock 17 in the back of his waistband. He peered around for the gold circle and turquoise swish of the post office logo. Mail service no longer operated from the city itself. But he knew he could get a package straight on a plane here. He crossed the concourse to the counter.

The secret policemen watched him. *They see your panic,* he told himself. *Be fucking cool.* Sweat needled his skin like drops of fat spitting from a pan. He glanced back at the doors. The porter perched on a cardboard box, picking his teeth. The Mercedes hadn't caught up. Yet.

Underwood flopped his forearm onto the post office counter. He fumbled out the package and took a flimsy blue airmail envelope from his shirt pocket.

The postal clerk was thin, with a tiny cartoon mustache and no chin, like the country's president in the faded picture hanging on the partition behind him. He took the letter and spoke.

Underwood pointed to his ears. He heard himself yell through the vibration in his jaw. "I'm deaf."

The clerk flinched. Underwood lowered his voice.

"Artillery shells." He gestured with his hands as though something blew out of both his ears. "Boom."

The clerk touched his mustache nervously. He produced a menu of postal services in poorly translated English. Underwood stabbed his finger at an express option. The clerk dipped his head and took back the list.

The letter was the nearest thing Underwood's wife and daughter would ever have to an explanation. The package was for Jeff Parry. He would finish this . . . if the stuff didn't finish him first.

Like it finished me.

The secret police turned toward the windows. Underwood followed their eyes. An old Mercedes sedan jerked to a halt behind his Jeep. The men who wanted him had arrived.

Underwood tossed his dollars over the counter in a sweaty wad. The postal clerk picked it up, puzzled. There was more than five hundred bucks. "Keep it," Underwood said.

Four men came out of the Mercedes, their postures alert, faces hidden by ski masks, short Belgian submachine guns at their hips.

"Please, see that this mail gets through."

The clerk noticed the action on the sidewalk and hid behind his counter. He shook his head.

"A lot of people will die if this package—" Underwood reached for his wallet. He pulled out a picture of Francine. His eyes had been cloudy and weeping for days because of his exposure to the stuff, but now they were crying for real. He leaned over the counter and showed the photo to the clerk. He picked up his letter and waved it. "For my little girl."

The clerk snatched the letter and the package. He crawled toward the sorting room behind the partition.

The armed men came through the door. Underwood zig-zagged in front of the abandoned car rental desks to draw their attention away from the post office.

The secret policemen wavered. They were here to pick up small bribes and confiscate a little Scotch. Gun battles were for people with everything or nothing on the line.

"Go." Underwood called to them. "Get out of here." He drew his Glock.

The gunmen opened up. Three quick blasts and the *mukhabarat* were down. The tallest of the gunmen yelled in English, "Finish them."

One of the shooters jogged toward the writhing policemen. Underwood lifted the Glock and shot him in the neck. *From twenty yards, with eyes full of tears and lungs like a nuclear test zone. You're good, Daryl.* He lowered the gun and retched.

Good shooting don't make you a good man. But you already know that, don't you, asshole.

The tall gunman leveled his machine pistol. He fired off a dozen rounds.

The bullets scythed through Underwood's shins. The back of his head hit the floor going down. His vision flashed and came back muted. The ceiling of the terminal was a long way up, shadowy and unlit. He closed his eyes.

The shooter ground his boot into the pulpy wound in Under-wood's leg. Pain like a shot from a three-million-amp railgun jumped him off the floor. He jerked and hit his head again.

The man squatted beside him. He lifted his ski mask. It was Lance. "Howdy, Daryl. What you doing at the airport? Going somewhere?"

Underwood could barely hear the words. He tried to accept what was coming. He must not fight it. He had to stay silent long enough for his mail to make the plane. He must allow his body to die now, even if his soul hadn't let go.

Lance brought his shoulders forward. His trapezius rose in a threatening triangle, lifting his shooting vest. He caught Underwood's chin and turned his head. "Oh, you done lost your hearing aid."

The mockery crept through Underwood's deafness. He snarled and choked.

"Let's roll, hombre." Lance grabbed Underwood's foot. He twisted the broken bone so the boot faced backward, and he hauled him across the floor to the door.

Underwood didn't have the breath to scream.

PART I

CHAPTER 1

Amy Weston stumbled fast along Twenty-Sixth Street, sensing her final breath. It was close. Closer with every step. She was skilled in recognizing the moment of extinction. She had tended to children scorched by white phosphorus in Libya and choked by nerve gas in Syria. Whenever a patient died, she counted down to her own end. She was counting now, as the gaunt man tracked her. The cowl of a green hoodie shadowed his deathly face, but his mouth showed amused, predatory intensity.

Weston hurried through the traffic on Ninth Avenue. Would he take her here? Surely it was too crowded. He gained on her. He didn't even try to hide himself.

One more block and she'd be at the US Immigration and Customs Enforcement office. Safe. For now.

Twenty yards behind her, the grim man's hand was in the front pocket of his hoodie. He had a gun there, she was certain, and it was for her.

Quanah had sent her to ICE because she insisted on dealing with a US government lawman. He told her any crime that involved the crossing of American borders was in ICE's jurisdiction. Weston had never heard of it. "Is Verrazzano one of the good guys?" she had asked.

Quanah mumbled, "You don't need a good guy."

The man in the hoodie picked up his pace. Weston went into a sprint. The memory of Quanah, his strength and love, overwhelmed her. She wouldn't have to run if he was here.

She collided with a young man chatting on his cell phone. She floundered across the sidewalk into the street.

A yellow taxi swerved around her and skidded to a halt.

The hooded man ran for her. He clutched his chest. His pale face contorted. Perhaps *he* was closer to death than Weston.

She scrambled into the backseat of the cab. "Go. Just go."

The driver was a lean Haitian. He rolled the taxi forward.

The traffic light turned yellow at the avenue. The driver braked.

"Go through the light," she yelled. "Twenty bucks. Twenty bucks to make the light."

The Haitian hesitated. Then he hit the gas and bounced across the avenue.

Weston stared out the back window. The tail was nowhere in sight. She wondered at the pain in his face and the hand on his chest. He was another of *them*. She knew it. It was in his lungs. Maybe it had gotten him too.

Halfway along the block, she tossed a bill to the driver and leapt out of the taxi.

She dashed for the north side of the street. To an old warehouse converted to office space.

A half-dozen people waited to sign in at the reception. She pushed past them, radiating such fear and tension that even a bunch of New Yorkers declined to call her out for jumping the line.

Weston pulled a folded copy of the *New York Times* from her bag as she searched for ID. She came out with a driver's license and tossed it onto the counter. She scribbled her name on the sign-in sheet. The guard handed her a sticker pass and dialed Verrazzano's extension. A music video howled on the screen above the newsstand by the elevators. "Will you turn that down?" the guard shouted.

The news vendor stared in confusion at his remote. He ticked at it with his thumb. The television volume rose.

"For Christ's sake, turn it *down*."

Visitors spilled through the revolving door from the street. But no man in a hoodie.

"You can go up. Sixth floor," the guard told Weston.

She flashed the sticker at a guard by the turnstile. She slapped the up button at the elevator bank. She was going to be okay. She entered the elevator. The doors started to close, the commotion of the television and the security line in the lobby receded. She exhaled. *So it wasn't my last breath*, she thought. *Not yet.* She fanned herself with the newspaper.

A sinewy hand jammed through the closing elevator doors.

Weston's scream sounded faint even inside her own head, drowned by the background clamor of the world she was trying to save.

The man in the hoodie slid through the doors.

Weston jumped into the corner of the elevator, pressing herself away from him. The man coughed hard. His skin was gray, his lips almost blue. *He is one of them.*

A woman skipped into the elevator. She gave Weston an *I-just-made-it* smile.

The hooded man put his hand on the newcomer's neck and shoved. Quivering and sick, he was still strong. The woman stumbled backward out of the elevator.

The doors shut. He advanced on Weston. His eyes were vivid emerald and his head twitched on his neck as though he were a bird.

She squeezed her eyes shut, but she couldn't stop seeing. The elevator was crowded with the dead. The refugee children, the rebel fighters, the helpless elderly. All the victims. They screamed for her to deliver their pleas to Verrazzano.

She barely felt the man's hands on her. They went into her clothing, searching her. He tipped back her head, thrust his fingers under her tongue. She choked on them, then he pulled them away.

Among the dead around her, she heard Underwood. Before he disappeared. Wheezing the fatal secrets of a malicious life, after she had told him he had just a few days left.

The hooded man brought his pistol to her chest.

CHAPTER 2

The afternoon shelling started as Nabil Allaf reached his office at the Military Intelligence Directorate. The impacts, two miles away in the Damascus outskirts, shook the room. Allaf flushed with a distant dread. He was brown as a rosewood coffin, the deep smoker's wrinkles like knots in timber, but it seemed like months since he dared to walk in the sun. He shut the window to close out the din of Syria's civil war and lit a cigarette. He had another battle to focus on.

The girl on the screen of his Blackphone was beautiful as only sleeping children can be. Her cheek rested against a fluffy panda. Allaf watched the image on the security-enhanced Android system and thought wistfully about his own features at that age. He wished his memories could be erased like this video, which was instantly expunged from its Swiss servers. Little Nabil never knew a night of rest. His father, the general, saw to that.

"You're ready?" Allaf said.

The phone camera in the girl's bedroom swung around. It filled with the massive, bald head of the Janissary. His features were as expressive as the front grille of a car. You might imagine you saw a personality in the headlamps and the sweep of the hood, but it was only an accident of design. Allaf had named his agent for the fighters of the old Turkish Empire, kidnapped as boys and made into slave soldiers with no past and a future that depended on loyal service. The Janissary closed his eyes briefly to signal his readiness and moved the camera back to the girl in the darkened room.

On his desktop computer, Allaf brought up Silent Circle, an encrypted video application run through secure Canadian servers. He had planted the same app on the cell phone of the man he wanted to call, attaching it to an innocent-seeming text message that released the code onto the operating system as soon as the man opened it. He dialed the phone.

"Yes?" One clotted syllable. The man on the other end of the line had been asleep. Allaf shook his head. It was before seven AM in New York, but the Syrian ambassador to the United Nations should've been up, preparing for a busy day of diplomacy.

"Morning of joy, O honored sir," Allaf said in Arabic.

"Morning of light." The man cleared his throat.

"May Allah bless you, Honored Abu Hafiz."

"A thousand blessings upon you, O honored sir." The ambassador waited for the caller to identify himself.

Instead, Allaf issued the first of his instructions. "Go to the bedroom of your daughter Nasrine."

He heard the stillness and shock down the line. Then he sensed the motion of air into the handset as the man left his bedroom and hurried across the hall.

Allaf turned to the Blackphone screen. The Janissary lifted the camera from the girl's face and held it in the direction of the door. The ambassador appeared, bulky and round-shouldered, silhouetted by the hallway light, his phone at his ear. He gasped and trembled.

"These are my instructions," Allaf said. "When the president of the United States makes his speech to the UN General Assembly, you and your delegation will walk out. You will immediately return to the Mission and stay there."

A pause. The ambassador waited for more. "And?"

"That's it."

"This is a major diplomatic demonstration you're talking about. What is it for? Who are you to demand this?"

Allaf laughed softly. "My friend will show you."

The Blackphone camera moved back to the girl. She stretched and mumbled, but she didn't wake up. The Janissary's Glock nestled between her head and the fluffy panda.

"O Abu Hafiz, I trust you have no more questions," Allaf said.

"None," the ambassador mumbled. "Take away the gun."

"May Allah lengthen your life." Allaf closed the Silent Circle app on his computer.

He watched the Blackphone screen as the Janissary shoved past the ambassador and went to the front door of the apartment. He swiped off the connection.

CHAPTER 3

Verrazzano waited in the foyer of the ICE field office for Amy Weston. On the floor indicator, he saw the elevator stop at two. Probably some T-shirt designer with a scrubby beard and distressed jeans jumping out at the Tommy Hilfiger offices with a tray of skinny Frappuccinos for the other fashion plates. The ICE field office was a single floor repossessed from a company that had been derelict in its taxes. When the agency was set up after 9/11, all the federal buildings in New York were jammed full. This was the first space that became available. Unlike other agents, Verrazzano didn't object to sharing the elevators with ad execs and fashion designers and, once in a while, with Martha Stewart on her way up to the office from which she brought America hearty cooking and perfect weddings. But security worried him. Sure, no one could get into the field office itself—there was a heavy door controlled with a remote switch by an armed guard. Almost anyone could, however, enter the elevators and come up to the foyer right outside the sixth-floor entrance to the ICE office.

He played his fingers against his leg, a lively riff from a New Orleans jazz classic. His mother used to be proud of the way he played Beethoven and Chopin on the piano, but it was Dixieland that got her on her feet. He soothed himself with it unconsciously.

The squealing wheels of the janitor's cart rolled through the security door.

"Morning, Leonard," Verrazzano said.

13

"'Java.'" The janitor lifted his finger and pointed at Verrazzano. "By Allen Toussaint. Recorded under the name Tousan back in 1958."

Verrazzano hadn't realized that he'd been humming the tune aloud. "You got me."

Leonard held out his palm for five. Verrazzano laid it on him.

"How's it going, Dom?" The janitor was two decades older than Verrazzano, nearing retirement. He set his cart by the elevator and stretched his back with his hands on his hips. "Allen Toussaint, oh yeah. You been playing lately?"

"I only play to calm myself down. And generally I'm icy cool."

"You're the icy ICE agent, man. But you're playing now." Leonard grinned. "So what's eating you?"

Verrazzano shrugged. The muted beat of the traction motor restarted, and the cab came up to the sixth floor.

"Toussaint also wrote 'Working in the Coal Mine,'" the janitor said. "I like that one. The one Lee Dorsey recorded. 'Lord, I'm so tired. How long can this go on?' I ask myself that every day, man. Don't you?"

"How long?" Verrazzano shook his head. It would go on forever. Which was as long as it would take for him to pay for the life he had lived. For the things he had done. "I never ask questions unless I don't know the answer."

The janitor laughed and rubbed the small of his back. "Yes, that's the truth. This shit just goes on and on. No reason to expect it to stop, no matter how tired you get."

The steel doors slid back. Verrazzano extended his hand to greet Doctor Weston.

She grabbed at him and fell to her knees. Blood slicked Verrazzano's palm.

"Ah, shit, damn." The janitor dropped his mop.

Her eyes were intense, focused on Verrazzano, not her pain. So that he would understand that her fear wasn't of death, but of what would happen to others after she was gone. He recognized that look. Maryam Ghattas had stared at him that way as she gripped his arms, before he shoved her to the stairwell floor and walked away fast into the Beirut street.

The janitor stumbled to the foyer and rapped on the bullet-proof glass. "Get some help out here. Somebody down."

The heavy security door unlocked with an electronic snap and the guard's feet pounded across the floor.

Verrazzano lowered the doctor to the thin, blue carpet. She was about forty. Her shoulder-length hair was light brown, but it was dark against her pallid skin. The blonde hairs on her upper lip quivered. She grasped at his sleeve. Her eyeballs bulged, the pupils tiny pencil-spots in moss-green irises. He gazed at them, desperate and shocked, as though she would take him with her when she finally closed them. The way Maryam Ghattas took away the life he led before her death in that stairwell.

He pulled away the folded copy of the *New York Times* clutched in front of her. Her chest was shot at least three times.

The guard reached the elevator. "Kinsella's on the way."

The best first-aider of all the agents in the field office. But even Noelle Kinsella couldn't save this woman. No more than she could save Special Agent Dominic Verrazzano. He nodded dumbly.

The janitor squeezed Verrazzano's shoulder. "Come on, man. It's okay."

The touch revived him. He yelled to the guard, "Shut down the building. All exits."

Weston pushed a sheet of paper into Verrazzano's hand. The note was bloodied, but the black ink hadn't smudged. He read her scrawl.

33.516388, 36.269086

He held the paper before her. "What is this?"

The security door clicked again. Kinsella rushed to the prone woman with a first aid kit. Her hair was long and dry, dyed the color of autumn leaves. It flew out behind her, and her gaudy jewelry jangled as she crossed the floor. Weston's wound bubbled and rasped.

"Hold on," Verrazzano said. "Doctor Weston, stay with me."

"Move fast." Her voice was like a whisper in a nightmare. "Got a few days. That's all."

The last air left her. She seemed to sink into the floor, as though she had been an inflatable doll, not a human being.

"What's happening in a few days?" Verrazzano leaned close to her. "Doctor, what's going to happen?"

Her eyes emptied of their urgency. A few days, a few years. It didn't matter. All deadlines were passed for her.

The janitor bent over his cart and cursed.

Kinsella ripped a chest seal out of its cellophane packing. The broadening shock channels of the bullets had gored Weston's vital organs. Kinsella's hands hovered above the woman, the thin fingers decorated with thick gold rings and freckles. The damage was so severe, she couldn't figure out where to place the seal.

Verrazzano stared at the sheet of paper. It was ragged along one edge, torn from a ring notebook. It was a map coordinate, written earlier with care. Bill Todd hurried into the lobby, his Glock 19 already out of his shoulder holster. He registered the body on the floor and the defeated posture of Kinsella with the chest seal. Verrazzano saw a flicker of despair cross his face before Todd switched on his habitual angular glare. Verrazzano knew the devastating memory that would be called to Todd's mind right now. But Todd was ready to go, and Verrazzano had to trust that he'd back him up.

Kinsella closed the doctor's eyes, brushing her bony hand over the woman's face as solemnly as if a thousand souls had expired.

Verrazzano and Todd leapt into the elevator.

"Shooter must've gotten out when the elevator stopped on the second floor." He hammered the button, and they dropped down.

CHAPTER 4

The fire alarm shrilled and echoed around the open-plan office on the second floor. Silver paint covered the bricks and beams, the exposed pipes and air ducts. The company logo of the famous clothing designer pulsated in gaudy red, white, and blue above the reception desk. Verrazzano rushed out of the elevator ahead of Todd. He swung his H&K MP7 across the lobby.

"Federal agent," he yelled at the receptionist. "Where's the fire escape?"

She stared at him, frozen.

"Where is it? Come on."

The receptionist raised a fashionably emaciated arm to point across the office.

Verrazzano sprinted past the horrified hipsters. The door to the fire stairs was open. He leapt through it. Todd followed him down, heavier on his feet, his features raging against the death he had seen upstairs.

They spun out into the ground-floor loading bays facing Twenty-Sixth Street. The space was massive, originally designed for the LeHigh Valley Railroad to house its rolling stock, lit by a high strip of dirty windows. The steel gates of the bays were shut, except for the closest one. Todd headed through it. He scanned the street. "No runner."

The pedestrian door in the farthest bay opened a crack. A man sidled through. Verrazzano spotted him.

"Bill, go for the corner," he yelled.

He took off in pursuit, leaping over boxes and pallets in the semidarkness. He burst onto Eleventh Avenue. The sidewalks were moderately crowded. Verrazzano picked out the pedestrian with the most purposeful stride, a guy in a green hoodie. He looked Army, like he was one click into a route march.

Todd reached the corner. Verrazzano dipped his head toward the hooded man. Todd jogged across the road to cut him off. A taxi braked suddenly and halted in front of him. Todd rapped the roof and called to the driver to move.

The hooded man heard him and looked back. Todd's cheap blue suit and rigid demeanor said law enforcement like a bottle of Cristal and a loose-kneed swagger said hip-hop artist. The target went into a sprint. Verrazzano cut fast across the avenue.

Todd shouted for the man to halt. He aimed his Glock, but the far corner was crowded with pedestrians waiting for the light to change. "Everyone out of the way."

The runner wavered down the block. He reached the stairs that spiraled up to the old elevated rail line where the city had built a new park.

Verrazzano and Todd were a dozen yards behind him.

He jumped onto the stairs and climbed up to the High Line. The ICE agents hammered up the iron stairs behind him.

When he made the top of the steps, Verrazzano smiled thinly. It still caught him off guard sometimes, being on this end of the chase. He was more accustomed to hiding, waiting out some African goon squad while they sniffed for the scent of his fear in the wild jungle.

The former elevated track north of the Meatpacking District was as neat as a city planner's sketch. The people on it gleamed like computerized illustrations of sweat-free joggers and first-time parents among the meadow plants and the benches of Brazilian walnut. The desperate, twitching fugitive couldn't hide himself up here for long. Verrazzano scanned the tall sprays of moor grass.

A hand extended through a brown clump of alumroot. It held a pistol. The muzzle flashed.

The joggers stumbled. The parents screamed. Todd dived to the ground.

Verrazzano shouted, "Everybody down."

Todd reached his Glock out before him, covering the undergrowth, whispering to himself words that Verrazzano couldn't pick up.

"Gunman, I'm a federal agent," Verrazzano said. "Put down your weapon. I don't want to shoot you."

The man rose out of the long grass like a seed floating on the gusty wind. His angular face collapsed.

Verrazzano saw something more than the resignation of a man who knows he'll never be free again. He had put away enough bad guys in the last four years to recognize *that* look. This was profoundly sorrowful, as if the man glimpsed all the evil in the world and understood his part in it. His hand hung limp, but it still curled around a Ruger LCP.

"Put down the gun." Verrazzano moved forward.

The man watched the clouds tracking fast overhead in the wind. "I got the four-ten."

"What's the four-ten?"

"Going to kill me."

"I'm not going to kill you."

"The four-ten is what's killing me."

"What's the four-ten?"

The man shook his head as though he were worried it would fall off.

Verrazzano closed the gap. He was only a few yards from the shooter. "Why did you shoot the doctor?"

"Who?"

Their voices were tender. They were talking about a subject they both knew. Killing. "The woman in the elevator. Doctor Amy Weston. Why'd you shoot her?"

The man's cheeks were pitted and ravaged. His soul seemed to reach out toward Verrazzano, burning and shuddering. Verrazzano had known every kind of bad guy there was—mass murderers, pimps, drug dealers, arms peddlers—and the corruption was never just skin deep. A world of filth flooded in with their crimes, inundating them. The only way for them to survive was to absorb it and make it a proud part of them. This wasn't an evil man. Verrazzano saw it written in his face, the struggle to vomit out the wickedness.

"What's your name?" Verrazzano said.

The man tilted his head to the side, as though it had never occurred to him that people had names.

"Give me the gun." Verrazzano held out his free hand to take the Ruger.

The man regarded his pistol with surprise, like a cell phone trilling an unexpected call. He dropped it in the bush.

Verrazzano took a long breath of relief. He bent for the pistol.

The man moved quickly. He leaped onto the top railing at the edge of the park and balanced above the street like a dancer sweeping into an arabesque.

"No." Verrazzano rushed after him.

The shooter crossed his arms over his chest and tipped forward. Thirty feet below, he struck the pavement headfirst.

His feet were still in the air when a city bus battered into him. It swatted his body ten yards down the street.

CHAPTER 5

Todd knelt beside the shooter's body. "He looks military," he said. Verrazzano checked respiration and pulse. The guy was dead military. He reached into the man's pockets. No cash. No ID. He rolled up the sleeves of the hoodie, looking for a company tattoo. Thick veins stretched over wiry muscle, but the arms were unmarked.

"I *would've* shot him," Todd said. "If it came to that."

Verrazzano knew now what Todd had been whispering about as he trained his gun on the undergrowth where the man hid. Talking himself through the dry mouth and the urge to shoot wide of the target. The natural compulsion *not* to take a life. The desperate need not to repeat a mistake for which he'd almost paid with his career a year ago. "I know it," Verrazzano said.

He reached into his jacket.

"I should've killed that guy," Todd said. "That guy in DC."

Verrazzano had read the internal inquiry, heard the gossip too before Todd transferred to New York. How he failed to neutralize a suspect during a shootout, how he let the guy run. During his escape, the suspect, a mope named Pangiottis, put a bullet in the back of another agent who was now going to walk like a ninety-year-old man until he actually was one. Verrazzano took out a knife with the blade folded into the black steel handle. "That's the thing about your head, Bill. You don't know how far it's going to let you go until your finger's on the trigger." He extended the knife. Its point curved like the talon of a bird of prey.

21

"What're you doing?"

Verrazzano heard the hint of shrillness in Todd's voice. "It's cool, Bill."

He twirled the thumbscrew to lock the blade in place and slit down the front of the hoodie. Underneath, blood soaked the man's white T-shirt. He cut the tee from the neck to the waist. A sparse vector of hair fuzzed in the dip between the pectorals. Still no tattoo. He ran his fingers under the collarbone and frowned.

A few passengers stepped out of the bus and stared, hugging themselves. The driver came forward, nervously.

With the flat of his hand, Verrazzano probed below the corpse's left collarbone. He braced his fingers around a protrusion about three inches by two. A vein appeared to snake away from it toward the heart. He pressed the tip of the knife on the skin beside the lump, pursed his lips, and drove down a half inch.

"Dom, you can't." Todd reached for Verrazzano's shoulder.

He turned on him with a glare so firm, Todd withdrew his hand. "We don't have time for the techs to process this body and send it through the system. Let me do this."

Todd took a hesitant step back.

Verrazzano sliced the skin around the bottom of the lump. He reached his fingers into the bloody pocket of flesh and yanked. He came out with a small silver disk a half-inch thick.

"What *is* that?" Todd asked.

"Pacemaker."

He cut through the plastic-coated wires that connected the pacemaker to the dead man's heart. The bus driver vomited in the gutter.

Verrazzano took an evidence bag from his other pocket and unfolded it.

Todd had his hand over his throat. "You can't just—"

"If you've got one of these," Verrazzano said, gesturing with the pacemaker, "you can't count on being treated in an emergency by medical personnel who have access to your records. But any doctor can get everything he needs to know by scanning this device."

Todd's eyes traced the blood in the folds of the plastic bag. "So, on that thing—?"

"All about our guy." Verrazzano pocketed the evidence bag. "Including his name."

Todd shivered. "Jesus fucking Christ, Dom."

Verrazzano folded his knife. "Wait here until NYPD shows up. I'm going to find out who this guy was."

CHAPTER 6

Roula Haddad hovered the black plastic interrogator over the pacemaker in the instrument tray. The printer on the desk pushed out a sheet of paper. Verrazzano grabbed it.

The pacemaker's data was displayed in tabular form. Pulse width, arrhythmia episodes, battery voltage. At the top was the name of the man from whose chest Verrazzano cut the device. "Lee Hill," he said. "Run a check on the name, Roula."

"Will do." She tapped at her keyboard to start the database search.

The computer expert for the New York field office had the magnetic beauty of a model, as if her exotic Lebanese features were perpetually lit by a fashion photographer's spotlight. Haddad's body was unlike the towering anorexics of the catwalk, though. Her center of gravity was low and her hips were wider than her shoulders. Watching her work was as mesmerizing as watching her walk. She toggled between three monitors and a dozen different sites and databases, and she always knew which one was about to spit out something vital. Verrazzano figured that if ICE tried to invent the perfect agent, the big suits in DC couldn't do better than an Arabic-speaking computer wizard whose beauty beguiled suspects so that they almost *wanted* her to bring them in. Let the ideal operative also be born in Beirut during the civil war so that she understood exactly what horrors unfold when law collapses and was, therefore, absolutely committed to ICE's mission to bust the bad guys.

"Take a look at this." Roula brushed her black ringlets from her brow and gestured to her second monitor. A scanned image of the dead doctor's final note glowed on the screen. "I pulled up those coordinates on satellite."

Her screen flashed to a white stripe of highway. Dusty rooftops. An open area of parched grass punctuated by the uniform puffs of planted trees. "The coordinates are for a place called Tishreen Park. In Damascus, Syria."

Noelle Kinsella entered the cubicle. "Damascus? The story Doctor Weston circled in the paper was about Syria." Her vowels were all pronounced through lips rounded as if to whistle, as Long Island as the Billy Joel fan club. There were agency regulations on women's hair, which should be no longer than their shoulders and tied into a neat ponytail. Kinsella hadn't read the regulations—or she didn't care about them. Or both.

"I'll call it up," Haddad said.

Kinsella folded her arms across her chest and whispered to Verrazzano, "How was Billy the Kid?"

Verrazzano gave her a warning look. "Agent Todd did just fine, Noelle. If I've learned one thing from my life, it's that everyone deserves a second chance."

"We don't all get what we deserve though, do we?"

"In the end, yes, we do."

She shook her head.

"Check it out." Haddad gestured to her screen. It displayed an image of the page from the *New York Times* the doctor had pressed to her wound.

The newspaper was folded around one particular story. Verrazzano read the headline. "White House to Spell Out New Syria Plan." He looked over the first few paragraphs. "The president's going to make a statement this week at the UN. Congress is pushing for increased action against Islamist groups and stepped-up military aid to the rebel forces we've been backing."

"The White House isn't on Twenty-Sixth Street and the West Side Highway," Kinsella said. "Why'd she come to *you*, Dom?"

"Amy Weston was a chemical-weapons expert. She just did a stint with the UN in Syria. A guy I know out there put her in touch with me."

"Syria gave up its chemical weapons. They did a deal with the UN a couple years ago. Why was Doctor Weston there now?"

"The UN keeps inspectors in Damascus to check that the Syrians don't develop *new* chemical weapons to use in the civil war."

"You think this Syria map reference could be for a chemical weapons dump?" Haddad said.

"Maybe. Before our shooter jumped off the bridge, he said the 'four-ten' was killing him. What could that be? Perhaps he blamed her for it. Thought she played a part in killing him, so he killed her in revenge."

"I'm doing a quick search for four-ten." Haddad glanced down her screen. "Nothing comes up that seems relevant."

"Four-ten." Kinsella touched her spa-tanned forehead as though it ached.

"Doctor Weston worked in chemical weapons. Could that be connected to the four-ten? Maybe to a chemical structure?" Verrazzano asked her.

"Chem weapons have much more complicated structures than that. They do have shorter numbers in indexes like the Chemical Abstract Service or the PubChem database. But even those are longer than 'four-ten.'"

"What about molecular mass or melting point? Those would be only a few digits."

Kinsella gave Verrazzano a smile of deep appreciation from her lips of deep purple. "Three digits, in fact."

She hurried to her cubicle, dropped into her chair, and reached for a row of books propped against her computer monitor. She pulled out a binder that was stamped with the logo of the Organization for the Prohibition of Chemical Weapons in The Hague. She flipped through it and ran her finger down a table of numbers in tiny print.

Verrazzano followed her into the cubicle.

She mumbled the names of the chemical agents as she cross-checked their molecular mass. "Tabun, sarin, soman, sulfur mustard, lewisite, VX, hydrogen cyanide, chlorine gas." She did the same with melting point and some other vital stats, then she pushed the binder away with a sigh.

"Nothing?" Verrazzano asked.

"Not a fucking sausage, hon. No four-ten."

Verrazzano leaned against the gray felt of the cubicle wall and closed his eyes to let the fear leave him and allow the focus to take its place. The outline of the answer to the puzzle crept into sight. "Whatever the four-ten is, we can guess that it's toxic, right?"

"If it was something Doctor Weston was worried about, I guess so." Kinsella had her elbows on her desk and her hands knotted under her chin.

"Let's aim for the top. What're the most toxic chemical weapons?"

"VX gas. Or sarin."

"How would you rate the toxicity of, say, sarin?"

"On a scale of one to ten? Oh man, it's a ten."

A scale. That was the last hint that filled in the outline for Verrazzano. "But one to ten isn't how you rate them."

"Okay, maybe I'd give it an eleven on a ten-scale."

"No, they're rated zero through four. By the Fire Protection Association. Zero means no health hazard. Four means short exposure can result in death."

Kinsella sat upright, alert and energized. "And these ratings are posted in a—"

"Fire diamond with only three numbers. So emergency responders know exactly what kind of hazardous materials they're faced with."

Verrazzano grabbed a notepad from Kinsella's desk. He sketched as he spoke. "A fire diamond includes a rating for flammability at the top. Let's say that's the one. Over on the right is instability. That's a zero. And on the left is the health threat. We'll put a maximum four here."

He showed the sketch to Kinsella. "That's the four-ten. Which chemical weapon gets marked with a fire diamond like that?"

Kinsella turned back to the binder and flipped to a different section. "VX is four-one-one. Tabun? No, that's four-two-one. Here, four-one-zero. Shit, it's sarin."

The very word sounded evil, like the hiss of a killer's knife through your veins. "Tell me about it," Verrazzano said.

Kinsella grimaced as though she'd just had a dose of the nerve agent herself. "Moderately high exposure kills you within a minute, tops."

"Symptoms?"

"Runny nose, tight chest, puke, shit yourself. Twitch, jerk, suffocate. Die."

"But the man who killed Doctor Weston said the four-ten was killing him. He didn't seem to have those symptoms."

"Could be he had very mild exposure. At that level, it'd take a while for the sarin to shut down the ability of glands and muscles to regulate themselves—that's how it really kills you. Whether it takes six months or sixty seconds, the organs get overworked and they can no longer sustain breathing."

Both agents took a silent moment to register the deadly nature of the substance they faced. To wonder which enemy wielded it and where they would strike.

"Noelle, see if you can track any recent references to sarin in our databases. Check with FBI too."

"You got it."

"See what NSA has. Maybe they scooped up a call or an e-mail. Push the Syria angle with them. That should interest them enough to cooperate."

Kinsella spun a heavy gold ring set with a fake amethyst around her finger. "Doctor Weston told you we had a few days. Before what, you reckon?"

"She was a chemical-weapons inspector. She wasn't talking about the sell-by date on a carton of milk."

"I get nightmares about terrorists bringing stuff like sarin into the city."

Verrazzano's smile was grim. "That's why we're lucky to be ICE agents. Other people get night sweats about public speaking and clowns—terrifying shit they can't do anything about. We get to toss and turn over money launderers and cybercriminals and people traffickers. But they're not as scary."

"They're not?"

"Sure. Because we get to arrest them in the end." He put a hand on her shoulder. "Sweet dreams."

CHAPTER 7

Martin Chavez twitched the controller of his wheelchair the way he used to worry the magazine-release button of his M16A2 on patrol in Baghdad. He read the letter over. Its dry, bureaucratic phrasing ripped him apart like the fiberglass rock stuffed with high explosive that sent him home from Iraq.

By the route all veterans knew. Via Hell.

Dear Mr. Chavez,
The agency has been impressed by your commitment and skills in your application and interview for the post of Computer Crimes Analyst, Cyber Division (GS4-1) in the New York Field Office. However, we regret to inform you that . . .

He had been sure this one was a lock. The interviewer told him they wanted to hire veterans. He carried her card in his shirt pocket for luck all month. He reached it out. It was embossed with a gold shield.

US Department of Homeland Security
US Immigration and Customs Enforcement
Homeland Security Investigations
Roula Haddad
Special Agent

Chavez had imagined his own name on that card. But now the weight of the government departments printed along the top crushed him—what was left of him. He jammed the card back into his pocket.

Special Agent Roula Haddad wanted to hire veterans. She didn't know what it was to *be* a veteran. She hadn't been tossed out of a Humvee by a roadside bomb. She hadn't lain in a dilapidated military hospital for a year, watching over and over the video of the attack that took her legs, posted helpfully online by the jihadis who carried it out.

He brought the heel of his hand down on the joystick and shot across the bedroom. The heavy wheelchair was a special Swedish design with a bulky electrical engine under the seat, entirely made of plastic so that it wouldn't set off metal detectors and force the occupant to undergo a humiliating pat-down. The letter fluttered to the carpet.

"Marty, I'm leaving in a couple minutes," Adela called from the bathroom. "What you want for dinner tonight?"

The 7 train rumbled along the elevated tracks outside the window. Chavez decided to wait for the next subway to pass. He'd do it then. The noise would cover the shot.

"You choose," he shouted.

He lowered his voice. "All I ever eat is shit."

He opened the closet and took his Beretta from the sock drawer. He zipped the wheelchair forward to push the drawer shut. He didn't need socks anymore.

On the armrest of his wheelchair was a picture of a soldier in parade dress, his breast bright with ribbons. Chavez touched it lightly, as though he were saying farewell to a beloved pet, a being for whom words were meaningless but whose understanding was absolute. He flipped it over and read it. "I've still got your back. Your buddy, Kyle." The soldier whose words had filtered strong and fierce through the death pooling in Chavez's lungs and brain, Kyle Massie had gripped his hand and bellowed encouragement while a horrified medic fumbled with the stumps of his legs.

Chavez checked the window, waiting for the cover of the subway's racket.

Kyle visited him often. Not out of pity. He came to thank Chavez for listening to his desperate voice. To thank him for living, for not dying when he held his hand.

On the windowsill stood a photo in a cheap plastic frame. The Chavez family at a Veterans Day parade after Martin's first tour. His wife hugged him around his big chest as though she was five and he was her favorite teddy bear. He had his hand on Ricky's shoulder. The boy was shy, but he glowed with pride. Daddy wore his medals.

The sweat on his neck burned. It seemed to eat through his skin and glut his throat with bile. His catheter bag was heavy against his hip. He ought to drain it. Jesus, he couldn't even pee any more. His eyes flooded. A man may imagine himself dead far more calmly than he accepts life as a deadbeat.

He laid the family photo facedown. He couldn't bear it. Adela loved him and Ricky was growing up fine. But Information Technology Specialist Martin Chavez, B Company, Ninth Engineer Battalion, was a worthless mess. He hammered his forehead with the barrel of the 9 mm.

The train rattled along the tracks. He racked a cartridge in the slide.

Adela flushed the toilet.

He put the gun against his neck.

The wheel of the 7 train screeched over the rail.

"Marty? You hear me, *papi*? I'll be right there."

So fucking selfish, he told himself. *You're going to let her be the one to find your body?* He couldn't do that to Adela.

He shoved the gun in among the socks. He'd finish himself somewhere else, while she was at work. He pushed the drawer to close it, but it skewed in at an angle and stuck. It was always Adela who cleaned up after him. Let it be someone else for a change. He jammed the drawer forward and cursed.

The bedroom door opened. "Let me get that for you, honey." Adela crossed the room.

"I can do it myself." He shoved the drawer and then pulled to free it. Shoved and pulled again, raging and red-faced.

The drawer flew out of its niche. His socks dropped to the carpet. They were all gunmetal gray. The pistol nestled among them.

Adela reached for the weapon. The handcuffs on her belt clicked against the anodized steel of the SIG Sauer in her holster.

"Give me that," Chavez said.

Adela eased the slide back a half inch and saw the brass casing of a shell through the ejection port of the M9. "You got one in the chamber, Marty."

He shrugged.

She noticed the ICE letter under her foot. She read it and stared at him, understanding what he had intended. "*Ai*, no. No, honey." She went onto her knees and slipped her arms around him in his chair. She pressed her face to his belly. He was fat now that he couldn't run for exercise. She was getting heavy too, as though all the misery he made her eat could be measured in calories. "Ricky needs you," she whispered.

"No one fucking needs me."

She whispered, "*I* need you, baby."

He wanted so badly to be alone, to go away and die. The worst part of it was that he had the things a man was supposed to require for happiness. This woman loved him. His boy was a dozen times brighter than anyone he'd ever known. He had a roof over his head. Everything else was window dressing, the extras from which a man draws status and the admiration or envy of other men. He was going to kill himself for that?

He even had Kyle Massie. A buddy who knew what he'd been through. A comrade who still cared.

He kissed his wife's brow, mumbling his regret incoherently. She gripped him tight. "You remember when Ricky was born?" she said. "You remember what you did?"

Chavez tried to reply, but a sob took him.

"You held him," she said. "You held your little boy."

The memory of the child in his arms, tiny and warm, black eyes staring up at his father's face. *He knew more than I did, even then*, he thought.

"You held him in your big, strong arms and said you were always going to look after him. He needs you, Marty. He's real smart and he talks so grown up. But he's just a little boy. He's helpless, like he was then. *He* needs you."

He hugged her as if the improvised explosives were about to go off underneath him again and these were his last moments.

The buzzer sounded at the front door.

"I'll get it." Adela pushed herself to her feet.

Chavez took his chair across the carpet. "You get set for work. I'll see who it is."

"Baby?"

He stopped at the door and craned his neck to see her.

"Taco night?" she said.

"I'd like that."

He crossed the living room. The locks were set low so he could reach them. He swung the door open.

In the austere glow of the corridor fluorescents, a towering man stood with his legs apart and his hands behind his back. His blond hair was short and combed to the side. His face was bony and tanned. He wore desert pants, high-laced work boots, and a brown leather jacket.

Kyle Massie saluted. "Specialist Chavez. Hooah."

CHAPTER 8

Verrazzano watched the surveillance tape. Haddad sensed the depth of his concentration. She wanted to put everything she had into this case. She wouldn't let him down.

On the tape, Doctor Weston entered the elevator and hit the button for the sixth floor. Her arms folded over her newspaper, she rocked impatiently on her heels.

A hooded man stepped in as the doors started to close. He jabbed the button board and coughed hard. The doctor huddled in the corner, frantic, trapped.

Another woman entered the elevator. The man shoved her out. The hood shadowed his eyes, but his gaunt cheeks and thin nose were enough for Verrazzano to recognize him. The guy from the High Line.

"Pacemaker man?" Haddad said.

"Yeah, that's Lee Hill."

On the video, Lee Hill thrust the doctor against the back wall of the elevator and snatched at her clothing, so that at first it looked as though he intended a sexual assault. Then his purpose became clear. "He's frisking her," Haddad said.

The man grabbed the doctor's chin and pushed his fingers into her mouth, rooting for something inside. Then he stepped away. He raised his pistol. The doctor covered her face with the newspaper as though it might shield her. A silent tremor shook the tape as the gun fired.

The recoil of the gun seemed to shiver through Verrazzano as if he had fired the shot. The way he had killed Maryam Ghattas. But it wasn't the same thing, not at all. Doctor Weston was alone when her end came. There was no child, no stricken innocent face to dog the dreams of her killer.

Amy Weston collapsed. Hill leaned over her, still checking for something.

"Whatever he wanted, it doesn't look like he found it," Verrazzano said.

Hill left the elevator on the second floor. The doors closed and the elevator rose.

"He's not a hit man. He didn't put one in her head." The tape rolled on. The doctor struggled to pull her notebook from her shoulder bag. She scribbled on it and dragged herself to her feet.

"How is she even alive?" Haddad said.

"What she had to tell me was important enough to keep her breathing until she passed on the message."

Doctor Weston swayed. She disappeared out of the frame as the door opened.

Haddad pictured the bloodied note, the map coordinates. What did they mean? Her computer gave a dull blip—the scan was complete. She clicked on a small image to blow it up. Verrazzano leaned over her desk. They stared at Lee Hill wearing camo fatigues.

"This is from the Department of Defense's personnel directory," she said.

"Bill was right. He was Army."

"No. Marines." Haddad read off the record on her monitor. "Staff sergeant in Afghanistan. Awarded the Navy Cross for evacuating wounded comrades under heavy fire."

Verrazzano glanced over the screen. "He's been out a long time. Last deployment was 2007 in Afghanistan. Left the Corps in 2008."

"Since then he's been working for private military companies. Most recently a new one. You ever hear of Molnir Partners?"

He shook his head. "Got an address for him?"

"In Queens. Lives with his wife, Jennifer Esquibel Hill."

CHAPTER 9

Massie picked up a DVD for the latest Tom Cruise action movie from the coffee table in Martin Chavez's living room. "You're kidding me, right?"

"Adela likes him." Chavez smiled.

Massie called into the kitchen, waving the DVD. "Adela, what the hell do you see in this tiny weirdo?"

She brought a cup of strong coffee for Massie. "He had me at hello."

"What is that? Is that a line from one of his girlie movies?" He tossed the DVD on the table and grinned. "I just don't get it."

She hustled back to the kitchen to pack her lunch.

Massie took a sip. "This coffee's awesome, Adela."

"You're welcome, Kyle, honey."

"You want to talk weirdoes?" Chavez knew that no movie star would ever measure up to Kyle's hero, the man on whom he modeled his clothing and hairstyle. He decided to have some fun. He pointed at Massie's cup. "Steve McQueen used to get coffee enemas because he thought it'd cure his cancer."

"Don't rag on the King of Cool, bro." He set the cup on the table and pushed his blue-tinted Persols to the bridge of his nose, smiling. "I've missed you, Marty."

Chavez glanced downward. Half of the Marty that his old comrade missed was, indeed, missing. Everything below the groin, to be precise. He screwed up his face, disgusted by his reaction, his sick, depressive, negative thoughts.

Adela came out of the kitchen. "I'll see you later, *papi*." She kissed Chavez's forehead and held his face.

"I'll be here," he whispered.

When the front door closed behind Adela, Massie bent forward, his elbows on his knees. "I know where you're at, man." He rolled up the cuff of his bomber jacket. His wrist was scarred across with what psychiatrists call hesitation marks. The traces of attempted suicides. "I've been there, bro."

Chavez swallowed. "How did you know?"

"I didn't lose my legs, and I didn't lose my eyes neither. I see what's going on with you. I did damn near lose my fucking mind. Nightmares, sweats. I was mad as hell *all* the time. Some dipshit spilled my beer, and I broke his teeth. I did ninety days for that in Indiana. I was a total piece of shit. I couldn't even kill myself. A real fucking loser."

"But you're good now?"

"I got a job with a private security firm. They found me help." He put his hand on Chavez's fingers where they gripped the controller of his wheelchair. "I want you to have the same protection, man. I want you to join us."

"A job?"

"You got it."

"No way. I don't believe it."

"Sure as shit. Look, man, I had to lose everything before I could accept help. Don't let it go that far for you, Marty. You've got to think about your wife and kid."

"I don't need anybody's pity."

"Right you don't." Massie got in Chavez's face. "You don't get no pity from me, man. You lost your legs, but you gained something too. You learned that your buddies won't leave you, even when everyone thinks you're finished. You learned there's someone who's got your back no matter what. Roger that?"

Chavez felt Massie's intensity enter him, burning with pride and love. He wiped at the tears in his eyes. "Roger."

"You ever hear these government assholes saying how they *served* as deputy secretary of state for some shit or other? Or guys on Wall Street *serving* as director of J. P. fucking Morgan. They don't *serve*. They *take*. Who really serves, Marty? Guys like you and me. Now it's time for *us* to take something back."

Massie took out a pack of Winstons and lit up. Chavez glanced nervously toward the kitchen, waiting for Adela to complain about the smoke. Then he remembered she had left for work. Massie took a long drag.

"We're bidding on a security contract," he said. "Once we get the contract, you'd be working indefinitely on it."

"Who's the client?"

"Cybersecurity's a big part of our pitch. That's where you come in. We present ourselves as a full-service security company. We've got guys who can stand around looking tough with assault rifles. We've got friendly faces to do pat-downs. We've got geniuses like you to stop hackers painting horns on photos of Ban Ki-moon."

"The UN secretary-general? The client's the UN?"

"You'll be working in the same place as Adela."

"Wait. Adela's going to lose her job?" Chavez said.

"What're you talking about?"

"Adela works in UN security. But the UN is hiring an outside firm to do security."

"The UN's getting additional security capability. They'll keep their in-house people."

"But you mentioned pat-downs. That's what Adela does."

Massie lifted his hands as though he had touched something hot. "Don't freak. The UN's putting up a new tower on the East River. We'll be doing security for that building. Adela and her buddies look after the old homestead. We get the shiny new ranch."

"Who're we working for?"

"You heard of Tom Frisch?"

"The Special Forces guy? Jesus, he's tough, yeah?"

"He's so bad, he ought to have his own arms control treaty."

Chavez remembered how soldiers talked about Frisch, the Green Beret who ghosted through the Baghdad alleys, leaving no trace of his presence but the neat holes in the foreheads of dead jihadis.

"Frisch put together a company specifically for this deal. Lots of experienced guys from Delta Force, Rangers, Marines. Specialist Chavez, we'd be honored to have you."

CHAPTER 10

Verrazzano parked at the corner in a blue Dodge Charger he'd drawn from the ICE pool. With Todd at the scene of Lee Hill's death and Kinsella trawling law enforcement databases for leads on the sarin, he was without a partner. A Lincoln limousine sat at the curb outside the home of the man who killed Doctor Weston. The unadorned brick row house looked like a tenement chopped down to two stories to resemble more desirable single-family homes farther away from the city.

A man came out of Lee Hill's house. A blonde woman leaned from the open door and waved to him. Verrazzano read her bright, lipsticked mouth. She said, "I love you." The man ignored her, looked up and down the street, and headed for the limo. He wore a blue suit without a tie. His hair was just beyond his collar, swept back over a thinning crown in oily curls. He had a mustache like a bootblack's bristle brush.

The limo driver started up the engine and drove down the block. Verrazzano reached for the ignition of his car but took his hand away. There might be nothing to it. It was probably just a visit from a friend who knew little about Lee Hill or what he had done. The wife was first, then maybe he'd question the limo driver.

He whispered the number on the Lincoln's plates to himself. He dialed Haddad. She picked up.

"Roula, I need you to check ownership on a Town Car. Plate number Delta-Papa-Charlie Seven-Eight-Nine." He got out of his Charger and started across the street.

"Registered to a Jon Ivin." Haddad read off her screen back at the ICE field office. "He hires out the limo with himself as driver. Address in Atlantic Beach."

"Text me the location. I might check it out after I've seen Lee Hill's wife."

"Hey, look at that. Jon Ivin's a veteran too."

"Was he in the Marines with Lee Hill?"

"Infantry."

"Tours in Afghanistan? Did he meet Hill there?"

"Negative. He was in Iraq."

Verrazzano recalled something he observed after he left the Army. Most vets had seen enough violence that they'd do all they could to avoid it. But a few of them liked it so well they couldn't live without it. Which side of that divide did Lee Hill and Jon Ivin come down on?

"Okay, thanks." He slipped the phone into his pocket.

He approached the door from which Hill must have emerged to murder Doctor Weston. He pressed the doorbell.

The woman who opened the door wore makeup thick enough to keep out the cold and a pink-striped tank top that strained to contain her freckled breasts. When she saw Verrazzano, the disappointment added twenty years. He sensed she'd been hoping for the limo driver to return. "Oh," she said.

"Jennifer Esquibel Hill?" He showed her his badge. "Special Agent Verrazzano, Immigration and Customs Enforcement."

"Oh." She put even more letdown into that syllable the second time around.

"May I come in?"

"I'm not an immigrant."

"I'm not here about an immigration issue. I'm in Homeland Security Investigations. May we talk inside?"

She stepped back to let him in. As he shut the door, she reached for a sweatshirt from the back of a puffy pastel chair. The tablecloth, the frilly lampshades, and the art prints were all pink as a six-year-old girl's bedroom. Lee Hill apparently hadn't made much impact on the decor of his own home.

Jennifer tugged at the hem of her skimpy, magenta shorts as though they might transform into more modest attire. "What's this about?"

Verrazzano positioned himself by habit in front of the window. The cream-colored blinds were down, but they were almost transparent. She'd see only his silhouette, and she'd wonder what she was missing in his expression.

"I'm sorry to be the one to tell you, Jennifer. Lee's dead."

The woman dropped into the puffy sofa and pulled a pink pillow over her belly. She buried her fingers in it.

Verrazzano sat lightly in an armchair. The room smelled of Play-Doh. He looked about for children's toys until he realized the scent was the woman's perfume. "Lee killed someone this morning, Jennifer. Then he took his own life."

He waited for her reaction, but she only bobbed her head mechanically.

"Did he ever tell you about a woman named Amy Weston?"

"He didn't have another woman. Lee wasn't like that."

"Amy Weston is the woman he killed."

She stared down at her fingers, wrenching the pink fringe of the pillow. "Lee killed a lot of people."

"Who else did he kill?"

"People in Afghanistan."

"Isn't that different? That was for the Marines."

"Later, too. When he left the Corps, he went overseas for private security firms."

"Back to Afghanistan?"

"Mostly to Syria."

Verrazzano thought of the map coordinates on the note the doctor scribbled before she died. Tishreen Park, Damascus, Syria.

"He was supposed to go out there again, but he got sick, and he couldn't travel no more." Jennifer's feet pointed toward the door. Verrazzano read the unconscious signal. She'd like to just get up and clear out of there.

"What was Lee doing in Syria?" he asked.

"Well, he wasn't there to visit the pyramids."

Verrazzano felt a moment of pity for the desperate woman and her dead husband. Perhaps Lee Hill had been no brighter than his wife. Whatever was supposed to happen with the sarin, its full consequences may well have been beyond the comprehension of the former Marine.

"Was Lee fighting for the Syrian government? For the rebels?" he said.

"He never told me nothing about it. He kept a lot of secrets."

"Did Lee say anything to you about sarin?"

"Who?"

"Sarin is a nerve agent."

"Does she work for the government?"

"Not that kind of agent, Jennifer. When was Lee in Syria?"

"He came back this time last year, around about. Why don't you ask Lee?" Then she remembered why Verrazzano was there, and she sucked in her lips as though her husband had messed up her life thoroughly, but not for the first time.

"Tell me about Jon Ivin," he said.

Her eyes startled. "I don't know that name."

Verrazzano rolled his tongue over his teeth thoughtfully. Only the worst Americans were able to disguise the shame that came over them when they told an untruth. Most Americans grew up expecting honesty from others and consequently were guilt-ridden when they engaged in deception. In less prosperous nations, the assumption was that everyone lied and the only way to avoid being taken for a sucker was to lie as well. The vocal cords of a dishonest American tightened with remorse, and the increase in pitch was like a shrieking klaxon to Verrazzano's ear. "Let me be more specific. What's Jon Ivin's connection to Lee?"

Her arms folded defensively under her breasts.

"Do you love Jon Ivin?" he said. "I don't read lips too well, but I think that's what you said to him when he left here."

She tried to pack away the outrage on her face. It was like getting an egg back in its shell.

"You want to tell me what Ivin's business was here?"

"He looks after Lee."

She spoke so softly that Verrazzano wasn't sure he heard her correctly. "He looks after you?"

"Not *me*. Lee. He looks after Lee."

"You said Lee didn't know him."

"I was confused. I meant Lee doesn't know why Jonny comes here. I mean, he *thinks* he does. But he doesn't know that—See, Jonny and me, we—"

"What did Lee think Jon Ivin comes here to do?"

"He thinks Jonny just comes to give him—give Lee something." She pulled at her shorts again.

"Money?"

She made her eyes bright, trying to appeal to him. She was like the happy photo a family distributes to the media when their daughter is abducted or murdered, telling a story of helplessness and loss. "Lee's been sick. It's been real hard for me, you know. Jonny brings compensation. From Lee's friends."

"What did Lee do for *them*?"

"Nothing. I don't know."

"Why did Lee's friends pay him compensation? Was he sick because of them?"

"They're just helping." She hugged the pink cushion to her stomach hard.

"Why did you call it compensation?"

"That's what Lee calls it. He's not just sick. He's dying."

Verrazzano hesitated, wondering if he ought to remind her that Lee was already dead. "Dying of what?"

"He's been weak a long while. The doctors discovered his heartbeat had gotten too slow. That's why they made him leave the Corps. He needed a pacemaker. We had to pay for that. The military didn't give us nothing. They just threw him out."

"But he *got* the pacemaker."

"Yeah."

"So his heart wasn't the thing that was killing him."

"Nuh-uh. He can't breathe right. He got something bad in his lungs and it hurt him."

"When?"

"I guess he got sick around about in April."

"Was he receiving medical treatment?"

"Out of a bottle of Wild Turkey."

"Is there anything in this house connected to Lee's work? Does he have a laptop? A tablet? Or any other property that might give me a clue about his death?"

"There was a box. Big wooden thing. Lee kept it in the basement after he got home from Syria."

"How big?"

"About as long as I'm tall. Too heavy for Lee to lift because of his lungs. But Jonny picked it up. He's strong."

Verrazzano pictured a transport crate for sarin canisters. It'd be about the size of this woman. "Where'd Jonny take the box?"

"It's by his bed in—" She curled over the cushion in shame. Verrazzano turned his eyes away as if she were naked. She mumbled, "It's at Jonny's place in Atlantic Beach."

CHAPTER 11

The Janissary swiped at the screen of his phone as Verrazzano left the house. Jennifer Hill shut the door. Her legs were thick, the way he liked them. He might go back there later to see her. On the phone he tapped the icon for Flight, a free download from Microsoft for its Xbox. But he wasn't playing games. Xbox included a Private Chat system that was effectively beyond the capability of law enforcement agencies to monitor.

Verrazzano reversed his car into the street. The Janissary started his engine.

He found an unused Private Chat channel on the Xbox interface. He tapped on Nabil Allaf's gamertag, Psycho Psyrian, and sent an invitation. He put his Toyota into drive and followed Verrazzano down the block.

A moment later, the military intelligence officer appeared on the screen. He wore a burgundy shirt and a bright floral tie. The hair was cut short and brushed back on his narrow head. His eyes fluoresced like scorpions under ultraviolet light. The Janissary never trusted Syrians with blue eyes. They were the genetic traces of old invasions, and those who bore them would always be marked as somehow not belonging.

He smiled at himself. He didn't trust brown-eyed people either.

Allaf said, "What?"

"The ICE agent left Hill's house." The Janissary's voice was rumbling and dry.

"Where's he going?"

Verrazzano's car passed a sign to the Grand Central Parkway.

"He'll go after Ivin," the Janissary said. "If I were him, it's what I'd do."

Verrazzano went up the ramp to the Parkway.

"If you were him," Allaf said, "you'd have stayed to fuck the woman."

"'Paradise is found on the backs of horses, in books, and between the breasts of women.'"

"You want to quote proverbs? Try this: 'Death rides a fast camel.' Focus on your job. Is everything prepared at Ivin's house?"

"The others are waiting for him."

"Follow. Make sure he goes there. Make sure he finds what we want him to find."

The Janissary flicked at the screen with a thick finger and ended the conversation. He sped onto the Parkway to keep up with Verrazzano. Three cars ahead of him, he picked out the silhouette of the ICE agent's head. He imagined the bullet he would put through it.

CHAPTER 12

The picture was ten feet by twenty on the wall outside the UN General Assembly chamber. "I recognize this," said the rugged, broad man. His voice was emphatic and warm. "I've seen this before. I'm sure of it, Andy."

Andreas Holtz linked his fingers behind his back. *These Americans, with their informality*, he thought. *Why do they always think they can call me Andy?* An Austrian who had filled UN posts in a half-dozen countries, he was confident that he was better able to express himself in foreign languages and to deal with people of different cultures than most Americans. Which was one reason he enjoyed showing them around the UN headquarters. The other was that, though they were in New York City, the UN compound was sovereign and independent. Tom Frisch was the alien now.

"You are looking at a version made in mosaic of *The Golden Rule* by Norman Rockwell." Holtz's English diction was precise.

"The guy who painted the turkey," Frisch said.

"*Freedom From Want*. That is the picture of which you are thinking. You are correct. That is also a Rockwell."

"*The Golden Rule*." Frisch smiled. "Do unto others before they do unto you."

Holtz was in his midforties, so tall that even with a stoop, he was a few inches above Frisch's height of six feet one. His thinning blond hair was combed back into a soft quiff. He felt an obscure nervousness in the presence of the former Green Beret.

The UN was a place where ideas were graded by a quantitative system, where everything was monitored and evaluated, where the things you knew how to do were called "competencies." Frisch wouldn't work that way, and that made him disturbing and attractive to Holtz.

He resettled his expensive, spruce-green eyeglasses on the bridge of his nose and tried to calm himself. After all, Frisch hadn't come to interview for a job in the UN protocol office. Frisch possessed exactly the competencies the UN lacked. He was one of the most decorated Green Berets in history. He served in the Persian Gulf, Bosnia, and Haiti, where a machete wound gave him the scar that his slicked-back hair barely concealed. His reputation was made in Iraq and Afghanistan, where he hunted al-Qaeda and its many offshoots. In those days, he grew a long beard and dressed like an Arab or a Pashtun. Now he wore a pink silk tie that shimmered like a rainbow trout in a summer lake. Holtz imagined Frisch's tanned fists shooting out of the sleeves of his blue suit to grab the fish from the water, ripping its flesh, eating it raw.

"I know we're not the only outfit bidding on this contract," Frisch said. "But we're the best."

"The selection process is clearly defined in the tender prospectus and—"

"*Process* isn't in my vocabulary. I'm going to tell you about me. I'm going to tell you about my outfit. I'm going to tell you what we *do*."

Holtz made a little snort of embarrassment. He poked at the top bar of his eyeglasses. Despite his preference for measured behavior and carefully formulated priorities, he was drawn to Frisch's easy, masculine style. Perhaps he simply wished to be friends with someone who molded the world to shape the life he wanted to live. Frisch never sat in a cubicle. He looked as though he may never rest long enough to *sit* anywhere. Holtz wanted to partake of the man's secret knowledge.

"I call my outfit Molnir Partners," Frisch said.

"Molnir is the name Thor gave his hammer. I see that you know your Norse mythology."

"I know my gods of war." Frisch made his gaze penetrating and intense. "Private security companies like to give themselves Greek or Latin names to make you believe what they do is high-brow and classy and bloodless. Molnir literally means 'the thing that smashes other things.' That's the name I chose. That's who I am."

"I see."

"The companies with the Greek and Latin names will give you process. Me, I'm going to give you five million bucks."

Holtz poked again at his glasses. He worked his lips, wondering if he had misheard. The confident grin on the American's face told him he hadn't.

"I'm sure of my ability to win a competitive bid," Frisch said. "But I'm a Special Forces guy. I don't fight fair. I fight to win. I pay you, I win. You got me?"

Holtz shuddered. It had never occurred to him that an American would offer him a bribe to win the security contract. Someone more senior, perhaps, might be paid off. It happened, he knew that. Then he realized that, no, he *was* the key man. He could take the money and deliver the contract. He started to speak, then he held back. Frisch grinned as if he knew what Holtz was thinking.

"Five million bucks," Frisch said. "And whatever else you'd need to ensure your security after the contract is mine."

"My security?"

"I get the contract. You stick around a while for appearance's sake. Then you quit this dump and go to your private island with a boatload of Brazilian girls."

Holtz tried to picture it. He had been a bureaucrat all his life, but now he could be a man like Frisch, a man with no rules. All he had to do was say yes. But the Andreas Holtz he imagined on the beach with the naked women was still wearing a suit and tie. He wasn't Frisch and he never would be. "I certainly cannot countenance such a—"

"Take the money, Andy." Frisch came close. "If you don't, I'm going to have to eliminate you. Maybe someone less principled will take over your position. I won't let you stand in my way."

Holtz sucked in a sharp breath. The American held his stare. Then he broke it.

Frisch laughed with sudden vigor. He poked Holtz playfully on the shoulder. "I'm good, huh, Andy? I had you, right?"

Holtz's smile was thin and shaky. "You are not bribing me?"

"If you change your mind about the money, you call me." Frisch moved toward the auditorium. "Meantime, I'm going to tell you why you should pick Molnir anyway."

Astonished and unnerved, Holtz followed him into the General Assembly Hall.

"You've got the annual session of the UN General Assembly here this week." Frisch gestured across the empty benches toward the podium and the green marble desk of the secretary-general. "My beloved president will be standing down there in a few days, telling us that time's run out for the Syrian government."

"Oh, I couldn't begin to guess what he'll—"

"I'm not guessing. I *know* everything worth knowing. What the good guys think. What the bad guys do."

Holtz wondered if the American president counted as a good guy in the mind of Tom Frisch.

"You've been with the UN twenty years, Andy."

The Austrian resisted the impulse to show his surprise. "I joined after graduate school."

Frisch reached out for the ID tag on a blue cord around Holtz's neck. He drew it close, examining it. "Chief of Safety and Security Department. You've been around. International Criminal Tribunal for the former Yugoslavia in The Hague. UN Assistance Mission for Iraq. UN Office on Drugs and Crime in Vienna. International Monetary Fund, Moscow office."

"You've done your research."

A school group bustled by them into the public gallery at the back of the chamber.

Frisch ran a finger across the back of the ID tag and let it drop. His grin was mellow and confident. He might have been chatting with Holtz at the quiet bar of an expensive hotel. "The other bidders on this contract are huge corporations with hundreds of guys guarding US embassies around the world and billions of dollars in government contracts. Molnir's a small, entrepreneurial company."

"What makes you think the UN wants to work with a small entrepreneurial company?" Holtz felt like a battered boxer who had finally landed a shot.

Frisch reached casually for Holtz's shoulder and clapped his hand down, laughing. "Andy, the world is changing. When the UN was founded after World War II, nation-states ran the globe. You had the Western bloc. You had the Soviet bloc. No crossover. That's not how things are today. Nation-states don't hold absolute sway."

Holtz glanced across the auditorium. Each of the 193 UN member states had a place at the long benches facing the podium. "Important decisions are made here."

"But not *final* decisions. Today the nation-state doesn't even have complete control over its national territory. Half the world is controlled by Russian oligarchs who aren't answerable to the law. Giant technology corporations reach into people's very thoughts in every country. Sugar companies get Americans fat and dead, but the lobbyists grease a bunch of Congressmen so there are no consequences or regulations."

Holtz felt like the nation-states Frisch described, his certainty leeched away by an ambiguous, new power. The UN's senior echelons pondered these same questions. How could its massive bureaucracy adapt to technological advances, to the new sources of wealth and authority transforming the world? Here was the answer, whispering to him, allowing him to see into the future. A future that belonged to Frisch.

"A country can't rely on an old-fashioned army anymore," Frisch said. "You've got to have a flexible force that isn't bound to a national identity or to the rigid rules of the conventional military. That's why I created Molnir. The UN needs me, Andy. Like a banana republic needs Kalashnikovs and Swiss banks."

"We already have contracts with certain private international organizations in the field of security." Holtz felt like a virgin talking dirty for the first time.

"Like what?"

"We were concerned that the US National Security Agency may have extended its monitoring to us. After all, they were tracking the German chancellor's text messages. Why not our secretary-general?"

"Who'd you hire?"

Now the virgin was being pushed to go all the way. Frisch's smile was conspiratorial and, Holtz thought, a little admiring. "You yourself pointed out that my last appointment before New York was in Moscow. I developed certain contacts there that I have maintained. You understand?"

"That's dynamite." Frisch gave Holtz a jab on the arm. "You're the shit, man. You hired Russians to dig out NSA bugs at the UN? That's awesome."

"Our consultants have found nothing so far."

"Well, you've got Russians on it, they'll find *something*. If they don't, you'll cancel the contract, and they're not going to let that happen. They'll squeeze you for every last cent."

Holtz's chin jerked back. The deed was done and the virgin felt used.

"Me, I don't squeeze," Frisch said. "I like to be generous. Look it, the US president's going to speak about Syria right here. I've got far more interesting things to tell you about Syria than he does. Molnir's in Syria *right now*, Andy."

"You're part of the civil war?"

"CIA wants to aid the Syrian rebels. But their fancy-pants operatives never took a course on how to do that at Yale Law School. So they pay me to get it done."

"What kind of aid?"

"Andy, I can pass along inside stuff to you any time. Don't you think the UN should know what's really going on there?"

"I suppose that I—"

"Are you familiar with Sun Tzu?"

"The ancient Chinese general who wrote *The Art of War*."

"I quote, 'Warfare is the way of deception.' You'd better live by that."

"I'm not at war."

"Your staff carry guns. If they weren't at the doors of this building, somebody'd come in and kill all the diplomats. So yeah, you're at war, Andy."

"But I am not interested in lying."

"Sun Tzu wasn't talking about *bad* lies. He meant you should trick your opponents so that your noble cause would win out. Maybe even without having to fight." Frisch faced the front of the hall. "When the president's at that podium, I want you to imagine how much more secure you'd be if you had me at your side, Andy."

They shook hands. Holtz didn't feel crushed by the man's grasp, as he had expected—only possessed.

CHAPTER 13

No one answered Verrazzano's knock at the limo driver's home. He walked cautiously toward the backyard. Under the spray of a sprinkler, the lawn edged the channel between Atlantic Beach and Long Island. A short, private jetty cut into the hazy, blue water. The straining stutter of an outboard engine approached. Then it cut off.

Verrazzano drew his Heckler & Koch and knelt down. The boards at the foot of the house were storm damaged and rotten. They reeked sweetly.

A small boat glided to the jetty with one man on board. The hull rumbled against the wooden pilings.

Another man descended the external staircase from the second floor of the house, a man who had chosen not to answer Verrazzano's knock moments before. "About fucking time," he said.

"Shut the fuck up and bring it down here." The boatman was black, his head shaved. The biceps that spilled out of the sleeves of his plain-gray T-shirt were as big as Verrazzano's thighs.

The man on the staircase tramped heavily onto the grass. He bent forward under a five-foot wooden crate balanced lengthwise down his back. He let the crate slip onto the jetty on its end, and he laid it flat. Verrazzano's adrenaline pulsed hard. He'd hefted enough weapons in his time to know what was inside.

The man patted the crate. "Hey, Clay. I brought you a nice, long dick to suck on. Just the way you like it."

Clay grabbed his crotch and said, "Tea bag me, bitch." The black man gave him a high five. "What's up, Slav?"

Slav wore an olive-green tank top. His skin was pale. His lats made a bodybuilder's V from his shoulders to his waist. He had a Beretta tucked into the back of his pants. He turned to survey the area. His nose had been smashed so often, it snaked down his face like a map of the Mississippi to a delta of broken veins. His buzz-cut head was pitted and whorled as though he'd been caught in an acid attack.

He stared at the corner of the house. Verrazzano ducked out of sight. Slav reached behind his back for his weapon.

Clay called out, "Hey, help me get this shit in the boat."

Verrazzano spun back onto the dirt path, his H&K braced. "Federal agent. Halt where you are."

Slav raised his pistol, but his movement was hesitant. "Slav, get in the boat," Clay called.

"I can waste him, man."

"Both of you, hands up where I can see them," Verrazzano shouted.

"Do not engage." Clay started the engine. "Get in the boat. We're out of here."

"God fucking damn it," Slav said.

"Get in the fucking boat."

"I *will* shoot you," Verrazzano called. "Put down your weapon."

Slav ran onto the jetty.

Verrazzano drew his finger back on the trigger and squeezed the safety built into the H&K's grip. He aimed for Slav's thigh to put him down.

The white siding of the house exploded inches away from Verrazzano's head. A gunshot. He threw himself onto the grass. The lawn sprinkler showered his face.

Another shot from the street, along the alley. The bullet thudded into the dirt by Verrazzano's feet.

Slav reached for the crate, but Clay dragged him back into the boat. "Leave that shit."

He let out the throttle. The boat reared into the channel. Slav tumbled into the bottom of the hull.

Clay fired a burst from a P90 machine pistol as Verrazzano scrambled across the lawn. He was in the zone where action over-rode all fear. Fear welcomed death, because death ended it. Without fear, you couldn't be killed. That's what the Green Berets had drilled into him, to persuade him to run into live fire. And, look, it worked, because he was still alive.

He raised his weapon. The boat bounced and kicked on the water. A round sizzled past him from the shooter in the street, so close it seemed to brush against him. He tumbled for cover again.

The launch disappeared around the bend in the channel. Verrazzano heard the wheels of a car pulling away fast from the front of the house. He sprinted along the alley. A silver Toyota rounded the corner toward the bridge. It was too far away for him to catch the number on the plates. He saw the profile of the man at the wheel, a massive bald head and a thick mustache. Then the Toyota was out of sight. He considered pursuit, but it was more important to know what was in the weapons crate.

He rushed across the yard to the jetty. He unsnapped the latches on the crate and flipped the lid up. He'd opened the same kind of box many times in front of glowering, mistrustful warlords in African jungles and on the windy steppes of the Caucasus—wherever Colonel Wyatt sent him. They always grinned with savage delight at the devastating tools he brought them. Inside was a BGM-71 TOW, a shoulder-launched, infrared-guided, antitank missile. Made in the United States.

Verrazzano crouched over the olive-drab barrel and peered at the stenciled description. If Wyatt had been in the boat, he wouldn't have run away. He'd have charged at Verrazzano, daring him to show a sliver of weakness.

He shook his head. It didn't matter if Wyatt charged or ran. If the colonel gave him a chance, Verrazzano would kill him. That was the only life he'd still take without compunction. Out of 7.3 billion candidates, having a death list of one wasn't so bad. "It sure is an improvement on the bad old days," he murmured.

Someone had tried to scrape away the serial number, but its outline was still there in black. He snapped it with his phone camera and sent the photo to Haddad. Then he dialed her at the office.

"Roula, trace that serial number." He listened to her fingers trill over the keyboard at the other end of the line.

"There's an alert out on this weapon," she said. "From Langley."

"The CIA? For this specific piece?"

"It's on a list of munitions captured by the Syrian government recently when they overran a rebel position near Aleppo."

Verrazzano put it together. "And the reason we know the government captured this weapon is because we gave it to the rebels in the first place. Right?"

"Looks that way. The entire list of captured weapons is US-made."

"So what we have here is a missile that we believe to be in the possession of the Syrian government, but it now happens to be in New York."

"I'll send a tech team to pick it up."

While he waited for the forensics techs to arrive, Verrazzano tried to figure out why the Syrian government would want to bring this weapon to New York. He didn't know anything for sure, except that their intention wasn't to return it politely to its original owners.

It was an hour before the techs took custody of the missile and heard his debrief. Only then could he leave the scene. He was trying to pick apart his theory as he slipped into the driver's seat of his car when Haddad called again.

"Dom, there's an alert over the Command Point Dispatch. A nine-one-one call came in from an address in Nissequogue, Long Island. The homeowner says a shooter is somewhere on his premises. Suffolk County police are responding."

"Okay. And?"

"The alert cross-references with an address I entered into the system. The call came from Doctor Amy Weston's home. The caller is Tyler Browne, her husband."

"I'm on my way."

CHAPTER 14

From a table at a sidewalk café, Martin Chavez surveyed the new UN tower, the girders and the scaffolding, the cranes perched forty stories up. He prayed Kyle Massie's security project would work out. He visualized himself rolling into the completed building to work. The sun warmed his face.

Adela rounded the corner. She brightened and came to him, rolling her broad hips in her unflattering uniform pants. Chavez was accustomed to trepidation in her eyes when she saw him. Now there was none. *For the first time in a while, I guess I don't look like I want to die,* he thought. It was as though a switch had flipped to reanimate the man Adela married. He thanked Kyle Massie for that.

"I love you, hon," he said.

His wife kissed his face. "You look excited, baby." She sat opposite him, shifting the pistol on her hip.

"I love the way you look in that uniform," Chavez said. "Like a sexy cop."

"I'm just a security guard, Marty."

"Then you look like a sexy security guard."

"I *am* a sexy security guard. What's the good news?"

"How do you know there's good news?"

The café was self-service, but a woman came from behind the counter with a tray. She put two cappuccinos and a pair of cream puffs on the table. "There you go, honey."

"Thank you very much, ma'am," Martin said.

The woman touched his shoulder and went back into the shop.

"I know it's good news," Adela said, "because you haven't wanted to meet me for lunch in months."

"So eat."

She bit into the pastry. "Mmmm, that's good. Come on, don't keep me guessing."

"I got a job."

Adela almost spat the cream over the table. "Honey, that's awesome. You're so cool." She squeezed his hand.

"I'm going to work with Kyle."

"Wow, that's great. Doing what?" Adela stroked the inside of Chavez's wrist. She did that when she wanted him. He wanted her too. In her dark-blue uniform. For the first time in months.

"I'm going to be working near you," he said. "Kyle and me, we're going to be point men on a bid by a big security firm to guard the new UN tower."

"Awesome, baby."

"It's not going to put you out of a job. It's extra security. Not replacement for the existing staff."

"Out of a job? Who said anything about that?"

"No one. I'm just saying, Jesus."

"Sorry, baby. I was worried."

"But you're happy?"

"I'm so happy, I want you to eat my cream puff." She wiggled her head, made a sexy face, and stroked his wrist again.

He laughed so loud he felt it down in his groin. His coffee spilled on the table. "Once we secure the contract, Molnir will take me on long term."

"What-nir?"

"Molnir. The company Kyle works for. And it's good money too." He reached for her fingers and gripped them. "I'm going to do whatever it takes to get this contract. Understand me?"

He saw that he was hurting her hand. "Are you with me?" He wondered why he needed so badly for her to approve.

She gave him the smile he had come to know well. The one that meant she was trying not to cry. She said, "I'm with you, baby."

CHAPTER 15

The Janissary chopped a few low branches and threaded them into a fan shape. He weaved them into the undergrowth in front of him to disguise his position. He rubbed the fringes of hair at the sides of his bald head to get the pine needles out. Then he sat with his bulky back against the tree, chewing on sunflower seeds, watching.

The house was all glass at the rear with a roof that swooped down from one end to the other like an airport terminal. Its modernity seemed out of place in the woods. There was no one inside. The Janissary had been through every room, turned out every drawer and closet as soon as he arrived from the shootout at Atlantic Beach. He hadn't found what he needed. Now he waited for someone to come who would find it for him.

A patrol car's light flashed red and blue through the windows from the front of the house. Someone must be around after all. They'd called the cops. The Janissary picked up his pistol and snapped it into a Tavor conversion. The Israeli-made frame transformed the Glock into an assault rifle. He sniffed, rolled his neck, and brought the butt to his shoulder.

The police officers came around the back of the house. They wore tan pants and shirts. One of them swaggered and chewed gum, striving for cool. The Janissary shot his twitchy, hyperalert partner first.

The cool cop didn't take cover. He stared at his dead colleague, shouting like a panicked kid. "Jesus, oh fuck Jesus."

"*Uscutt, ya manyack,*" the Janissary whispered. *Shut up, ass-fucker.* He pushed the wad of seeds into his cheek with his tongue, set the red laser guide on the cop, and put a bullet through his throat.

The silence of the woods quivered with the calls of fleeing birds. The recycling bins outside the kitchen door hid the dead cops from anyone inside the house. Whoever had phoned for help might still be around, watching. The Janissary decided to leave the bodies where they were.

A grackle fluttered down to a rock. The Janissary reached out a handful of sunflower seeds. The bird hopped toward him, almost as large as a crow, black and lustrous. It gripped his forefinger with black claws and pecked at the seeds. He stroked its iridescent green neck. "I have only seeds. Ah, but you'd like to have a mouse, wouldn't you? With blood in it."

Back in the Syrian mountains, he used to watch the grackles float on the thermals over the rocky slopes when he played with his brothers. That was thirty years ago. Before the president sent tanks to put down an Islamist uprising and to kill anyone who happened to live near a mosque. Like the Janissary's family. He ran to the mountains after the government soldiers came to his village, alone in the world but for the birds. He learned how to lure them to him with beetles and lizards. Eventually they sought him out, led him to sources of water, warned him of the approach of strangers. They watched over him, as if they were the spirits of his departed brothers.

"So you found me all the way here in America." He smiled gently under his heavy mustache and whispered to the bird in his hand. "Keep me company a while, my darling."

The grackle nestled in the branches of the hide.

CHAPTER 16

The peace of the woods was isolating and threatening when Verrazzano got out of his car. He crunched across the gravel, past a parked Porsche and a Suffolk County police cruiser with the light bar still spinning red and blue. The steep roof of Doctor Amy Weston's house angled down above walls of dull, gray paneling. The neighboring properties were three hundred yards away through the dense beeches and pines.

Verrazzano knocked on the heavy stainless-steel door. He peered into the frosted sidelight. No one came. But the county cops must be about—and the driver of the Porsche. Whoever that was. The quiet suggested none of them were in a position to respond. They were either too scared or too dead.

He forced his breath to slow, to deepen. It all came down to breathing. In Colonel Wyatt's special unit, Verrazzano did months of training in survival tactics in the Amazon and East Africa, sniper school, hand-to-hand combat, and emergency medicine. He learned weapons electronics and systems hacking when he and Quanah posed as arms dealers, entrapping gang leaders and minor despots across the Middle East and the Caucasus. He spoke Arabic, Russian, and Serbian, as though he only wanted to talk to the real bad guys. But he survived because he knew how to stop his lungs from cutting off the oxygen to his brain. It preserved his lucidity, so he made good decisions that kept him alive. He drew his H&K and went around the back of the house.

The rear wall was glass, displaying the two stories like a doll-house. He twisted the handle on the kitchen door and found it locked. The lock was a plain pin tumbler. Verrazzano put his lips close and blew a quick, hard puff of air to clear the lock of dust and grit. He took out his keys and found his bump key. Each of the notches on the key was filed to the same length, except the one nearest the tip, which protruded an extra eighth of an inch. He pushed it halfway into the cylinder. He twisted the stainless steel doorknob.

He shoved the bump key all the way into the lock. The sharp movement sent all the pins jumping. For an instant they met the upper set of pins and the lock was aligned. He was already twisting the knob so the lock snapped open before the pins could drop again.

He opened the door slowly. "Anyone home? Federal agent."

The ground floor was a high-ceilinged, open-plan living room and kitchen. Verrazzano went quickly through the house. Two bedrooms, a mezzanine office with a drawing board and two desks, no basement. Every room was ransacked, strewn with clothes and papers. The beds and sofas were slashed, the stuffing ripped out.

A gunshot snapped in the trees.

Tension and purpose burned through Verrazzano. The dog-woods eddied in the breeze. The ground crackled with dropped leaves. But there was no sign of the shooter. Verrazzano jumped out through the kitchen door and threw himself into cover behind a row of plastic trash containers.

He fished inside a recycling bin until he came up with a plastic soda bottle that hadn't been fully emptied. He weighed it in his hand. It needed to fly against the breeze. Even half full, it wasn't heavy enough.

He unscrewed the cap, grabbed a handful of dirt, and fed it into the neck. He repeated the procedure three times until the bottle's weight would carry it through the wind. He replaced the cap and scanned the trees. He whirled the soda bottle above the lawn. It crashed into the branches.

The undergrowth crunched. The shooter was moving, taking the bait. The bottle rolled across the leaves.

Another snap of dry foliage, a hesitating footfall. Verrazzano squinted at the place where he heard the movement and shifted toward it. From his new position, he saw the two county cops on the other side of the recycling bins. *Dead,* he thought, and that was all the thought he had to spare for them. He heard another rustle in the trees.

He dashed across the grass and pitched himself onto his stomach in the undergrowth beneath the trees. His mouth was dry, his body responding to the fear his mind refused to acknowledge. Even without the dead cops, he'd have known his life was on the line. He could always tell, as though fatal intent glowed brighter, like heat on a thermal scope.

A flash of skin shone with sweat from behind a spray of branches—a well-prepared hide. Verrazzano waited to see the skin again. This time he got a clearer view through the membrane of sunlight refracting between the branches. A bald head and a thick mustache. The man who fled the Atlantic Beach shootout in the Toyota.

Verrazzano came onto his knees and raised his pistol. He opened his mouth to call for the man in the hide to surrender.

A gun barrel dug cold into the back of his neck.

"Stay where you are." A cultured voice, quivering with tension, unused to threats or guns. But the pistol was steady enough. "Don't move or I'll blow your head off."

The gun barrel twisted against Verrazzano's neck. A hand in the center of his back pushed him flat and patted the sides of his body. The guy was no pro. He even failed to notice that Verrazzano still held his Heckler & Koch.

"What's your game?" The gunman tried to make his patrician lockjaw sound tough.

"I'm a federal agent. My badge is in my back pocket."

The man reached for Verrazzano's wallet. "There's someone here, a gunman. He killed those cops. What're you doing in my home?"

"Are you Doctor Weston's husband?" Verrazzano turned his head. "Tyler Browne?"

The pistol jammed harder into his neck. "Don't move." The man opened the wallet. "You're the one." He let his gun hand drop to his side.

Verrazzano looked about for the bald shooter in the trees. He wanted to track him, but he needed to find out what Doctor Weston told her husband about her work in Syria, about the deadly thing she tried to pass on to Verrazzano. He dragged Browne deeper into the bushes, out of sight. "Your wife came to see me this morning. She said she had important information."

"Where is she?"

"I'm sorry to tell you this. Doctor Weston is dead."

Browne's face looked as though it had been drawn by a child, with patches of red on his cheeks and his head completely circular. He licked his lips like a man searching for an excuse he knew would convince no one. His chest convulsed. He pressed his fists to his temples. "Amy, my Amy."

"Mister Browne, there's someone out here. Someone dangerous. You know that. You have to let me do my job now."

"She was just so good." Browne stared into the trees, pale, beyond caring for his safety. "I told her this would happen."

"Sir, she was dying when she got to me. She'd been shot. Right now, I need to find out what she knew that made someone kill her. Help me."

Tears dropped off Browne's chin and spotted the dry dirt on Verrazzano's jacket.

The loud hard call of a grackle broke through the trees. *Chlaaack.* A bullet snapped a thin branch above Verrazzano's head. Browne tried to rise, but Verrazzano held him down. "Don't move," he whispered.

He dragged himself through the undergrowth, pressing his face to the earth until he came to a small outcrop of limestone. He inched up the rock. From the top he looked down six feet on a sniper's hide. He launched himself from the rock and dropped lightly, his pistol braced to shoot.

The dirt of the hide was smooth where a man had lain in wait. There was no one there. Verrazzano revolved slowly, legs bent, crouching low. He tried to identify the shooter's line of retreat.

But it wasn't a withdrawal. It was a trap.

The underbrush rustled behind him. He came about fast. His eyes were so wide the light breeze seemed to penetrate the sockets and freeze his brain.

The brush crackled again. To his left this time. He strained to locate the movement.

A dry twig snapped. Verrazzano advanced toward the sound.

"Stop." A single word from behind, spoken with the unhesitating force that had been missing from Browne's grip on the gun at Verrazzano's neck. The voice was metallic, scalding cold, like ice on a burn. A hand reached for Verrazzano's pistol and took it.

He started to turn. The voice simply grunted in a tone of command and disapproval. He stayed where he was.

The speaker's restraint confirmed Verrazzano was dealing with a man of special talents. Even a hitman could rarely resist a few scornful words to make of his victim something less than a human, to neutralize the guilt that every person experiences when he or she takes a life. To make it merely the disposal of a worthless thing.

Verrazzano heard long, calm respirations through the nose of the man with the gun. Soft and deep, like the combat breaths Verrazzano took when he needed to overcome adrenaline. *Why doesn't he kill me? What's he waiting for?*

A skittering rush through the brush ahead of him. *He's trying to figure out what that is. Figure out whether I'm alone. As soon as he does, I'm dead.*

A rock the size of an apple rolled out of the ferns. Kicked by an approaching foot. Or thrown as a diversion.

Verrazzano sensed a tremor of uncertainty in the air. He readied himself, watching for the instant of carelessness that came when even the most bloodless man was distracted.

The swish of a swinging length of wood, and the man behind him growled with sudden pain. Verrazzano started to move even before the impact. He felt what was coming. Thousands of hours of close-combat training attuned him to the paths of nearby limbs and weapons so that he could anticipate where and when the blows would land. He flipped about, took a long step, and grabbed for the gun.

But it was gone. The gunman's senses were alive to the same whispers of electricity impelling Verrazzano's muscles.

Tyler Browne tottered into the hide, leaning over the fallen branch he had used to strike the gunman.

The shooter reeled across the clearing. He had the heavy, rounded muscles of a laborer—none of the trim showiness of gym-made beef. He snarled beneath his big mustache and worked his jaw and blew hard. Verrazzano went at him.

The man opened his jacket. He reached inside and flicked his wrist. A black mass flashed toward Verrazzano. The wings of the grackle battered against his face, unexpected and nightmarish.

Verrazzano ducked away, his heart thundering with the beat of the grackle's wings. The bird flew into the trees.

The gunman made a hammer fist and struck Browne on the back of the head. The short man's lights went out. He slumped onto the leaves.

Verrazzano took a hook kick to his ribs. He slipped inside the blows and moved in close. His weight projecting upwards, he brought the flat of his hand under the gunman's chin and thrust.

The man grunted. "*Kuss ukhtak.*" *Fuck your sister's cunt.*

He's an Arab, Verrazzano thought. Even as he fought, he tried to figure the man's place in the unfolding scheme. Tishreen Park, Syria. Sarin gas. Doctor Weston's warning. *Move fast.*

The Arab's right hand came to Verrazzano's throat and closed over his windpipe. He drove his other fist over and over into his kidneys.

Verrazzano's jaw clamped shut. His temples throbbed. He strained against the man's grip on his neck. It got him nowhere. The Arab held firm.

He felt himself weakening, and he knew it was because of his agitation. He remembered what Colonel Wyatt told him back in the Georgia woods, bawling into his ear as a Special Ops guy from Montana strangled him in hand-to-hand training. *You can't fight him with the muscles in your face. Use the muscles that can beat him.*

He elbowed the Arab in the solar plexus and then hit his neck with his forearm. Then he struck above the ear with the outer edge of his hand.

The man grabbed Verrazzano's collar as he went down, pulling him close and butting Verrazzano's nose with his massive, shining forehead. He tossed him against the rock.

Verrazzano landed on top of Browne's body. He blinked to clear the jagged colors from his eyes. The unconscious man's pistol dug into Verrazzano's side. His vision returned. He wrenched the gun away from Browne's grip and lifted it.

The Arab threw himself into cover behind the big rock. The leaves crunched under his rolling body.

Verrazzano struggled to his feet. His legs gave out. Dark lightning flashed through his head, and he dropped onto his side, retching on the leaves. He scanned the trees and extended his gun arm. The Janissary was gone. But not far.

Verrazzano slapped Browne's cheek and hauled him up, his arm under Browne's shoulder. He struggled across the lawn. With every step, he expected to be shot down. Each footfall exploded under him as though he were treading out his own life.

They went into the house and crossed the big, exposed living room windows to the mezzanine office. Verrazzano dropped the Venetian blinds and peered through them toward the trees.

"Is he gone?" Browne asked. "Has he given up?"

"Guys like that never give up." He took out his cell phone and dialed Haddad.

Preparatory sketches for political cartoons filled the wall of the office. Verrazzano recognized the style. They featured obnoxious Republican elephants dumping their bulk onto a reedy Uncle Sam. One of them was unfinished on an angled drawing board. Around the room, files had been tipped out of the drawers. Papers sprayed across the floor. On his knees, Browne made little stacks in the mess as if he intended to tidy up.

Haddad came on the line. "Roula, I'm at Doctor Weston's house," Verrazzano said. "I'm with her husband."

"You got there in time." Haddad breathed out the sentence in relief.

"Getting out of here isn't going to be so easy. I need backup from Suffolk County PD. There's a suspect in the woods around the house. He's armed and very dangerous."

"Suffolk PD already sent a couple of guys to respond to the nine-one-one call."

"They didn't know what they were walking into. They're dead."

"Ah, shit. Okay. What else do you need?"

"I'm good for now. Get them here as soon as you can." He hung up and turned to Browne. "Is that your Porsche outside?"

Browne looked sick. The luxury car must have seemed like a worthless frivolity to a man who had lost the most valuable thing in his life. "I'd just parked it when I saw that guy going across the lawn. The guy you fought in the woods. He came out of the house, and I called nine-one-one as quickly as I could."

"Where'd you get the gun?"

"My wife bought it. I had it in the car. She told me to keep it close."

"So you took the gun and went into the woods after the guy?"

"I should've just driven away after the cops went round the back and I heard them get shot."

Browne shuffled the papers. Verrazzano watched him. The guy hadn't done too badly. He had eluded the Arab gunman.

"I thought, if I was lucky, I might get him to tell me who's been threatening my wife," Browne said. "Or I'd kill him."

"Pray you never get that lucky."

"I thought you were him."

Except for the lack of a mustache and bald head, Browne hadn't been far off. Verrazzano was grateful the cartoonist hadn't shot him right away. "Doctor Weston bought the gun yesterday? Because she believed she was in danger?"

"*I* believed she was in danger. *She* believed she was doing the right thing."

"What *was* she doing?"

"Getting herself fucking killed," he yelled.

"Mister Browne, please stay calm. I need your help." Verrazzano glanced over to the trees. Maybe he should go out there and track the guy. But he didn't want to leave Browne alone.

The husband's head rocked side to side. He slipped into a daze. "Oh, Amy, baby." He shuddered, then he seemed to firm himself from the ground up, until his shoulders and neck were straight. "She got back from Damascus yesterday. She went out to buy the gun then."

"Why did she bring her information to me? Why not one of her bosses at the UN?"

"Her friend Quanah Jones convinced her you were the one who'd work hardest to stop whatever it was." Browne's face was soft and quivering, but his eyes were like transplants from a harder man. "So why don't *you* tell me?"

Verrazzano stayed quiet, waiting for Browne to break his stare.

The toughness leeched out of Browne's eyes and grief replaced it. This wasn't a real hard man. No one could keep up that act. It was like being bullied by yourself.

"She showed me a document," Browne said. He glared at the files strewn around him, as though their disturbance represented a last degradation of his wife's spirit. He whispered her name again.

Verrazzano stared at the disordered papers. "Which document, Mister Browne?"

Browne pulled a USB drive out of his hip pocket. "She uncovered something in Syria. A man who'd been exposed to a nerve agent."

Verrazzano had a flash of hope. The Arab gunman hadn't found what he wanted. It must be on the drive. "A rebel fighter?"

Browne held out the USB drive. "An American."

Verrazzano took the small plastic drive. If the Arab was looking for this, he'd be back. *Where the hell is Suffolk PD?* he thought.

Haddad would've called for backup right away. He scanned the lawn and the fringe of trees again. "Can we read this USB now?"

"Whoever they are, they've stolen Amy's hard drive and her laptop. Mine too."

Verrazzano imagined the dead doctor, giving up only so much information to her anxious husband as she peeled away the layers of a horrifying conspiracy, menaced by the shadows in the woods as he was now. Waiting for her meeting with the ICE agent. Trusting him.

A yellow legal pad poked from a heap of photocopied scientific articles on the floor. Verrazzano slipped the pad out and brought it close to his face. "Mister Browne, watch the garden for me. If anything moves, shout out."

Browne went to the corner of the window.

Verrazzano flicked on the Anglepoise lamp and directed the beam across the surface of the legal pad.

"What're you doing?" Browne said.

"The top sheet has been torn away," Verrazzano murmured. "But the pen made an impression on the next page."

He fiddled with the lamp until the sidelight illuminated the grooves in the page. It read, "TomFrisch4464."

Verrazzano reached into his pocket, took out a palm-sized notebook, and copied down the words. He beckoned to Browne. "Is this Amy's handwriting on the legal pad?"

Browne leaned close. "That's Amy's writing. Who's Tom Frisch?"

He's my past, Verrazzano thought. *At least I hoped he was.*

"Frisch is a former Special Ops guy, Mister Browne."

"Special Ops? Amy wasn't into the military. And what're those numbers after the name?"

The silence outside heightened somehow. Verrazzano's senses lit up. It was the extreme vigilance of the moment before danger, too late to stop whatever was about to happen, but an instant of calculation—a split second that might keep him alive. He dived at Browne and took him to the floor.

The window blew in. Glass splintered around the office.

A hot sliver of metal fizzed on Verrazzano's temple—shrapnel from the wire bundled around the charge inside a grenade. His brain seemed to descend through his neck and down his spine.

Into darkness.

CHAPTER 17

His eyes stung and blurred when he came around. His brain busted against his skull in all directions. A hand reached down and ripped his shirt open. Verrazzano flailed to defend himself, blind and drowsy. A needle drove into his shoulder. The hand held him firm as the hypodermic went down. Then the grip loosened.

Verrazzano scrambled backward. Who was this? What had this person put in him? He wiped at his eyes with his shirt.

"Don't do that." Browne's voice was unnaturally calm. He sat on the floor, cross-legged and still. "Your clothes are saturated with nerve agent. You'd better strip. Take some of my clothes instead. Wash your eyes." He rolled a bottle of mineral water over the pine boards.

Verrazzano poured the water into his eyes. His vision cleared.

A spent autoinjector syringe lay beside Browne. "After he blew in the window, he tossed in another grenade to make sure. But it wasn't a regular grenade." Thin mucus glistered from his nostrils and ran past his mouth. He wrapped his arms around his chest, wincing. "I started to feel my lungs seizing up. I know enough about Amy's field of expertise to understand that this was a nerve agent."

Verrazzano gaped at the injector pen. "Atropine?"

"To block the nerve agent from hitting the muscle receptors. Without it you'd be dead within a matter of minutes."

"Christ." Verrazzano lumbered to his feet.

Browne held up the orange syringe. "This stuff gets its name from Atropos, the Greek goddess who cut the thread of life for those fated to die."

"Your wife kept a supply of atropine here?"

"No." Browne laid the injector softly before him. "She only left one."

Verrazzano froze. "And you gave it to me?"

"You have to find these bastards. It's up to you." Browne rolled suddenly onto his side, retching.

"She must have another dose here." Verrazzano went to him. "You're going to be okay. Stay with me."

"Don't touch me," Browne wheezed. "I'll be dead in the time it takes you to go upstairs and put on uncontaminated clothing."

"I'm not leaving you."

"I made a calculation. If I saved myself, I'd be able to draw some fucking cartoons about chemical warfare for the newspapers. Big deal. *You* can actually change things. Just go do it. Find these people. Find out why they killed Amy."

"I'm going to get you out of here."

"Your friend Quanah told Amy to come to you because you'd do anything to complete your mission. So will I. Even if I have to die for it, I'm going to help you finish what Amy started. That's why I gave *you* the atropine instead of taking it myself." Browne convulsed, bucking and twisting.

Verrazzano leapt down the stairs and wrenched open the freezer. He tossed the contents onto the kitchen floor. Peas, pizza, ice cubes. There had to be another dose of atropine in there. Chicken Kiev, meatballs, Chunky Monkey.

He heard Browne's breath stutter and rasp, fighting the paralysis of his lungs.

He ransacked the fridge. Milk, olives, cheese. *I won't let him die.* He dragged everything onto the linoleum. Eggs, juice, lettuce.

No atropine.

The office went silent. Browne was dead. Verrazzano doubled over like a runner at the end of a race. A race he had lost. He still had some running in him—he just had to have.

He found a pair of scissors in a kitchen drawer and cut away his T-shirt, so that he wouldn't have to lift the contaminated cloth over his face. He stripped off his other clothing. He took the USB drive from his pocket and held it tight in his palm.

He ran up the stairs, panting and sweating hard. He jumped into the shower, rinsing his eyes in the stream of water. When it got hot, he soaped and scalded his body.

He was once just as deadly as the nerve agent that killed Browne. He changed his life, but he didn't know yet if he had changed *himself.* If some new Colonel Wyatt came and ordered him to do something dreadful, maybe he'd carry out the orders and make excuses for himself later. Some people didn't get a second chance, like Tyler Browne. Others didn't deserve one, but they got them anyway. He let the water fill his mouth and splash across his chest.

He rushed into the bedroom. From Browne's closet, he grabbed underwear, jeans, socks, shoes, and a T-shirt. He pulled on the clothes and slipped the USB drive into his pocket.

He went to the front door. A green pea coat hung on the rack. He was cold to the core of his torso, scarred by the nerve agent even as the antidote fought it off. He slipped the coat over his shoulders.

An engine started up outside the house.

Verrazzano yanked the front door open.

A silver Toyota passed the bottom of the drive. The bald, mustachioed Arab Verrazzano had fought in the trees swung the car toward the river road. *He figures the house didn't contain what he was looking for,* Verrazzano thought, *and anyhow, he'll have another crack at me soon enough. Unless I get to him first.*

He ran to his Dodge. He yanked at the driver's door and cursed. His keys were inside the house with his discarded clothing. He hammered the roof with frustration as the Toyota accelerated away. He spun about to go back for the keys.

Stomping over the gravel drive, he shoved his fists into the pockets of the pea coat. His fist brushed against a plastic key fob. The locks of the Porsche snapped open.

The cockpit of the German sports car was all supple dark leather and bright gadgets like a tiny bachelor pad. The acceleration of the V8 pinned Verrazzano to his seat as he flashed past the russet leaves and silvery trunks of the fall woods. He pushed the car hard as the road curved along the narrow Nissequogue River. A long, straight section opened up ahead of him. Empty. He thumped the heel of his hand against the steering wheel. The Toyota had vanished.

His lungs constricted like the slow kill of a boa, a symptom of exposure to the nerve agent. But the atropine was working. He wasn't dead. The pain would go away. The danger wouldn't. He needed to focus on the case. If he couldn't track the Arab in the Toyota, he at least had to get Doctor Weston's USB drive to the ICE field office. Browne's phone was in the dashboard phone dock. He dialed Haddad.

"It's Dom."

"What've you got?" Her voice was hushed. The cubicles in the field office didn't encourage excitable talk.

"Check something for me. Tom-Frisch-four-four-six-four. One word, no spaces, upper case T Tango, F Foxtrot. Frisch ending with Sierra-Charlie-Hotel. Roger that?"

"Roger."

"Check if it's a Skype address or some other online identifier."

"I'm on it. Is Doctor Weston's husband with you?"

"He's dead. Killed with some kind of nerve agent. I was exposed to it—"

"Dom, oh my God."

"Weston's husband gave me a shot of atropine. I'll survive. Someone took away computer equipment, maybe documents from Doctor Weston's house. He killed her husband, tried to kill me. Probably the same guy killed the Suffolk County cops."

"Did you see who it was?"

"Middle Eastern male. He cursed in Arabic."

"Don't tell me what he said. I'll blush, *habibi*."

"Hey, I'm a gentleman. I'll do a full description of the guy when I get to you." Verrazzano gagged and coughed. He blinked against the stark sun off the pavement as he pulled onto the Long Island Expressway.

"Dom, are you sure you're okay?"

The dial on the dashboard clock flashed one PM. *Move fast,* Doctor Weston had said. *Got a few days.* Verrazzano wished he had an exact deadline. He turned away from the clock. He'd know soon enough how little time he had.

"I'm fine." He hung up.

He tried to close his mind to the chaotic possibilities and dangers ahead of him. He focused on driving, on breathing. On simply being.

Colonel Wyatt once found Verrazzano meditating like this. "You're trying to follow your breath to calm yourself?" Wyatt crowed. "Try *not* breathing. You want peace and tranquility? You'll find it when you're dead. Being alive is all about pain and suffering."

"That's exactly what the Buddha said."

"Then we're doing holy work, you and I. We deal in pain and suffering."

Not any more, Verrazzano told himself. He cut around a semitrailer in the slow lane and came up behind an Isuzu truck. On the Porsche's dash, Browne's cell phone trilled. The screen showed a call on Silent Circle. Verrazzano wondered if Browne downloaded the privacy app to avoid unwanted attention from people who disliked his political cartoons. He took the call.

A deep bass voice vibrated through the speakers. "I did not consider the possibility that you would survive." An Arab accent. The man who fought him in the woods behind Browne's house. The man who *hadn't* found the USB drive that was now in Verrazzano's pocket.

"That was a failure of imagination on your part," Verrazzano said.

A breathless chuckle. A gap in the traffic. Verrazzano spun the wheel and rounded the Isuzu truck.

"If I get another chance to kill you," the Arab said, "I will not fail again."

Verrazzano hit the gas. "If."

The Arab hung up. The Porsche shot toward the city.

CHAPTER 18

The Molnir Partners reception area was done out with faux marble columns and walnut panels. The leather of the claret wing chair by the elevator was as pristine as the sand on a Seychelles beach. Anyone who ever came into that office was tough enough to stand.

Anyone but Chavez.

He ran his wheelchair across the jade wreaths inset in the white Carrara floor. The receptionist was a sixty-year-old woman with wide shoulder pads in her jacket, a peroxide perm, and sharp, hazel eyes. She reached out for a shake with a hand the color and texture of drying tobacco.

"I'm Zissel. Kyle told me you'd be coming. Welcome aboard, Marty. Go straight to the end. You can't miss it. It's the office with the dumbass inside."

She buzzed the security door. "Hey," she barked.

Chavez halted.

"You've got some schmutz on your lapel, hon."

He brushed away a spray of confectioner's sugar that had dropped from the pastry he shared with Adela at lunch. His wife would like a blousy, cranky old girl like Zissel.

Massie's office looked along Forty-Fourth Street to the United Nations building a block away. He was stretched out on the low heating cabinet by the window with his hands folded on his stomach, like the funerary statue on the tomb of a dead knight in a

European cathedral. Chavez wondered if his friend rested in that spot because he liked it or because there were no chairs in the room.

Massie sprang off the heating cabinet and noticed Chavez's examination of the Spartan room. "I can't get used to comfort, man. I guess I tried to turn this place into a bivouac, even though it's an office in Manhattan."

He beckoned Chavez to the window. He knelt beside the wheelchair and pointed along the block to the UN tower. "They're talking about war in there this week, man. War in Syria. War in Iraq. In Ukraine. Israel, South fucking Sudan. Shit, why *are* people so damned surprised every time a war starts up? It's more common than a no-hitter in the major leagues. All those UN bastards know to do is talk, man. You and me, we got shit to accomplish."

He pulled a laptop from the desk drawer and spun it toward the computer expert on the desktop. "Take me down the street." He nodded toward the UN tower and winked.

Chavez's last job had been to defend the Army against hackers. But he could just as easily wear a black hat and bust into the system of a big organization. *So that's the mission*, he thought. *Well, did you expect to be designing a sales page for the Molnir website?* A job was a job, and he always got his done. "Where'd you get this laptop?"

"Don't worry. It's not traceable. And it's going in the river tonight." Massie squared up to him. "I want to ask you a question before we take this any further."

"Okay, man."

"The job is solid. The UN contract, I mean. But to *get* the job, we're going to do something with implications. Maybe legal consequences."

Chavez got it. To bid on a UN contract, Molnir would want to know that its bid was better than the competition. To *know* it, not just to hope. That meant illegal access to the UN system. He mustn't show reluctance or scruples. Special Forces men didn't waste time asking you to do something a second time.

"Yeah, Kyle. I got you."

"I played by the rules all my life. Rough, but by the rules. You did, too, man. But we came home and got treated like shit."

"I hear you."

"We're not going to hurt anybody. We're not going to steal." Massie watched the UN tower as though he were addressing it directly. "We're taking back our dignity."

Chavez set his hands on the keyboard of the laptop. "You want to see the rival bids for the UN security contract?"

"Not right now. I don't want the FBI assholes dragging us away in handcuffs."

"I can do it securely."

"Easy, tiger. I want you to figure out exactly how we're going to get into their system. Then, on Wednesday, you and I will pay a visit to the great center of international diplomacy."

"We're going to hack into their computers from *inside* the UN? That's risky, man."

"Go ahead and check their systems to make sure it's possible. See if you need any specific equipment when we go in."

"If we get caught in there, Kyle, my wife could lose her job."

"But if we *don't* get caught, Adela can *quit* her job. We're going to be set up for life. See, we get a percentage, not a salary. The contract's worth fifty million bucks, give or take. You get two percent."

"A million bucks?"

"A million a year. Anyhow, we ain't going to get caught. Taliban couldn't catch me. Neither could al-Qaeda. No way I'm going to be taken by a bunch of four-eyed paper pushers with graduate degrees in international relations. Let's work."

Chavez called up the site where the bids were to be submitted for the security contract. "This is going to be simple enough."

"How do we get in?"

"Cross-site scripting. Most web frameworks don't protect against it." His voice slowed as he watched the browser react to his touch at the keyboard. "I can insert data by JavaScript, and it won't be filtered."

"They don't know to guard against that?"

"I guess they decided not to bother. It's pretty uncommon. This site relies on HTML encoding to protect it. But that doesn't catch data that's output inside of a script tag."

"Whatever. It's vulnerable, right?"

"We can get into the website. We can read the submissions other companies have made for the security contract. We can be sure that our bid beats everyone else's."

"You're the man."

Chavez toggled his heavy wheelchair around to face Massie. "We're just going to roll into the UN and do this?"

"Not exactly. That's your responsibility too."

"I don't get it."

"Buy your wife some roses and get her some chocolates or whatever the fuck she likes best. I want you to make her real sweet."

CHAPTER 19

Verrazzano rumbled down the RFK Bridge to Manhattan, the skyline dipping behind the redbrick projects of Harlem. When he joined the ICE field office in New York, he had come home to the city where he was born. For two decades he tried to convince himself he didn't miss the place. But he was a New Yorker. He pined for the city even as he walked down Broadway. He couldn't get enough of it. He wanted to be everywhere at once, just as New York was every city all in one miraculous space. No crisis or threat could take that feeling from him. New York wasn't scared of anything, and Verrazzano relished his part in backing up the city's magnificent balls. Driving into Manhattan reassured him. Sometimes people felt betrayed by the city. But Verrazzano knew it had his back.

On the dashboard dock, the cell phone connected to Damascus. A bass voice resounded out of the electronic interference on the line. "This is Quanah Jones."

A delivery truck slipped lanes and came within a foot of the Porsche. Verrazzano hit the brakes and jerked the wheel to the right. The looping off-ramp seemed narrower than ever before, as though the city had squeezed an extra column of traffic onto it.

"It's Dom," he said through his teeth.

"Yeah." Just one word. From a man who didn't care if people liked him.

"Doctor Amy Weston is dead."

Myriad voices on other satellite connections ghosted through the space in the air. Some of them may even have been voices from the past, when Quanah was Verrazzano's partner in Colonel Wyatt's special unit—assassinating people Wyatt claimed would carry out a new 9/11. Until Quanah ran and Wyatt sent Verrazzano to kill him. All those old voices spoke now too. Quanah said only, "Yeah?"

"Who knew she was coming to me?" Verrazzano pulled up at the light on 125th Street, heading crosstown.

"You and me. And whoever killed her."

"How did *they* find out?"

"You think I had something to do with her death, Special Agent?"

Verrazzano accelerated along the street, past the projects and the barred-in school buildings of Harlem. "No, I don't think that."

Doctor Amy Weston trusted Quanah. Verrazzano had trusted his word, too, when it meant the absolute destruction of who he thought he was. He needed someone dependable in Damascus, and there was no ICE agent on the scene. "I'm going to send you map coordinates for a location in Tishreen Park. Doctor Weston gave them to me as she died. I don't have any other specifics. I need you to check the place out. Can you do that? Tell me what you find there?"

"Will do." The voice was unemotional, robotic.

"Quanah, the doctor isn't the only one who died today. I don't know what this is all about yet, but it's dangerous. Be careful."

"I'm reaching into the drawer where I keep my Tough Motherfucker Face."

Verrazzano smirked. Quanah had made a joke. They both knew he kept that face in his pocket.

The Porsche crossed Broadway and sped onto the West Side Highway. Quanah's narrowed eyes and strong jaw seemed to float before Verrazzano, as he weaved through the cars heading south along the twisting Hudson bank of Manhattan. Then he was back in Beirut, on the Corniche. The water was the Mediterranean, and he was driving Quanah toward an empty lot in Karantina to kill

him. That was when Quanah told him the real story of Maryam
Ghattas. Told him Wyatt wanted her killed because she headed a
parliamentary committee that was about to accuse the Shia militia
Hezbollah of murdering the Lebanese prime minister. The prime
minister had negotiated a secret peace deal with Israel and was
about to sign it when he was killed. Hezbollah figured peace would
be bad for business, and so would a public report by a respected
lawmaker accusing them of assassinating a popular prime minister. So they paid Wyatt to rub her out. Wyatt assigned the job to
Quanah, who refused and went underground. It could've all been
a pack of lies designed to save Quanah's skin, but Verrazzano had
heard them with the instant clarity that confirmed they were not.

In the Porsche, Verrazzano spoke into the clamor of static on
the mobile line. "When we were in Beirut, Quanah—"

"I sure do appreciate that you didn't kill me like Wyatt told
you to."

"There's something else."

"You killed Maryam Ghattas. I know that, Dom. She died the
day after I told Wyatt I wouldn't do it. I didn't have to be chief
of intelligence to figure it out. I'm sorry about it, Dom, because
she was a good lady. She'd have told everyone the truth about the
assassination of the prime minister. But it couldn't have saved
the peace deal. Not once Prime Minister Karami died. The chance
for peace died with him. That's the bottom line."

The bottom line. The truth. There was always time for that.
Verrazzano gripped the wheel hard. "It was me. I was the one who
killed Karami."

Silence from Quanah. The line filled with bursts of squealing
feedback, as if the confession were too much for the digital channels to bear.

"Wyatt told me it was policy. From DC. The State Department and the Pentagon wanted the prime minister dead," Verrazzano said.

"Don't make excuses for yourself. None of the shit Wyatt pulled
was policy, Dom. None of the shit *we* did for him was policy."

"I know it. I know it now."

"How many wars have they had between Lebanon and Israel since then? Maybe if there'd been peace with Lebanon, the Israelis could've done a deal with Syria too. There'd have been no fucking civil war. No Islamic State. No four million refugees. None of that shit. How many people died over there because you just went off and did what Colonel fucking Wyatt told you to do? Without asking questions?"

"More than I'll ever know."

"You going to tell me you die right along with them every time or some shit like that?"

Verrazzano slowed for the light.

"Aw, fuck it. I'll get you what you need from here, Dom." Quanah spat his words out with disgust. "But don't ever let me hear your damned voice again." He hung up.

Verrazzano swung Tyler Browne's Porsche off the West Side Highway and drove up the ramp into the parking garage at the corner. He cut the engine and sat still. His hands wouldn't come away from the wheel. In the mirror he could see down the ramp to the river. There were times he'd thought of dropping quietly under the water forever, but now he climbed out of the low seat. He took the garage elevator up to the ICE field office.

CHAPTER 20

The 7 train ground along the track behind the apartment. Chavez heard his wife's rolling footsteps in the corridor. Adela entered, pushed the door shut with her foot, and put a brown paper shopping bag on the table. She trotted across the carpet with her arms out wide. "There's my sexy computer expert." She hugged him.

He gripped her shoulders, driving his fingertips into her flesh. *One million dollars*, he thought. *And one million ways it could all go wrong.*

"I bought some wine to celebrate your new job, baby. Ricky texted me. He's gone to shoot hoops with the guys." She pushed herself against his belly and tried to give their kiss some tongue. "You've got me all to yourself."

His meeting with Massie had sapped the sexual excitement he felt at lunch. The prospect of breaking the law made him too nervous to relax into love. He pulled away.

"It's okay if you don't feel like it," she said.

"We'll see, baby. It's been a long time. I guess I'm kind of nervous. Come sit down."

She perched on the sofa and reached out to hold his hands. Reluctantly, he gave her a couple of fingers to grab onto.

"You really got me going at lunchtime. You're so damned sexy," he said.

She grinned and murmured as she leaned down and brushed her lips across his neck.

"You trust me, baby?"

"Of course I do, Marty. Why do you even ask that?" She made her face playfully disapproving. "You going to do something bad?"

He looked away.

"Marty?" She saw that her joke had hit a raw nerve. "Baby?"

"No, baby, nothing bad. Am I a bad guy?"

"Nuh-uh."

"Then don't you worry about your man doing anything wrong. I'd never put what we have at risk. Not for anything. You know that, right?"

"I know it."

"I wouldn't give up what we have now, even if you told me I could have my legs back."

"Baby, don't say that."

"I just want you to know that it's the most important thing in the world to me. You and Ricky. Our home, our family. Everything I do is to protect it. I would kill to protect it." He smiled. "I would eat your mother's *ropa vieja* to protect it, and that woman cannot cook, may God bless her."

"Don't be mean to my Mamma."

"It's true, though." He laughed. "She cooks some seriously bad shit."

"It's true, *papi*. Yes, it's true."

They kissed. He felt his power over her and it made him enjoy the physical contact where at first he had been hesitant. But he couldn't let go of what he had on his mind. He needed to get her to agree to his plan before he took her to bed.

"I've got to have your help with the new job." He heard the resentment and pain in his voice. She pulled back. The lines either side of her eyes contracted. She caught it too.

"We're going to do something, Kyle and me." His voice was firm. He was taking back the pride he lost. He had refused no sacrifice, and he was owed. By everyone.

Except her.

"I've got to get into the UN building. But no one can know that I'm there."

She let go of his hand. Her cheeks were usually so animated, so fleshy and alive. She looked suddenly like a Botoxed Vegas crooner.

"If you help me inside, I can compare the other bids and make sure we beat them. Then Kyle and me get the job for sure. I'll take the train to work every morning with you."

"That'd be nice, baby." She sounded strangled, on edge.

"I can't go into the UN building as a regular tourist, because I'd have to show identification. Right?"

"That's right." Just a whisper.

"Any breach in the computer system could potentially be linked to me, because of my background in the field. My connection to Molnir would come up, and the whole deal would be shot."

"I guess."

"You've got to get me a visitor's ticket without recording an ID. You can do that, can't you, baby?"

She was nodding her assent, but it looked to Chavez like a case of palsy.

"You're going to help me through the metal detector too," he said.

Her eyes snapped to him in shock. "What're you going to do, Marty?"

"I'm not going to carry a weapon." He couldn't help reacting angrily to her suspicion, her lack of trust. But he needed to be persuasive. "You believe me, baby, yeah?"

"Sure, yeah. I do."

"I've got to bring some computer equipment through the metal detector. My chair is all plastic compounds, so it doesn't set off the alarm. But I'm going to hide the computer hardware in the chair. That'll trigger the alarm. I don't want to take out the hardware to be examined. Because then any network infiltration that's detected is going to get tied to me eventually, see? So you've got to give me the override key."

Her hand went automatically to her waist. "Baby, that has to stay on my belt the whole time."

He reached under her belly. A black disc the size of a quarter was hooked onto her belt by a tiny carabiner. He unfastened the clip, his face close to hers. He listened to her breath, felt her stillness and anticipation. He was reminded of the first time he had put his hand into her pants when they were sixteen.

But she had wanted him to do that.

He yanked on the clip and the disc came away. "See, it's not a *part* of you. You're just the same with it off."

She lowered her head.

"I'm going to explain to you how we'll do it, Adela. You're listening to me?"

She rocked her head, crying silently.

He breathed out hard in exasperation. "Without this contract, I don't have a job, Adela. Are you hearing me? *Are you hearing me?*"

"Yes, baby."

Her stillness smothered his anger. He'd have felt less blameworthy if she'd argued with him. His frustration and fear welled up. Some days it made him suicidal. Now, instead of ending his life, he was just going to ruin what was left of it. A tear dropped to his cheek.

She saw it and shook her head. "You're more man than anyone I know, baby." She cradled his face between her gentle hands and caught his tears. She had read him. She knew this wasn't about money.

CHAPTER 21

The forensics tech drew a syringe of Verrazzano's blood, squinting through thick glasses to check that he had fifteen milliliters. He wrote the agent's name along the tube with a black marker. "Why don't you spell it like the bridge?" He stowed the test tube in a desktop refrigerator.

"I do."

The tech bent over Verrazzano's ID. "You've got *two* Zs here."

"Yeah, like the Verrazzano Bridge in Rhode Island."

"Smartass. I meant the other bridge." With plastic tweezers, he yanked a hair from Verrazzano's scalp.

"The one in Maryland?"

"Jeez, how many bridges got named for that guy?" The tech slipped the hair into a test tube and sealed it. "Do you get to cross without paying the toll? Because of your name?"

"I never crossed it."

"You're kidding."

From the window of the lab, Verrazzano glanced down the Hudson. Named for the Florentine who was the first European to explore the bay back in 1524 and misspelled because some bureaucrat in the sixties thought it looked too Italian with a double *Z*, the Verrazano-Narrows Bridge arced over the water between Brooklyn and Staten Island. "I'll cross it when they correct the spelling."

He picked up the thin file Haddad gave him on his way back to the field office. She had downloaded the footage from the surveillance camera on the patrol car of the cops who died at Doctor

Weston's house. The video showed a heavy Arab whose features matched the databased biometric details of an assassin called the Janissary.

"We'll test blood and urine first." The tech's voice was deep, orotund, and breathless, somewhere between a torch singer and Orson Welles.

"Will that tell you if it was a nerve agent?"

"It'll tell us exactly which nerve agent it was. They all have distinctive components."

The Janissary's real name wasn't known. The file connected him to assassinations in Lebanon, Iraq, Turkey, and the Gulf states. He might be an agent of Syrian intelligence. Other sources said the Janissary hated the Syrian government so profoundly that he appeared to have some deep personal grudge. Was the Janissary working for Syria now? The weapons at the house in Atlantic Beach had been in the hands of the government. But those were Americans transporting them, not Syrians. And if the Janissary had something against the Damascus regime, what was his role?

"How long will the results take?" he said.

"You'll get them this evening. Are you experiencing shortness of breath?" The technician certainly was. He gave off a sulfurous stink like a steel foundry from his Russian cigarettes.

Verrazzano tried to answer in the negative but wheezed instead.

"Okay, so that's a check," the tech said.

Verrazzano coughed.

"You just answered my next question too." The tech removed his surgical mask.

"I always cough. I drink too much coffee. It makes my throat dry." Verrazzano stared at a grainy photo of the Janissary. It was from a hotel surveillance camera in Dubai. The Janissary took out a South African arms smuggler and an unlucky Romanian hooker who happened to be in the guy's room. He strangled them with a short length of plastic cord. CIA sources reckoned the hit was for a rival arms trader. But they didn't really know.

"The one dose of atropine should be enough," the tech said. "Your symptoms look to me like aftereffects that'll work themselves out if you get some rest. But you need to see a physician. You should have an EKG to check heart function and blood pressure." He handed Verrazzano an orange syringe. "Recognize this?"

"I don't need it."

The tech pushed the autoinjector into Verrazzano's pocket. "If you start twitching or losing consciousness or have real difficulty breathing, zap it into your arm fast. It administers a single dose. Don't waste any time."

"How about a spare? So I don't have to decide between saving myself or saving a friend."

"Everyone saves themselves."

"Not everyone." Verrazzano thought of Browne calmly waiting for his end.

The tech pulled off his latex gloves. "I guess it depends who else you have to live for. I'm going outside for a cigarette."

Haddad opened the door of the lab. "Hey, Dom. How'd the tests go?"

"I'll find out tonight. If I'm still alive."

"Just in case you're about to die, hurry up and come see what I found."

He weaved through the tall cubicles on the Homeland Security floor behind her. She sat at her desk, and he leaned over the desk beside her. She tapped an arrow key to activate the blank screen. A scanned page, typed with signatures at the bottom, opened up. It started with the words "Sworn before me, Amy Carla Weston, MD." The text continued in the first person.

Verrazzano leaned close. "Is this supposed to be an affidavit?"

"It's the only document on the key disc you brought back from Doctor Weston's place." Haddad scrolled down. "It's dated last week and sworn by a guy named Daryl Underwood. We've got ourselves another veteran."

"Where'd he serve?"

"Six tours in Afghanistan."

Six tours. Jesus, what these guys went through. "Afghanistan? Like Lee Hill, the man who killed Doctor Weston." Verrazzano squinted at the screen.

"Underwood claims to have been exposed to a chemical agent."

Verrazzano sniffed. His nose was still irritated from his exposure to the nerve gas. "How?"

"It's right here." Haddad paged down. "He's in charge of a store of weaponized nerve agent in Damascus. I guess this is what Doctor Weston was intending to tell you."

"Looks like it."

"Why didn't she just get this information to the UN security people while she was still in Damascus? Why come to you?"

"The UN security guy in Damascus figured we'd work quicker than official UN channels. If you think ICE is a slow-moving bureaucracy, you've never seen how the UN works." He dropped into a chair. "Right now we have to find this guy Underwood and track the nerve agent. It's got to be connected to the danger Doctor Weston mentioned before she died."

"You might have to go to Syria if the nerve agent is really there."

"If it is, it's a contravention of the deal Syria made with the United Nations to give up all its weapons of mass destruction."

"Not exactly. According to Daryl Underwood's testimony here, the nerve agent doesn't belong to the Syrian government."

Verrazzano rose out of his slouch. "Then who?"

"Daryl Underwood's employer."

"Which is?"

"Same company Lee Hill worked for. Molnir Partners."

Verrazzano thought of the name and number he lifted from Doctor Weston's legal pad. The unstoppable Special Forces guy who ghosted through war zones snuffing out the targets Wyatt gave him. "Who runs Molnir?"

He knew the answer before Haddad spoke it. "Tom Frisch."

It had been a long time. But the adrenaline rippled through him as though it were happening now. As though he were bursting into Wyatt's headquarters in Beirut, seething with rage, feeling used after Quanah told him the truth about Maryam Ghattas. After Verrazzano realized that his assassination of the Lebanese prime minister had been intended to destroy the peace deal with

Israel. He found no one there except Frisch, smug with all the secret knowledge the officer class denied to men like Sergeant Major Verrazzano.

Frisch would know things now that Verrazzano still couldn't even guess at. He thought of the Arab in the file. The Janissary. He knew his history, remembered the Janissaries, the young boys kidnapped into slavery and trained as mercenaries. It could've been him too. Trained to fight so well he'd forgotten that he didn't own his own future, his own life. Until the enormity of what he had done reminded him that the future was his.

Now it was his turn to remind Tom Frisch.

CHAPTER 22

The receptionist studied Verrazzano like a breeder assessing a stallion on a stud farm. She fondled a pack of Winstons as he crossed the marble floor of the Molnir lobby.

"I get off in a half hour." Her voice was fifty-a-day rough. Her inhalations sounded like a vacuum cleaner.

Verrazzano hoped she was joking. "I'm on a case. I'll be working late. But if the cigarettes don't kill you by the weekend, let's do brunch." He gave her his card.

"With an incentive like that, I'll quit." She tossed the Winstons over her shoulder. "What's the case?"

"Daryl Underwood."

"When you find him, tell him to call his girlfriend." She poked at her chest. "You want to see Tom?" She read his card. "Verrazzano, like the bridge?"

"No, like the explorer who was eaten by cannibals on Guadeloupe."

"I'm kind of a man-eater myself." She dialed and spoke into the phone. "A special agent from ICE to see you about Daryl. Did you kill him, Tom? Because this guy looks like he's here to take you downtown."

Verrazzano wondered if the tension showed through the joking mask he had tried to wear. It didn't matter. Frisch knew what he looked like when he was at his worst. But the knowledge went both ways.

"I'll send him in, Tom," the receptionist said. "Do me a favor—take him prisoner and make him my sex slave."

She pressed the button for the security door. "Through that way. Pick me up Sunday at eleven for brunch. I'm a cheap date. I'll do anything after two drinks."

"Then the mimosas are on me."

She laughed so hard, the bag on the vacuum cleaner seemed to burst.

Tom Frisch waited at the end of the corridor. At least this time, Verrazzano had come looking for him. The last time they met, he had been after Wyatt, and the colonel had left Frisch to tell his hitman that the unit was disbanded. Back then Frisch was wearing the heavy beard he used to go undercover everywhere from Morocco to Afghanistan. In the office suite, he was clean-shaven, the corridor's entire length was a cloud of his cologne, and his shirt and tie looked to be worth a month's paycheck for an ICE agent.

Verrazzano walked toward him as the receptionist gagged and hacked with laughter.

"Zissel hit on you?" Frisch's voice was warm and soft. Same as it had been when he told Verrazzano that his suspicion was true—that Wyatt's unit was no more than a gang. That everything he'd done to protect the United States had really been for the benefit of terrorist militias, Russian gangsters, and the colonel's Cayman Islands bank account.

Verrazzano said nothing. He ignored the hand Frisch held out to him.

"Zissel gives me no bullshit," Frisch said. "That's what I want. From everyone."

"Fine. I'm fresh out of bullshit today."

Verrazzano followed Frisch into a corner office decorated like the library of a London gentlemen's club. Frisch took a seat before a tall drinks cabinet. Expensive scotch glimmered in the crystal decanters. Propped against the side of the desk was the giveaway that this office didn't belong to a gentleman—a black bag identical to one Verrazzano had carried around Europe and the Middle

East. It was specially designed by the Tula Arsenal, south of Moscow, to hold its 9 mm sniper rifle. The gun's Russian name was *Vintorez. Thread cutter.*

Verrazzano didn't sit. "Your guy Underwood. I have a document dictated by him last week in Syria."

Frisch spun his chair to the drinks cabinet, reached out two tumblers, and poured a measure into each. He slid one across the desk to Verrazzano and took a swig of his own. Verrazzano left the glass where it was.

"I don't get it," Frisch said.

"I don't like whiskey."

"Syria. I don't get why Daryl Underwood was in Syria. I brought all my best guys back here to New York a couple months ago. We're bidding on a new UN security contract. If we get it, it'll be our first really big score. The prep work is intensive. Daryl was on his way back here for that project when we lost contact with him."

"Back from Syria?"

Frisch turned his glass around slowly on the leather desktop. "Okay, yeah, we've been conducting logistical ops there since last year."

"For whom?"

"For *whom?* That's good grammar. You been taking classes, Sergeant Major Verrazzano?"

"Answer, please." He didn't say *sir.*

"That's classified."

"You mean it's illegal."

"You're going to lecture me about legality? I know your background better than you do. I was Wyatt's scout in the Special Forces. I picked you out and turned him onto you in the first place."

"So it's all your fault."

"Ain't nobody's fault but your own, Verrazzano." He sipped the whiskey. "You did shit for Wyatt he wouldn't even have asked *me* to do, and he used to call me his Mad Dog. You know what he calls you?"

"Let's get back to Syria."

"Lethal Lapdog."

"There are covert US weapons shipments to non-jihadi rebel groups in Syria. It's no big secret. That's you doing that?"

Frisch smirked. "Some."

"You and Wyatt?"

"I don't know what the fuck Wyatt is doing now, and if I did, I would be sure to do exactly the opposite. That way I'll stay out of jail and I won't get whacked by some guy from South Sudan or any other place because he thinks I caused a revolution in his bumfuck country or a genocide against his motherfucking tribe."

"If it's not Wyatt, you're playing some other connection? Maybe it's something real, something legal-illegal from the Pentagon."

Frisch refilled his glass. "Washington wants the right local militia in Syria to come out on top, whichever the fuck that one is today. Just so long as the Islamic State doesn't get the upper hand, right? Until someone at Foggy Bottom decides maybe *they're* not as bad as the next bunch of assholes." He grinned. "I guess that's when they'll call Wyatt back in from the cold. Anyhow, Underwood was in country a while, but mostly I keep him here with me. He's good with budgets and personnel. I mean, don't get me wrong, the guy could snap your neck. But he kind of prefers to fire people."

"Where does Underwood live?"

"Zissel can give you the exact address. I believe his place is up the Hudson valley. Beacon, or somewhere around there."

"Underwood was exposed to a nerve agent in Syria."

The grin was gone. "Is he okay?"

"The nerve agent belonged to you."

"What the fuck? No way."

"It belonged to Molnir."

"I *am* Molnir, Verrazzano, and I can tell you I don't mess with that shit."

"Not what Daryl says."

"I told you I don't want bullshit."

"And I told you I was fresh out. Underwood made a sworn statement to a UN official. He was guarding a Molnir arms dump in Damascus. Chemical weapons."

Frisch drained his glass a second time. "You know how Special Forces work. I run my shop the same way. It's all about initiative. My guys put together their own ops. They don't run them by me first, because that way I can't put the kibosh on them. They just go with it. If it pans out, they're golden. They take a percentage—a big one. If they fuck up, they fight their way out and work off whatever it costs me to save their ass."

Sometimes Verrazzano wished ICE functioned that way—every time he had to fill out Form 293 to pay an informant or Form 151 to process an arrest. "So you're washing your hands of Daryl Underwood?"

"If he was fucking with chem weapons in Syria, it was without my knowledge. For all I know, he'll report to me on whatever he's doing soon enough and I'll be able to clear this up for you."

Verrazzano took the glass of Scotch. He examined the drink. A pause in an interview was a prompt to the guilty, to make them fill the silence with chatter. But Frisch stayed quiet.

The lights in the UN tower were shutting off beyond First Avenue as the staff went home for the night.

"If Underwood was working his own operation," Verrazzano said, "he'd have brought in other Molnir operatives to help."

Frisch raised his hands, palms out. "I don't owe you anything, Verrazzano. I feel bad for what happened to you—"

"But you've got enough other shit on your conscience."

"Don't fucking push me." Frisch took a long breath. "Here's what I'll do. Because you got the shaft from Wyatt, just like I did. I'll talk to the guys who're closest to Daryl Underwood. I'll be happy to do that for you."

Verrazzano glanced about the plush office again. This was where he'd have been now if he'd continued on the track of entrepreneurial violence. He liked his cubicle at the ICE field office better.

He set the whisky on the desk and went to leave. Frisch rose and extended his hand once again. This time Verrazzano took it. The shake was wary and combative, like the touch of gloves before the bell in a boxing bout.

At the door he turned to Frisch. "Where's Wyatt?"

"I told you, I don't want anything to do with that asshole."

"I don't think that's the case." Verrazzano touched his fingers to his forehead as though he were puzzling something out.

"What the fuck are you talking about? I haven't seen him since he skipped out on us in Beirut," Frisch said. "You and me both, remember?"

"It's the Lethal Lapdog thing."

"What? I was just razzing you about that. Don't be a pussy."

"I'm not offended by the nickname. But you said, 'You know what he calls you?' Not what he *called* you."

"I did? Slip of the tongue, brother."

Verrazzano nodded slowly. "Yeah, I guess. A slip of the tongue's the kind of small mistake that could cost you your life on a special op. I wonder what it's going to cost you, Frisch."

He went into the corridor. Frisch was lucky to be dealing with a federal agent, because it meant a slip of the tongue wasn't evidence enough for Verrazzano to take him down. But he was unlucky, too. Anyone who made a mistake would soon make another one, and Verrazzano felt sure that when it came, Frisch's error would lead him to the sarin.

Or to Wyatt.

CHAPTER 23

The Underwood house was a narrow two-story with cream siding, dark-brown window frames, and an aura of decrepitude. Verrazzano brought his face close to the cloudy windows and peered inside. "Someone's there."

Kinsella knocked for the third time and waited, stroking her long hair and turning it between her fingers. "Maybe they died of boredom." The main drag through Beacon had seemed closed down when they drove into town. The shops and cafes, which had a reputation for a rural kind of Brooklyn-style hip, appeared to have no more life than the abandoned rail yards and cement silos.

Verrazzano drew his Heckler & Koch. He put the edge of his hand to the window to shield his eyes from the last of the daylight. "I'm sure there's someone—"

A flash of flame lit the room. The windowpane burst outward.

Verrazzano flew back. His head slammed against the cast-iron railing of the deck.

Another explosion erupted from the windows upstairs.

Kinsella rushed to Verrazzano. The sudden heat flushed his face a deep red.

A muffled thump inside the building. Another room went up in flames. The fire caught at the canopy above the deck.

Kinsella lifted Verrazzano with a hand under his arm.

"Go around the back, Noelle. Someone was in there. They must've gone out the rear."

"You're hurt."

Verrazzano shoved her away. "Around the back. *Now.*"

Kinsella hurried across the lawn, her Glock drawn and raised.

The fire cast cavorting shadows over the yard as it spread through the rear of the house. The beams creaked like an old bed under a troubled sleeper.

"There's no one here, Dom," Kinsella called.

Verrazzano stumbled to the back of the house, calling into his cell phone for the emergency operator. He touched the nape of his neck. Blood slicked his collar.

"That's a nasty cut." Kinsella examined him. "You hit your head badly when you fell."

"Better me than you. That blast would've burned your lovely red hair right off."

A Lincoln headed down the street past the house. Verrazzano felt fuzzy and hot. This was a neighborhood of yellow Mustang convertibles and fifteen-year-old Hondas, not limousines. He tried to read off the Town Car's plate number.

Kinsella's fingertip raked his scalp. "Hold still, Dom. I see some glass in the wound."

Verrazzano winced and blinked at her touch. His eyes clouded purple and bright gold.

When his sight cleared, the Lincoln was gone.

CHAPTER 24

The arc lights of the fire truck filtered through the lingering smoke after the blaze was controlled. Verrazzano and Kinsella strapped flashlights around their hard hats and went through the front door. The furniture, floor, and walls of the living room were uniformly blackened. Verrazzano lifted his nose, trying to catch a scent. "You smell accelerant?"

"Gasoline. Remember the way it blew out the windows? It hit the whole room all at once. The flames didn't work their way around slowly like they would in a natural fire."

"I heard other ignitions after the first blast. The arsonist must've set a device in each room."

Verrazzano went up the stairs. The front bedroom was thoroughly burned out. Flames had charred the foot of the door to the other room. Verrazzano pointed out the scorched wood. Kinsella registered it with a frown. Floor-level flames indicated fuel had been poured on the ground, another arson tell.

Verrazzano yanked the door open in three tugs. They came into a room barely bigger than the single bed along the wall. It was partially burned. The scent of gasoline was strong. The accelerant hadn't burned off.

"The window didn't blow," Kinsella said. "It's double-glazed and the door's a bit too big for the frame. The room's airtight. The fire used up all the oxygen and snuffed itself out."

Everything was black and white—the covers on the bed, the desk and chair. In a black frame on the wall, "F. U." was painted in gothic letters on a white background.

"That's friendly," Kinsella said.

"The daughter's initials. This must be Francine Underwood's room."

Verrazzano picked up a photo from the desk. The flames had tinted the image to the color of steak sauce and warped the plastic frame, but it was still recognizable as a shot of a man in desert fatigues with his arm around a skinny girl in her middle teens. She hugged the soldier, who scowled at the camera as though it had called attention to something that shamed him.

"Francine and her father." Verrazzano showed the photo to Kinsella.

"Looks like one unhappy pappy."

Outside the house, a woman wailed. Her keening reached the front door, but heavy footsteps and mumbling male voices gathered around her and took her away.

"The unfortunate lady of the house must've come home," Kinsella said.

Verrazzano sensed someone behind him. He turned. A lanky girl with greasy hair and prominent teeth stood on the landing.

"Francine?" he said.

The girl lifted one shoulder, as if her name barely mattered to her. She fiddled with the waist ties of her black hoodie. "This was the nicest room in the house. I'm glad the rest of the place got burned."

"We'd better talk to your mom," Kinsella said.

"She's too strung out. We've been by the river. She had a bottle of Jägermeister."

"I guess it's been hard on her. And on you. Your daddy being out of touch."

"He hasn't been out of touch." She sucked at her back teeth. "Daddy sent a letter. He said we could go to his friend when we needed money and stuff. But Mom doesn't want anything to do with those people anymore."

"Those people?" Verrazzano said.

"The guys from Daddy's work."

"Molnir?"

"Who's Molnir?"

"Doesn't matter. Go on."

"Daddy said his buddy Jeff would look after us."

"What's Jeff's last name?"

"Parry. He lives in Brooklyn."

"May I see the letter from your father?"

The woman outside bawled. The girl winced at her mother's anguish. She pulled a blue airmail envelope from the pocket of her hoodie and handed it to Verrazzano. The letter was addressed to Francine and postmarked Damascus International Airport, Syria. Verrazzano read it.

Sweetie,

This is like my will. Go to Jeff. He's the only one I trust. I've done some stuff that was bad, but I've tried to make it better. I met someone here, and she's going to help take care of it. She's a doctor. Maybe she'll explain to you one day. I can't write more. Jeff will look after you. Don't trust the others. Love you.

Your Daddy

Verrazzano handed the note to Kinsella. She read it and said, "Why didn't your daddy address this to your mother?"

The weeping on the deck turned to a scream, refusing the murmured sympathy of an emergency worker. Francine stared at Kinsella. The ICE agent lowered her eyes and bagged the note.

"Did you contact Jeff Parry?" Verrazzano asked.

"I phoned him. He said to come see him in a couple weeks."

"Why not now?"

"Read the back of the envelope."

Verrazzano took the evidence bag from Kinsella and turned it over. In a shaky, almost indecipherable hand, Underwood had scrawled, "Baby, do NOT go to city. NOT safe."

"Why isn't the city safe?" Kinsella asked the girl.

She went to the wall and traced a finger over her initials in the frame. The interview was over.

The ICE agents left the house and got into their Ford.

"The attack's going to be in New York," Verrazzano said. "That's why the city isn't safe."

Kinsella gripped the wheel hard and pulled away. "Jesus Christ."

"We have to find Underwood. Find out what he knows about the attack."

They drove through the orange light of Main Street. Verrazzano's meditation readings told him that "the world is what you are." Right now he struggled to see how he could save it from the criminals who made it what *they* were.

Kinsella turned the Ford south along the river.

The world is what you are. If Verrazzano was still alive in a few days, the world would be closer to justice. If he was dead, perhaps the world would be too.

His cell phone lit up. "Verrazzano."

"Hey, Special Agent." Quanah sounded as though he was still wearing his tough motherfucker face on the other end of the line in Damascus.

"You checked out those coordinates in Tishreen Park?" Verrazzano said.

"Affirmative."

"What'd you find?"

"I'm pretty sure I found Daryl Underwood."

"Great. I believe he knows something about the planned attack. Someone just tried to burn down his house. I want to know who'd do that. What does he say?"

"He tells a hell of a story."

Verrazzano wondered at the vicious tone of Quanah's voice. "Give it to me."

"You know how badly I *don't* want to see you?"

"I know it."

"Then you understand how serious I am when I say that if you want an answer to your question, you'd better jet on over here to Syria and see for yourself."

"I don't have time for that, Quanah. We've got kind of a deadline."

"Right you do. Whereas Daryl Underwood is just plain dead."

PART II

CHAPTER 25

The white Jeep slithered through the confusion at the edge of the Casbah. From the passenger seat, Verrazzano watched the residents of Damascus scurry and wail like extras in a biblical disaster epic when the flood came. Every city had its characteristic background din. The rush of freeway traffic was never out of earshot in Los Angeles. New York City had the distant honk of a taxi. After six years of civil war in the ancient Syrian capital, the hubbub of alarm was its constant.

During the long flight from New York, Verrazzano fretted that this trip was a diversion for which he hadn't time. But the body Quanah found in Damascus was a significant lead, and so far they had no more specific deadline than the "few days" the doctor had mentioned. So he sent Kinsella to track Underwood's buddy Parry in Brooklyn while he visited the city where he had often been at his worst, in the company of a man he had once been sent to kill.

"You located him pretty quick," he said.

Quanah tapped a warning on the horn of the Jeep. The square outside the old Hijaz Railway station was thick with yellow taxis and heedless pedestrians burdened by heavy sacks. Quanah wore his black hair in a tight ponytail. His eyes were narrowed and probing, as though gazing out over the sage with his Comanche forefathers. He had barely spoken since he picked up Verrazzano at the airport. Even now, his voice sounded hollow, as though it emerged directly from his chest somehow against the will of his tight jaw. "The grid reference you gave me is for a square area thirty-two feet across. Most of that was taken up by hundred-year-old olive trees. Only one spot had been disturbed. I dug there and bingo."

"What condition was he in?"

"He'd been shot in the lower legs, and his ankle was badly broken. He'd been whacked around. A lot of bruising to the ribs and the small of his back. Someone wanted information out of Underwood—if it is Underwood."

"Was he buried alive?"

"Negative. His airway didn't have a lot of dirt in it, far as I could tell. He had a nasty grimace on his face. Like he'd taken a look at the world and seen it for what it was. That could be fatal, don't you think?" Quanah punched the wheel softly with his big, leathery fist.

Verrazzano tried to lighten the man's mood. He needed Quanah to turn his focus outward to their mission. "You should get out of Damascus. It's making you too dark."

"You think? Maybe I'll quit the UN and go work somewhere chill, like Hawaii."

"Maybe you should."

"Don't fucking believe it. This city is made for me. It's thousands of years old, which means more people died here than you could even imagine. People like you and me, Dom, we belong here. With the dead. They're the only ones who know what it's like to live with the memories we got. Don't tell me you don't feel them all around you?"

Verrazzano was quiet. He felt them all right. "Remember what Wyatt used to say? 'The thing about the past is—'"

"'It's all ahead of you.' Yeah, I remember."

To Verrazzano, this city was a signpost on his own immoral path through the past. In Damascus he first sensed the horror that later engulfed him when Maryam Ghattas died. Colonel Wyatt sent him here to whip a man into line, the Palestinian arms trader who sold them the bomb that killed the Lebanese prime minister. Marwan Touma tried to haggle for a bigger payoff once he learned who the victim was. He ran his crooked business from a storage space on Straight Street, the walls decorated with framed photos of his handshakes with PLO chiefs and left-wing European politicians. As he sat across the desk from Verrazzano, snuffling at baklava and grumbling about his finances, Touma's phone rang. The little Palestinian leered, only his bottom teeth showing, and handed the receiver to Verrazzano. "It's Colonel Wyatt," he said.

Verrazzano took the phone. He heard Wyatt's deep voice, his Tennessee diction so precise, it seemed to be drawn from an old public information announcement. "Has Marwan learned his lesson?"

"I do not have that impression, sir."

Touma opened the top drawer of his desk. Verrazzano leaned forward warily. Touma took out a folded pouch. He lifted a syringe of insulin and waved it apologetically at Verrazzano. He pinched a fold of fat from his stomach and drove in the needle.

"No matter. This isn't about teaching *him* a lesson," Wyatt said. "Give him the phone."

Touma laid the syringe on the desktop with a shaking hand. He took back the phone and listened. "That's bullshit, Wyatt. Come on, man, you put me at a big risk because you didn't tell me who you were going to kill. Now I deserve—What?" Touma's face dropped and he started to shake. Verrazzano knew it was something in Wyatt's tone that cowed him. He protested some more, but his words sounded thin. Wyatt cut him off again, then Touma said, "What does that mean? Okay, okay." He lifted his eyes to Verrazzano. "Colonel Wyatt tells you, 'Meat eater.'"

It was Army slang for a Special Forces soldier sent on a violent mission. It meant Wyatt wanted Touma gone. Verrazzano drew the H&K from his belt.

"Please," Touma whimpered.

Verrazzano shot twice. The first bullet brought down a picture of a very youthful Touma with Vanessa Redgrave. The second smashed into the couch. Touma stared at him. Verrazzano took the phone, dropped it on the desk, and picked it up again.

"Report," Wyatt said.

"He's soon at room." A *dead* body. Soon to be at room temperature.

"Do you know your Bible, Sergeant Major?"

"Some."

"Saul persecuted the disciples of Jesus. He went to Damascus to track some of them down. On the road, Christ appeared to him and struck him blind. Saul took refuge in a house on Straight Street, the same place you are now. Then God sent a man to cure him and give him back his sight. Saul became the apostle Paul. Given that, what did you learn there, Sergeant Major?"

"That you're God, sir."

"See, you're not blind anymore."

When Verrazzano hung up, Touma collapsed before him. "If you ever need anything," he said, "I'll try to do it. Really, if I can, I'll try."

Verrazzano laughed. In the Middle East, a highly qualified promise was all you could expect for a life spared. The last he heard, Touma had a new name and face, but he was still in Damascus. He wondered where he was.

Quanah's Jeep cleared the square and took off past Damascus University.

"These streets are chaos," Verrazzano said. "Is something going on today?"

"People got to hurry to find food during the day. Makes them kind of volatile. If the militias get you on the street at night, they'll rob you and kill you and say it was because you collaborated with the government. Or the government guys pick you up and accuse you of being on a mission for the rebels. Those guys will turn your testicles to toast."

The Presidential Palace ran along the scrubby ridge above them. A series of limestone rectangles, it looked like a fancy high school or a provincial art museum.

"Where's the spike you found with the body?" Verrazzano asked.

Quanah reached into the map pocket on the driver's door. He handed over a dull steel skewer. It was ten inches long with a heavy sphere the size of a golf ball at one end and a sharp point at the other. Verrazzano examined the patina of oxidation in the metal and the brown-black gobbets of dried blood in the inlay.

"It was on top of Underwood's body," Quanah said. "Like someone tossed it there before they buried him."

Some of the blood had been scratched away. For the tests Verrazzano requested when he got the call from Quanah in New York. "The doctor's checking if this is Underwood's blood?"

"Results should be at the clinic with the body."

Verrazzano tapped the skewer lightly against his palm. "How well did you know Doctor Weston?"

Quanah squinted into the early afternoon sun. He turned south onto a busy four-lane road. "As well as I've known any woman in the last twenty years."

Verrazzano thought of Browne choking on the nerve agent at Weston's home. "You know, she had a husband."

The wheel jerked in Quanah's hands. "Listen, motherfucker, I'm not going to take lessons in morality from you, of all people."

"Okay, you're not. Just go on."

He breathed loud through his nose. "What it is, you get out on one of these humanitarian missions and no one else understands what's going on the way you and your colleagues do because you're the ones on the ground. Soon enough, you're next to each other in bed. You share this real deep purpose in your work, and it makes the love real intense."

The light turned red. A woman came to the window of the Jeep. She waved a bunch of coriander at Verrazzano and pleaded with him to buy it. Her skin was the color of tea, lined and pouched like a bulldog's snout, but her teeth were white and even. Despite her complexion, Verrazzano figured she was younger than him. In war zones, he had watched peasant women move overnight from fresh girlhood to craggy old age. He gave her a thousand Syrian pounds, about three bucks on the black market. He pushed the coriander back at her. She went away muttering, massaging her hip.

"Amy investigated chemical-weapons incidents in the civil war here. Attacks too small for the White House to care about but big enough to leave a bunch of kids with permanent lung damage." Quanah pulled away from the light. "She'd tell me about it and we'd—we'd just feel how goddamned awful it all was. Together. She couldn't explain it to her husband over in the States. With me, she didn't have to explain. Amy was going to leave her husband. For me."

Browne injected the last of the life-saving atropine into a stranger, though he knew it'd mean his own death, so that his wife wouldn't have died in vain. The wife who had been about to leave him. If he had known less about how the world really was, Verrazzano would've disliked Doctor Amy Weston for that. But the more criminals he snapped the cuffs onto, the harder he found it to lay ultimate blame. If he forgave people for their malice, perhaps he might be pardoned for his past.

Quanah jolted the car off the pavement into the sandy lanes of Yarmouk, a neighborhood slung together for Palestinian refugees a half century ago. The cinderblock apartment houses were gray and ragged and unsound, like a smoker's teeth. Sewage pipes, shattered by shell blasts, delivered their filth into pools of scum. Yet the mosquitoes were still thirsty. Verrazzano slapped at a bite on his neck. Blood is the most prized of all nourishment, whether you are an insect or an insurgent.

Quanah pulled up by a wall graffitied with cartoons of martyred gunmen. A sign in the light blue of the UN marked the entrance to the clinic. "Amy was stubborn."

"Like you."

"Until she got herself killed." Quanah climbed out of the Jeep. "That's where the similarities end."

CHAPTER 26

Chavez watched a dumpy man in a rumpled suit tumble off his stool. The man dragged himself to his feet and peered at the clock behind the bar. Two AM. He reeled out to the street. Through the door swinging behind the drunk, Chavez glimpsed a dead-end sign on the sidewalk. The second word had been sprayed out. He drew an *A* for Adela in the condensation on his glass.

Kyle Massie drained his beer glass with a loud gasp of pleasure. "Drink up. That's an order. You got a few things to get out of your system, don't you?"

Across the barroom, a bony Korean in wraparound shades shot a frame of pool alone. Salsa played on the radio in the kitchen.

"Hooah." Chavez tipped his glass and drank until the brain freeze stopped him.

"All *right*, compadre." Massie whistled the riff to "Tequila" and flashed two fingers at the listless bartender, a Cuban with a gel fauxhawk and an ebony soul patch under his lip. He took the Cuervo from the shelf and poured.

Massie slid the small, heavy glass to Chavez. "*Uno, dos, tres.*" He slugged back the tequila and shook his head, as though he'd taken a punch.

Chavez did the same. "Damn, I can almost feel my legs again."

Massie grabbed Chavez's head and kissed him on the brow. He called to the bartender. "*Dos más, amigo.*"

The bartender poured two more measures. Massie swallowed his shot and gestured for another one. Chavez hammered the empty glass down and giggled. The Cuban left the bottle in front of them and disappeared through the kitchen door.

"This feels good." Massie glared at Chavez, his damp eyes intense and fierce. "Being here. Together on a mission. You've got my back and I've got your back. That's what I live for. I haven't had it in so long. Not since, you know . . . not since Iraq. No one who wasn't there understands. Thank you for giving me that feeling again, Specialist Chavez."

They toasted and drank. Massie poured a double measure for each of them. "You got to meet the boss. Balls like a rodeo bull. Brain like fucking Einstein."

Chavez laughed.

"Seriously. This thing he invented—Tom Frisch invented a briefcase that damn near kills you, you try to steal it."

"No way."

"Here's how it happened. He goes down to some fucking looney tunes place like Bogotá to make a deal a couple years ago. Some asshole rips off his briefcase. Big Tom decides, never again. So he rigs up a case with an electric alarm."

"Like it beeps or something?"

"Better'n that. He keeps a—what do you call them things? A transponder. He keeps a transponder in the breast pocket of his suit jacket. Always has it there, always carries the case. Someone takes the briefcase more than a hundred paces from the transponder, the alarm zaps six hundred volts through the handle grip. Puts you on the ground, twitching like a hillbilly with fleas."

"Shit." Chavez snorted into his glass.

"Frisch is the man." Massie downed another shot. "But *you're* the man this week."

"Aw, come on."

"To you it's just like a few clicks on a computer keyboard. But to a shitkicker like me, you're a wizard. You've got magic knowledge that's hidden from the likes of me."

"Thanks, man."

"Lucky you didn't lose your hands in Iraq too." Massie punched Chavez's shoulder.

Chavez brought the tequila to his lips. "Yeah, that was lucky."

"Oh, Christ, man. I'm sorry." Massie linked his hands on top of his head.

"Don't worry about it, Kyle."

Massie stared down at the bar. "After you got shipped out, something happened to me."

Chavez watched Massie suck at his underlip.

"I got it both ways. I got PTSD. Everything I remember is a nightmare. Makes me blow up over nothing. But I got a traumatic brain injury too. Fucked up the part of my brain where I store memories, so I keep forgetting important stuff. Can you believe that?"

"Kyle, you only need to remember one thing. You're a good guy. You got that?"

"I drove right over a fucking IED and I didn't even know I was hurt. The Humvee was all busted up, and I was fine. I figured, 'Well, that happened.' And I went off to have a beer. Then I started getting these gaps. I'd be standing in the mess tent and I'd think, 'How'd I get here?' Or I'd start stripping down my weapon and somebody'd say, 'Hey, Kyle, you just cleaned that.'"

"Did you get treatment?"

"I tried to get sent to some clinic the Army's got out in California, but they wouldn't put me on the priority list because I didn't have 'polytrauma,' whatever the fuck that is."

"That's just not right, man."

"I hooked up with Tom Frisch. He sent me to a specialist, did a brain scan. Guess what, bits of my brain got shaken so hard against my skull by the explosion that they just disintegrated." He closed his eyes. "I had this high school teacher used to say to me, 'Kyle Massie, you got half a brain.' Turns out, asshole was right."

"Kyle, that's not so."

"That's what Tom Frisch told me too. Said he knew I was still good to go. Showed faith in me. I'd fucking do anything for that man."

When the bottle was empty, Chavez and Massie went into the early morning street. Massie leaned against the *end*-less *dead* sign in the sallow light of a buzzing streetlamp. "You got a spare wheel-chair, Specialist? I'm as good for walking right now as you are."

Chavez belched. "Uh-uh. My wheelchair is my only carriage." He sang a few lines from "No Woman, No Cry."

Two men loitered on the sidewalk. One was white with a wide Slavic face. He wore a red bandanna on his head and sat on top of a newspaper vending box. The other was black and muscular. His Yankees cap was pristine, the brim angled to the left.

The bandanna man lifted himself from the box. The action showed his powerful arms. He trotted toward Chavez. "I kick *dogs* that sing better than you, faggot."

Chavez struggled to focus on the advancing man. "What the fuck?"

Massie stumbled forward. He pointed at Chavez. "This veteran is an American hero, asshole. You'd better—"

The man in the bandanna smacked Massie to the ground without breaking his stride. The black man jogged over and kicked Massie in the guts.

Chavez shoved hard on the joystick of his chair, rattling toward his friend.

Bandanna man skipped out of his path. He jabbed Chavez on the nose with the heel of his palm. Chavez's head sprung back and bounced forward. He spewed tequila down his front.

The black man grabbed the joystick. He spun the wheelchair, laughing. Chavez plunged at the man's arm, biting down on the wrist. The black man howled. He pummeled the back of Chavez's head, but Chavez held on.

He felt a hand in the small of his back. With a quick shove, the hand dropped to his withered buttocks. The black man jerked his fist under Chavez and wrenched at his testicles. The guy wasn't squeamish. He was a street fighter. He'd do whatever it took. Chavez let go of his bite.

The black man shook his forearm. "Motherfucker."

The bandanna guy unclipped the belt that secured Chavez to his chair. "Move over, asshole."

Chavez raked his fingers down the man's cheek as he tumbled to the sidewalk. A thin streak of blood ran from the wound. "Son of a bitch," the man hissed.

The black guy jumped into Chavez's empty wheelchair. "I'ma burn rubber." He moved off so fast, the chair lifted into a wheelie on its heavy frame. The other man followed him into the side street.

Massie staggered along the block. "Going to nail those fuckers. They can't take your fucking chair. Going to show them who we are, man."

"Kyle, help me up," Chavez called. "You're in no condition to fight. Leave them."

Massie reached a Beretta from under his shirt at the back of his waistband. He struck a 007 pose. "Who said anything about fighting?" He loped around the corner.

Chavez propped himself against the outside wall of the billiard club. The tucked ends of his pants dragged behind him. He tried to make them neat, but his fingers were clumsy with alcohol.

The subdued electrical whine of the wheelchair approached. Massie came fast around the corner, leaning back in the chair, his legs high before him. He whirled the Beretta above his head.

Chavez craned his neck. The thick, cushioned backrest of the wheelchair had been carved open at the top. "What the fuck did they do to my chair?"

"I'll fix it, man. Let's get you back up here." Massie gripped Chavez unsteadily beneath the arms and lifted him into the chair. "You should've seen them run when they met my little nine-millimeter friend." He put his hand on Chavez's shoulder. "I told you, I've got your back."

CHAPTER 27

Gurneys lined the corridor of the UN clinic, spread with sheets so filthy, they'd have made the gorge rise in a street whore. Injured men in their twenties lay on them smoking cigarettes. Their relatives brewed tea on camp burners. A dozen young men with slim hips and smoldering eyes loitered outside the dispensary, which doubled now as an impromptu morgue. They stared at Verrazzano with the undisguised contempt of the truly hopeless.

A Syrian woman in her thirties bent over a tray of test tubes on the counter. She wore a white lab coat, large spectacles, and a black headscarf pinned beneath her pale chin. Quanah greeted her and asked her to fetch the doctor. She went out with her head down.

By the shuttered window, a body lay under a pink shower curtain. The plastic was peppered with mold from the damp bathroom where it used to hang. The fungus made it more alive than the corpse it concealed.

"That's our guy," Quanah said.

Verrazzano raised the sheet. The dead man was a muscular Westerner of medium height. His ribs and joints were bruised. His broken foot dangled off the gurney at a shocking, unnatural angle. He wore a goatee trimmed close. His face was lean and sour. He hadn't found peace, even in death. Verrazzano lifted the foot back into place.

Elevated blood pressure ticked in his neck. He coughed and immediately thought of the effects of the nerve agent the previous afternoon, a little dash of destruction in him, faint yet undeniable, like the bitters in an Old Fashioned. He shook his head. He was being paranoid and a hypochondriac. It didn't surprise him. He was standing over a man who suffered a terrible end. He countered the adrenaline with slow breaths.

From his pocket, he took the Department of Defense personnel photo of Daryl Underwood. He held it beside the dead man's face. It matched. The Pentagon records said childhood surgery left Underwood with a scar on the right of his abdomen. There it was, hiding in the sparse layer of fat the dead man carried. He should also have a mole above his left buttock. Verrazzano lifted the man's hip and found the mole. The sweat on Verrazzano's hand turned the residual dirt of the grave to mud, imprinting the marks of his fingers on the cold skin. He wiped his hand on his cargo pants.

He scanned the ID document again. He reached for Underwood's right ear and poked his finger inside. "No hearing aid."

Quanah touched the Leatherman pouch on his belt, an unconscious soothing gesture. "I dug him up at night. I didn't see any hearing aid."

"No matter. We've got enough to ID him."

The lab technician returned with a file pressed to her chest. "The doctor will be here shortly. Meanwhile, he told me to give you the blood test results."

"From the skewer?"

She ran her finger down a checklist as she spoke. "The blood on the skewer is human. It tested negative for all nerve agent identifiers. As you requested, we examined it for sarin and there was none present."

"Was it this man's blood?" Verrazzano scanned Underwood's body for puncture marks from the skewer.

"This man was type O. The blood on the skewer is type B." The woman's English was very proper and controlled. Though she was small, she seemed to occupy a larger space in the room than Verrazzano. He recognized the energy that kept someone going through a war. Without it, you fell into depression and rage, and then you died.

"So the blood on the skewer is from someone else," Verrazzano said. "B is a pretty rare blood type."

"Among people of European ancestry, yes. But it's common in Arabs. There are almost as many type B Arabs as types O and A."

"Did you run DNA?"

"Our testing capabilities are not advanced in this regard, but we have done our best." She turned to a second page of test results that showed a long series of short, black lines like a bar code—the DNA sequence. "The blood is from a male. The marker we get from his Y chromosome is mostly found in Syria, though it's also present in nearby locations like Turkey and the Caucasus."

"The blood on the skewer is from a local?"

A doctor slouched through the crowd outside the door. He wore medical scrubs spattered with blood. His hair curled like a wet-look perm. His black mustache drooped almost as much as his heavy jowls. His eyes were pouched and sunken.

The lab technician lowered her head deferentially. The doctor gestured for her to continue. She cleared her throat. "The genetic marker in the blood is specific to members of one particular religious sect."

"Sufis." The doctor took out a pack of cigarettes. "Islamic mystics. Mainstream Muslims sometimes accuse them of worshipping more than one god." He shook a last cigarette into his fingers and crushed the pack. As he lit up, he stared at Verrazzano through the flame. "That means they don't like them."

"Sufis do not marry Muslims who are not from the Sufi sect," the woman said. "At least, it is very rare."

Verrazzano had met Muslims who'd want their daughters to marry a Sufi the way a Kentucky cracker would like his baby girl to breed with Snoop Dogg. "Meaning that this type of DNA stays within the Sufi community?"

The lab technician nodded emphatically. "It follows that what we found is the blood of someone descended from Sufis and who is therefore probably still a Sufi now."

The surgeon whispered thanks to her, and she left the room. He took another drag on his smoke. "Mister Quanah, welcome." His voice was so deep that it seemed to creep across the floor and vibrate up from Verrazzano's feet through his entire body. "You've brought me another fucking American."

He stared at Verrazzano and blew smoke from his nostrils. "Unfortunately, this one is alive."

Quanah kissed the doctor five times, going from cheek to cheek. "Good to see you, Doc. Sorry I don't have more corpses for you. I know you were delighted to receive a dead Yankee."

"A novelty among all these dead Arabs." The doctor dropped his cigarette and stepped it out with his sandal. He extended his hand to Verrazzano. "I'm the fellow who tells people that their loved ones have gone to sit beside Allah in Paradise." He paused. "In Syria, you understand, that means I'm a physician."

Verrazzano shook the doctor's hand.

"Mister Quanah, did you bring this gentleman here to tell us that the Americans finally decided to help the people of Syria? To stop the government murdering us? Or is it only the Islamic State whose murders are bad?" The doctor reached out his hand and let Quanah slap it to celebrate his joke. He turned back to Verrazzano. "You're not upset that I hate America?"

"Get in line." Verrazzano gestured to the sullen young men glaring at him.

That earned him a big slap on his hand too and a rumbling, smoky laugh. "I'm in charge here, so I am allowed to cut the line," the doctor said.

Verrazzano drew back the shower curtain from Underwood's corpse. "Would you give us your findings?"

"It is my medical opinion that this man is suffering from a common condition in these parts. I call it Damascus Syndrome, or Syrrhea. To be precise, he's dead. Don't worry about him. A dead man will never be lonely in our city."

"I need to know how he died, Doctor."

"I can tell you what killed him and when. But that's hardly the answer to *how* he died."

"It'll help identify the people who did it so I can prevent something very bad that I believe is about to take place."

The doctor lowered his chin. "Someone always smiles when a man dies, no matter how beloved he was. It is the way of our species to derive pleasure from the extinction of another man's spirit." He looked up. "You know who he was?"

"A former US serviceman named Daryl Underwood."

"Was he a spy?"

"I don't think so."

The doctor pretended to look surprised. "He helped our friend Doctor Weston. Surely she is a spy."

"Doctor Weston was a chemical weapons inspector for the United Nations."

"If you say so." Then the doctor became still. "Was?"

"She was murdered in New York yesterday."

The doctor wasn't laughing now. "This man—Tell me his name again?"

"Daryl Underwood."

"Mister Underwood was beaten very severely as you see from the extensive contusions. He was shot in both legs with resulting tissue damage and shattered left tibia and fibula. But he died of exposure to a nerve agent."

Verrazzano felt his lungs constrict as though he were once again breathing odorless death in the house on Long Island. "Can you be more exact?"

"Sarin gas. His blood shows high levels of isopropylmethophosphonic acid, or IMPA. It's produced when sarin mixes with water in the body."

"Is there any other possibility?"

"IMPA is an absolute determinant of the presence of sarin. Nothing else produces it."

"How big was the dose?"

"Moderate and not prolonged."

Small enough that he didn't die right away, Verrazzano figured, *but large enough that Doctor Weston couldn't keep him alive.* "Where could he have been exposed?"

The Arab took a new pack of smokes from the back pocket of his scrubs and lit up. "Both sides have used chemical weapons in our civil war. Eventually, you Americans decided to act after an attack on a neighborhood in the east of the city."

"By the government."

"Maybe. Maybe not. Anyway, it killed fourteen hundred people. Just like that." The doctor snapped his fingers. "Your White House concluded that this was a naughty way to snuff people. They put pressure on our beloved president."

"That's when Doctor Weston and the UN came over?"

"The UN shipped away Syria's nerve gas for decommissioning, and Washington let the government and the jihadis go on killing us in more acceptable, conventional ways."

"Neat deal," Quanah said.

"Works for everyone, right?"

"Not quite everyone." Verrazzano stared at Underwood's body.

The doctor took a long drag. "It looks like our friend here came across some sarin that the UN didn't know about."

"Doctor, I appreciate the work you've done."

"My work is never done. There's always someone else to usher through to the other side." He picked up a clipboard from the counter and scribbled across the bottom.

Quanah came close to Verrazzano. "You had the map coordinates from Amy's note. That led to Underwood's body. You got the USB drive with Underwood's story about his exposure to a nerve agent, and now you have confirmation of that from his body. But there's no new lead here. It's a dead end."

Verrazzano shook his head. *Dead* and *end* didn't go together. In a body, there was still decomposition after death. In a trail of facts, some divergence was always missed. "We need to find out more about what Doctor Weston was working on. Maybe she tracked the sarin further than we know."

The doctor covered Underwood's corpse with the moldy shower curtain. "Why don't you ask Hussein?"

Quanah shrugged. "I tried last night. Couldn't locate him."

"Who's Hussein?" Verrazzano said.

"Amy's driver," Quanah said. "Went everywhere with her."

"Doesn't the UN office know where he is?"

"He's not a UN driver. Amy hired him privately. With the UN, you have to fill out three different forms every time you take a car out of the garage pool. With Hussein, Amy could travel without reporting her whereabouts."

"You can be sure where you'll find Hussein today." The doctor beckoned to one of the young men in the doorway. "At the Rifa'i Mosque for the *dhikr*."

"What's that?" Verrazzano said.

The doctor lifted the lids of the patient's eyes and peered close. "A ritual they usually perform in March for the birthday of Prophet Muhammad's son-in-law. But last week, the government broke in on their prayers and beat them up. They're going to do the *dhikr* today as a protest."

"Who're *they*?"

"The Sufis."

Verrazzano recalled the type B blood on the skewer Quanah found with Underwood's body. From a man of Sufi origin, probably still a member of the sect. "Doctor Weston's driver is a Sufi?"

"Quite an ardent devotee, in fact."

"You didn't know?" Verrazzano asked Quanah.

The UN man glared. "You don't give me orders, and you don't have the right to chew me out. Anyhow, I don't talk religion with these guys. Once you bring up that kind of shit in the Middle East, it gets ugly."

Verrazzano went toward the door. "Let's go to the mosque."

"You'll like the ceremony," the doctor called after him. "It's *pret-ty* crazy. The Sufis get themselves into a mystical trance. Then they pierce their cheeks and hips. With metal skewers."

CHAPTER 28

Parry saw the postal service van pull up outside his row house in Bay Ridge. The driver hitched up her shorts and studied her clipboard. She lifted the roll door in the side of the van and took a package the size of a closed fist from the sack. She checked the address and stepped briskly across the sidewalk.

Parry went into the hallway. A gold silhouette of George Washington's head on a purple background decorated the frosted glass of the front door. The delivery woman's form loomed in the porch. She pushed the bell. Parry opened the door while the woman's hand was still on its way to her nose for a scratch.

She recoiled and gawped at his shirtless torso. It was hard and muscular, tattooed in a patchwork of tiny illegible copperplate, big Celtic knots, writhing Chinese dragons and ideograms. He looked like a page from a medieval sorcerer's spellbook.

"Package for Jeff Parry?" the woman stammered.

He reached for the package. When he saw its origin on the waybill—Damascus International Airport—his face grew harder than his ridged abdominals.

"Sign here." The woman held out a clipboard.

Parry ignored her. He shut the door.

He slipped a box cutter into the crumpled wrapping. His focus was absolute. Every step now was mission critical. He was entering a realm in which anyone he met might kill him. He'd been there before, but never so alone.

From the package, he drew a silver, plastic ellipse and a thin, transparent tube. A behind-the-ear hearing aid and a connection that went directly into the ear canal. It was Daryl Underwood's signal to him.

He spoke into the earpiece as if his friend might hear him. "So long, man."

No one else would understand the significance of the hearing aid. Underwood had told only Parry what it meant. He looked about at the shabby room, the unwashed clothing strewn over the armchair, the bedsheet furrowed by wrestling nightmares of combat. Determination crossed his face like a cloud. Underwood was gone, that was all. Nothing was good or bad. It only *was*. Until it wasn't. Once you knew that, you could kill, and you could live with it—until you lived no more.

He closed his fist around the hearing aid. With his other hand, he pulled a rucksack from the upper shelf of his closet. He rooted behind a stack of unfolded T-shirts and came out with a few bundles of cash. He stuffed them into the rucksack and put another in the pocket of his jeans.

"Where you going, Jeff?" A smiling, cruel voice from the doorway.

Parry turned quickly, swinging his fist at the voice.

CHAPTER 29

The siren of an ambulance keened away down the avenue beyond the end of the block. Todd and Kinsella went up the steps to the front door of the house. A sticker in the frosted glass bore the profile in gold of America's first president.

"Purple heart." Todd pointed a thick, ruddy finger at the sticker. "Parry was wounded in action? Was that in his file?"

"Yeah, it was." Kinsella gave him a scornful sidelong glance.

"I must've missed it." He put his face to the glass and cupped his hands to see inside.

"Be careful. Last time I saw someone do that, he got a close shave from ten gallons of gasoline, and he was a lot better looking than you in the first place. Parry's file also said he expressed feelings of anger toward the Army. About the way vets get treated."

"So he got screwed by the military. Join the line."

"Right behind you, huh?"

"Nope. I'm as gung ho as I was on the day I first pulled on a National Guard tunic."

"Hooah." She rolled her eyes.

Todd was about to come back at her when the ambulance turned the corner. It pulled up in the middle of the street. An NYPD patrol car followed. The ambulance driver jumped out. "Did you guys call nine-one-one?"

Kinsella brought her Glock out of her shoulder holster. "Aw, fuck. We got to break it down."

She stepped away from the door, drawing her weapon. She leaned back and dropped her weight forward as she kicked.

The door smashed open. The ICE agents charged into the hallway.

The house was silent. But the silence in the rooms at the rear seemed louder. Kinsella rushed back there.

A man lay on the floor. He was shirtless, his chest pale except for the colorful plethora of tattoos and the small hole over his heart, pink and red and flinty gray, where the bullet had entered. The pocket of his jeans bulged.

She came to her knees beside the corpse. She grabbed a latex glove from her jacket, fumbled it on, and reached into Parry's pants pockets. "Sorry I don't have time for foreplay, hon." She brought out a bundle of twenty-dollar bills in a white paper band. She turned it in her hand, examining it.

She heard a whine almost too high-pitched to pick up. She shook her head as though her ears were full of water. She wondered if the explosion last night at Underwood's house damaged her eardrums. The noise could be the constant whistling of tinnitus.

The band on the pack of bills was printed with two words in a futuristic font that reminded her of a Star Wars movie poster. She showed it to Todd.

The noise puzzled her. It seemed to lift and wane.

Todd read the band around the bills. "Freedom Coin?"

"What the hell is that fucking sound?" Kinsella turned the dead man's left arm. She bent close to the wrist. The reedy whine emanated from the closed fist.

Todd knelt beside her. "I hear it."

"It's electronic." Kinsella peeled back the dead man's fingers.

"This is Parry all right," Todd said. "Those are his tattoos. I memorized a couple of them from his file."

Kinsella lifted a small, silver hearing aid out of the palm and held it between her long, bright-red fingernails. She spun the volume dial, and the battery-test tone halted.

She held the hearing aid toward Todd. "The file didn't say Parry was deaf."

CHAPTER 30

The Sufis rocked rhythmically, beating their chests, chanting the name of God on the outbreath and, as they inhaled, affirming that He lived. *"Allah hai, Allah hai."* The men with the strongest build stood near the doors of the mosque, expecting trouble. The sect was known for criticizing the abuse of political power. That never made it popular with the men at the top. During a civil war, such criticism was a pronounced liability.

Quanah spoke quietly with one of the young guards. He came over to Verrazzano. "They've been getting into the trance for a few hours already. They'll start the piercing soon. Amy's driver is part of the ceremony. We'll have to wait until afterward to talk to him."

The sheikh of the mosque wore a thick, white mustache teased away from his cheeks in wide sweeps. He approached an impassive young man with raddled skin.

"That's Hussein," Quanah said.

The sheikh held a foot-long silver skewer like the one Quanah discovered with Underwood's body. The blackened patina within the scrollwork suggested the great age of the metal. He ran the skewer between his lips to moisten and bless it.

Hussein's ill-shaven jaw twitched as the skewer touched his cheek. The sheikh eased the metal into the skin beside Hussein's mouth. The point emerged from the other cheek. The young man's eyes were remote and withdrawn. The skewer passing through his flesh symbolized his devotion to God, a proof that divinity transcended pain and the body. The sheikh repeated the procedure on two seven-year-old boys. Their delicate faces showed no sign of a wound.

The chant gained in intensity. The crowd knew Hussein was ready for even greater union with God. The sheikh lifted a skewer topped by a sphere of olive wood the size of a baseball. He rested the point against Hussein's hip, held the skewer parallel to the floor, and beat it with a circular mallet. The contact resounded like a kettledrum. The length of metal disappeared through Hussein's robe into his hip. The sheikh let go of it. Hussein seemed to Verrazzano to be suspended, as if some force took hold of the skewer and used it as a handle to lift him.

The older men slid skewers through their own cheeks. Hussein held his head back, transfixed like St. Francis in a Renaissance portrait.

"Allah hai, Allah hai."

The sheikh drew out the skewers from the young boys and squeezed the wounds to heal them. The boys drifted away, trickles of blood along their slack jaws.

Hussein pulled the spike from his hip. He raised it with both hands, like a priest with the last of the communion wine, and returned it to the sheikh. The crowd broke up.

Verrazzano sensed the changed atmosphere as the Sufis headed for the exits. In the trance, their bodies were beyond pain. But even God couldn't erase the dangers outside in Damascus. A shell exploded a mile away. The shock wave rolled under Verrazzano as he approached Hussein. It felt as though he were crossing the deck of a ship.

Hussein wore an expression of exhaustion and disembodiment. He removed his long, black robe. Beneath, he was shirtless. He sat on the floor against the wall and picked up a white T-shirt. He slumped as though he hadn't the energy to lift it over his head. His stomach was a constellation of small, round scars, like the bare spot left by the surgical removal of a mole. They were concentrated over the oblique abdominals, just above the hipbones. Now that he was close, Verrazzano saw bruises on Hussein's face and chest. These injuries were different from the incisions of the skewers. He had been beaten.

"Doctor Amy is dead." Hussein stared at the carpet. "They didn't tell me. But I knew."

"They?" Verrazzano asked.

"They came to the mosque last night." Hussein closed his eyes, all his energy spent. "When I pierced my body today, I prayed for Doctor Amy. My devotions soothed her departed spirit. She is almost free now."

"Almost?"

"She will not be free until it is done." Hussein looked at Verrazzano for the first time. "That is up to you."

The Sufi was still on some mystical plane, seeing more of this world than others did.

"What am I supposed to do?" Verrazzano felt as though he were consulting a guru rather than interviewing a witness.

"Doctor Amy cared for our people. I loved her." Hussein watched Quanah. "Though not as you did."

Quanah lowered his head.

"Do you have your famous Leatherman?" Hussein held out a shaky hand.

Quanah popped the flap on his belt. He slipped the steel tool from the pouch and handed it to Hussein.

The Sufi levered the tiny saw, can opener, and scissors out of the handle before he found the knife. He put his forefinger and middle finger to his belly and pinched around one of his scars. With a long exhalation, he cut a half inch below the skin. Blood squirted across his hand.

Verrazzano jerked forward. "What're you doing?"

Hussein laid the Leatherman on the carpet. He reached a finger into the wound and brought out a square of black plastic the size of a thumbnail. He wiped his blood on his sweatpants and handed the plastic to Verrazzano. A blue logo at the center of the square was inscribed with the letters *GPS*.

"A tracking device?" Verrazzano said.

Hussein compressed the edges of his new wound. "Doctor Amy implanted this in me. Put it in a cell phone in the place where usually you put the SIM card. It will show you a map with the location of its twin, which is hidden."

"Hidden where?"

Hussein shrugged. "This device will show you that."

"Why did she put it . . . in there?" Verrazzano gestured at Hussein's stomach.

"She asked me to keep it. I suggested she conceal it where I would never lose it."

Verrazzano looked at Hussein's bruises again. "Can you describe the men who came to you last night?"

"The way they looked? Or the condition of their souls?" Hussein smiled faintly. "They were the men who took Daryl Underwood from the airport."

"You saw that happen?"

"Doctor Amy asked me to track Underwood. I waited outside a storehouse in the Casbah while they tortured him. I heard them demand the location of this GPS device."

Beyond the door of the mosque, someone shouted—a man, his tone mocking and hateful. Then came laughter. A murmur of concern rumbled through the Sufis who remained inside. Verrazzano glanced toward the entrance. A few young men went into the small hallway to peer out. Hussein coughed, and Verrazzano turned back to him.

"Underwood didn't give you up?" Verrazzano said.

"He didn't know I had it. He gave the device to Doctor Weston. She didn't tell him what she did with it."

Verrazzano imagined Underwood's torture, his broken leg probed and twisted. He couldn't blame a man for spilling what he knew in the face of such pain—everyone did. Underwood had given up his connection to Doctor Weston. The killers had been looking for this GPS device when they murdered her in New York—her killer had frisked her as she lay dying. When they didn't find it, they ransacked her home in search of it.

A gunshot outside the mosque. The men inside hurried to shut themselves in. Another Sufi entered, making calming gestures with his hands.

"What was that?" Quanah said.

"The local gunmen letting us know they are tough enough to fire a gun in the air." Hussein's perspiration glowed gray in the fluorescent light. "I tried to help Underwood. I crept inside the warehouse while the torturers took a break. I gave him one of the skewers we use for this *dhikr* ceremony. I thought he might fight his way out with it. It was all I had to give him. But perhaps he was too near death to use it."

That's why the skewer in Underwood's grave had Sufi blood on it, traces left over from a previous ceremony. Verrazzano saw the next connection too. "You followed them to Tishreen Park after they killed Underwood. You gave Doctor Weston the map coordinates for Underwood's body."

Hussein inclined his head in assent.

"The thugs who beat you, how did they get to you?"

"They must have seen me following them when they buried Underwood. But they found nothing." Hussein gestured at the blood on his abdomen. "To them, the place where Doctor Amy buried this thing in me looked like any other scar from our ceremony."

The tiny GPS device on the end of Verrazzano's finger was warm from the Sufi's stomach. But the ICE agent felt colder than Underwood's corpse. "Give me your phone," he said to Quanah. "I need to keep my line open to the field office back in New York."

Quanah tossed him his cell phone. Verrazzano slipped the GPS chip into the SIM-card slot and powered up. He gestured at Hussein's wound. "Quanah, there's a medical facility at the UN headquarters, right?"

"It is nothing," the Sufi said.

"We'll take you there anyhow. Patch you up." Verrazzano reached out to help Hussein to his feet.

The cell phone screen flashed a login form. Verrazzano groaned.

"Password?" Quanah said.

Verrazzano shook his head. "It's activated by a soundwave pattern. When it registers a particular sound that matches a soundwave already recorded on the phone, the GPS chip is activated. Then it'll show us where its twin device is. We have to hope the twin is hidden with the sarin."

"What the hell is the sound that activates the chip?"

"A military guy like Underwood wouldn't just leave things in the hands of a civilian. He gave the GPS chip to Doctor Weston, but he must've told someone he trusted about the soundwave that activates this device." Verrazzano tapped the phone against his chin. "We have to figure out who that was."

They helped Hussein to the door. When they came out, the sunlight was bright. It gleamed off the windscreen of a big Ford truck. In the back of the truck, a half-dozen men lounged, their faces wrapped in red-and-white checkered kaffiyehs, Kalashnikov assault rifles across their laps or braced against their hips. A man stepped out of the cab. He leaned against the hood and pulled the kaffiyeh off his face. His beard was long, square, and black. He grinned at Verrazzano, his teeth showing the color of old floor tiles.

"*Ahlan wa-sahlan*," he called out. His voice was ragged with cigarettes, coffee, and dust.

"*Ahlan bik*," Verrazzano said.

"Aha, you speak Arabic. Westerners don't speak Arabic very often. Usually this means you are a spy. Are you a spy?"

"You think I'm undercover as a clueless asshole? Sorry, but that's the real me."

The gunman laughed and lit a smoke. His eyes flickered from Verrazzano to Hussein. They were instantly devoid of humor. His features rippled as hatred, opportunism, and anticipation passed through him.

Hussein stumbled forward toward Quanah's UN Jeep. "Let's go to your car."

"Who's that?" Verrazzano followed.

"Abu Jihad. Our local gangster. He takes money from the Sufis. For protection."

"Protection from whom?"

"Mostly from him." Hussein climbed into the backseat of the Jeep, holding his belly.

As Quanah pulled away from the mosque, the gunman watched them go. Verrazzano looked back as they turned the corner toward the UN headquarters. Abu Jihad was climbing into his truck to follow them.

CHAPTER 31

The Freedom Coin homepage had a big, blue "Get Started Here" button known to online marketers as the "call to action." Roula Haddad was pretty sure it was a call to illegal action. She held her phone in the crook of her neck, with Todd and Kinsella on the end of the line in their car outside Parry's home. As she figured out how to get into the Freedom Coin system, Haddad caught them up on what the company did—or claimed to do. "It's a virtual bank. People don't keep actual money in it."

"Imagine that." Kinsella laughed. "I've had a virtual bank account for years and I never knew it."

"You deposit money. The company converts it to something called Freedom Coin dollars. You send Freedom Coin dollars anywhere in the world and you cash them in with a local moneychanger. Because it's not a real currency, there's no reporting and no restrictions on amounts."

"Sounds like a nice way to launder money."

Todd talked out the idea, nailing it down for himself. "Like, if Parry does a mercenary job in Africa, say, his pay goes through the Freedom Coin system as *virtual* currency. He runs over to Freedom Coin's office to pick it up as *real* dollars."

"All under the radar of IRS or Treasury," Haddad said.

"Can you get into the system, Roula?"

She tapped at her keyboard. "It's pretty secure. The company's network runs on a second-generation onion router. The data Freedom Coin sends—"

"Like details of a money transfer, say?"

"Yeah. That data's wrapped in a series of encryptions. Freedom Coin sends it to your e-mail address, but it goes through different routers all around the world on the way. At each stage, there's a different key, a different level of decryption. It's all aimed at disguising the ultimate destination."

"Like a suspect trying at every corner to shake an agent who's tailing him."

"You got it. The sequence of routers changes with every message, which makes it hard to intercept. Each router strips a little bit of the encryption, like the skin of an onion."

"But by the time it gets to its destination, it's decoded."

"The people who make this kind of software say it protects privacy. But if you're *that* concerned about keeping something private, it's probably because you're worried you'll go to jail for it." Haddad played her knuckles against her desk. "I'm going to go for it head on. Let's see what happens when I click on the call to action."

She hit the big button and talked Todd and Kinsella through what she saw. "It asks if I want to access the system through a mobile phone or through a Windows program. Okay, let's take Windows. Now it wants me to log in. It needs my name and birthdate."

"That's it?" Kinsella said. "Doesn't seem like much security for a financial firm."

"If a virtual bank asks for too much verification, crooks are going to take their dirty business elsewhere. They'd worry we might find a way to access their background information by tapping into Freedom Coin's data, so they keep the details light."

Todd's voice came over the phone, suddenly alert. "The name Verrazzano found at the doctor's house before it burned down."

"TomFrisch4464. I couldn't match it with a Skype address or any e-mail system."

"I'm looking through the case file now." Todd found what he wanted. "I've got a biographical summary of the Molnir chief executive, Tom Frisch. Here it is—date of birth, April 4, 1964.

TomFrisch4464 is his name and birthdate. Enter it in the Freedom Coin system."

Haddad called up the access dialogue box for Freedom Coin account holders. She plugged in "TomFrisch" as the user name and typed "4464" for the password. The box flashed a red advisory: "Sorry. Your account is temporarily unavailable."

"Are we in?" Todd said.

"Nope." Haddad stared at the screen.

"Damn."

Haddad came upright in her chair. "Wait, this is great. It proves Frisch *has* an account. The computer doesn't say, 'Who are you?' It says, 'Hello again, Mister Frisch. Sorry for the inconvenience, but see you soon.'"

"Shall we bring him in?"

"Frisch isn't going to be easy to break down. If we bring him in now, he'll just clam up. Let's see if we can get more on Molnir, maybe from Freedom Coin. I'm sending you the company's address in Borough Park." She pasted the address and sent the text. "Head over there. I'll meet you outside."

Haddad gathered her gear and went to the lobby.

CHAPTER 32

Todd took the ICE car from Bay Ridge through Dyker Heights and down to Borough Park. "Why'd you join ICE, Noelle?"

Kinsella gave him a look like he'd asked her why she never had children. "Seriously? Now?"

"I'm trying to be friendly."

"Be a friend and shut the fuck up."

Two Hasidic men dodged through the traffic. Todd weaved around them. "Jeez. I was only asking."

"And I'm only telling you to mind your own business."

He glided the Dodge Stratus around a double-parked delivery truck and sighed. "The guy had a stutter."

Kinsella frowned at him. "What?"

"You act hostile to me because of the bust in DC. Because I didn't shoot that guy Pangiottis. Well, I didn't shoot him because he had a stutter. So now you know."

"What kind of fucking reason is that to—?"

"I shouted, 'Put the gun down.' He said, 'D-d-d-don't sh-sh-sh-shoot.' But not because he was nervous. I could tell it was like a real tic. Like he obviously spoke that way all the time."

"He had his fucking gun on you, and you didn't shoot him because he stuttered?"

"I couldn't do it. I figured, you know, someone beat him when he was a kid or something. Maybe he was bullied, you know?"

"Well, aren't you the liberal soft touch."

"I just thought, it's not his fault. He's a scumbag. But it's not his fault. And I couldn't shoot him."

He cut onto a side street. Kinsella giggled softly.

"What?" Todd said. "What's funny?"

"D-d-d-don't sh-sh-sh-shoot." Kinsella laughed and doubled forward.

Todd laughed too.

"I'm a sc-sc-scumbag, Off-ff-ff-icer." Kinsella's laughter was out of control.

"Okay, okay." Todd's laugh was lower but relieved.

Kinsella let her head drop back and moaned out a last long laugh. She was quiet a moment. "I joined ICE because of nine-eleven."

Todd stopped laughing.

She turned to him. "Oh, come on, don't look so fucking serious."

"Were you there? At the Twin Towers? On nine-eleven?"

"No, I fucking wasn't there." She looked suddenly as though she had never laughed. "This is the address. Pull the fuck over."

Todd pulled up and cut the engine on the Dodge fifty yards from a two-story house with tan bricks and white cornices. "That's the address Roula sent us. That's Freedom Coin."

"It's not exactly the Bank of America Tower." Kinsella's cell phone rang. She picked up. She was aware of Todd examining her. She knew she should've blown off the 9/11 question calmly. Instead, she lost her control, and now he knew there was something about it that needled her deeply. "Roula, we're here. What's your ETA?"

The background noise on the line suggested Haddad was on the subway headed through Brooklyn. "About fifteen minutes away. Tech messaged me right now with a trace on the hearing aid."

Kinsella touched her jacket pocket. Inside was the hearing aid she'd found in the dying man's hand. "Is it Parry's?"

"Based on the serial number you gave me, it was issued by a VA hospital upstate. To Daryl Underwood."

"Did he leave his hearing aid at his buddy's apartment by mistake?"

"If he did, he was walking around completely deaf. This was Underwood's only device, but his other ear was severely impaired too. He was waiting for the VA to pay for another hearing aid. He'd had the tests. He just needed to get a new device fitted. The VA takes a crazy long time to fulfill stuff like that."

"I'd better let Dom know about this. Did you tell him Parry was dead?"

"Not yet."

"Okay, I'll inform him of that too."

"Thanks. I'll be with you guys shortly."

Todd played his fingers on the wheel impatiently and stared at the Freedom Coin offices. "Doctor Weston told Dom we only have a few days to stop whatever it is that's going down. Maybe we should just go right in. We don't have a lot of time to play with."

"We'll wait until Roula gets here. If the Freedom Coin people have something to hide, they might try to wipe their computer system when we come through the door. We'll need Roula to recover data if that happens."

Todd shook his head. "If only we knew how many days Weston meant."

"We'll find out—and I don't mean the hard way. I've worked a lot of cases with Verrazzano. He always gets it done." She smiled. Her teeth were crooked, as disordered as her hair. "I'm going to zip around the corner and get a coffee from the deli before Roula gets here. Want anything?"

"I don't have change."

"Maybe the deli takes Freedom Coin dollars." Kinsella put on her Tifosi running shades and left Todd in the Dodge.

In the deli, the charcoal scent of toasted bagels was in the air from the last breakfast orders. Kinsella asked for an everything bagel with lox, onions, and full-fat cream cheese. All the most powerful flavors. Her taste buds were dying off in droves—the gin-and-tonic holocaust.

As she waited, she saw herself in the mirror behind the counter and grimaced. She pretended to study the tuna and the herring in the refrigerated counter, vowing to cut back on the booze. She felt weak for having to make such a promise and weaker for knowing that it was just air. At the ICE Academy, the body-language instructor told trainees to remember that a face may lie, but eyes can't. That's why people wear shades. Without the eyes, our ability to read a face is reduced to the clichés of a bad movie or a fashion ad. Kinsella with her shades on: cool, tough broad. Shades off: unresolved sorrow and loss leaking from pale-blue irises. "I joined ICE because of nine-eleven," and "No, I fucking wasn't there." She may as well have been, since a part of her died that day too. The part that would never have quit mourning for someone who *did* die there. She ordered a coffee with milk and sugar, her voice husky and whispering.

She picked up her order and left the deli. The neon Budweiser sign of the dive across the street started to flash as if it had turned on just for her. She sipped the coffee and cradled the hot cup. She felt better. Caffeine and a pair of shades was all she needed to right herself. And a few good leads on this sarin case. She took out her phone to dial Verrazzano.

She waited for the sounds of the war zone on the other end of the line.

CHAPTER 33

The Sufi lay quietly in the backseat, his fingers compressing the gash in his stomach. Quanah drove the jeep toward the UN compound. He twisted his lips in frustration. Verrazzano knew that look. It was how men reacted when they hit a roadblock in their heads. Verrazzano never got hung up, never charged headlong over and over at the very point where his thinking broke down. He always stepped back and looked for a way around, for a different solution.

He refused to believe the clues had run out. He was so close. He had the GPS chip that he believed would lead him to the sarin stockpile that Underwood had guarded. But he didn't have the soundwave that activated it. He had tried putting the phone on mic in front of Hussein's mouth as the Sufi spoke. He held it out of the Jeep's window under the loudspeaker of a mosque for the call to prayer. Nothing. He dialed Doctor Weston's extension at the UN office and waited for her incoming voice mail message, all the time watching through the back window for Abu Jihad and his gang of gunmen. Again, nothing. The GPS didn't activate.

"Remember what Wyatt used to say? 'The solution lies within.'"

Quanah glanced at him and said, "Fuck Wyatt."

Verrazzano's smile was thin. "He also used to say, 'Recognize that you're ugly enough to have known the answer all along, and even the worst thing in the world will suddenly appear to be the obvious solution.'"

"Well, he'd know. Wyatt killed men in every conflict that involved Americans since Vietnam and about half of those that didn't. He was the worst thing in the world."

"That's why I paid attention to him. So did you."

"Too damn long."

The Army trained Verrazzano to be a soldier. But Wyatt showed him how to function like a private operative. Such a man carries the fire of life in his hand, Wyatt said once, because only he really knows what it is to snuff it out. The colonel thought deeply enough to impart some philosophy too. If it was only the squeezing of a trigger, he said, the job could be carried out by the stupidest of men. But a good operative must be more than a machine, and he certainly couldn't be an idiot. He must have the spark of a god in him. To decide life and death. To change the future of mankind when he took out the president of a republic or a designer of revolutionary software or a gangster's rival. He neither built nor destroyed. He simply changed what was to come. He created the transforming energy in the cosmos that drove the planet on its axis. In its turn, the cosmos helped the assassin.

"I bought the philosophy, and I followed Wyatt's orders," Verrazzano said.

"Until I told you the truth about the Ghattas woman in Beirut. The truth about that bastard."

Verrazzano touched his fingertips to the dashboard, tapped them through the opening bars of Mozart's Adagio in B minor. He wondered if he'd really eradicated Wyatt's thinking. He searched for the power of the universe to help him—looked for a way to move it within himself. "You know as well as I do, Wyatt's riding this Jeep with us right now," he said. "He's in my head."

"Don't tempt me. I'm just about ready to blow your brains out already. If you've got Wyatt in there . . ."

Verrazzano laughed, and Quanah smiled reluctantly.

"He's in your head too, Quanah."

The smile was gone. "I've thought of putting a bullet through that too."

The Jeep crossed the bridge over the parched Barada River. Verrazzano's phone buzzed. He glanced at it and picked up. "Noelle, what's new?"

"Underwood's buddy Jeff Parry is dead." Kinsella panted down the phone line. She was walking. "I found him with a bullet in his heart less than an hour ago."

Quanah turned the Jeep into the UN compound. He waved to the bulky Syrian guards at the gate and pulled across the courtyard.

"Where are you now?" Verrazzano said.

"We're about to go into a financial office in Borough Park. A virtual bank by the name of Freedom Coin. Parry had a roll of dollars bound in one of their paper bands."

Hussein moaned as he lifted himself upright. Quanah opened the door and helped him out. They shuffled away to find the medical officer.

Verrazzano gave a thoughtful hiss. "A roll of dollars?"

"Yeah, it's not much," Kinsella said. "But that's pretty much all there was. Except for the hearing aid. Parry had it, but it's registered to Underwood."

Verrazzano had assumed Underwood's hearing aid was lost in the grave when Quanah dug him up. Instead, it had surfaced on a dead man six thousand miles away. "Parry borrowed his friend's hearing aid?"

"Parry wasn't deaf. The thing wasn't in his ear. It was in his hand. I only found it because of the noise it was making."

Verrazzano snapped forward. "What kind of noise?"

"The switch was turned to the battery-test setting. It's like this high-pitched whine."

"Do you have it with you?"

"It's in my pocket."

"Get it out." Verrazzano pulled up the GPS app on Quanah's phone. Once again, it demanded the soundwave to activate the login. "Play the tone back to me, Noelle. Down the line. Hold the hearing aid by your phone and turn on the test tone."

"Got you."

A thin squeal keened from the phone. Verrazzano stared at the GPS app. The login icon was still. The phone slipped in the sweat of his palm. Five seconds of the test tone and nothing. He tightened his fingers around the handset. "Come on," he whispered.

Quanah stumped across the courtyard. He opened the door of the Jeep and slipped into the driver's seat.

The dialogue box on the cell phone disappeared. The tone matched. The device was logged in. A map filled the screen: Damascus, the skein of alleys and streets around the Casbah at the center and on the slope of Mount Qasioun from the Presidential Palace, a throbbing blue dot.

Verrazzano showed the map to Quanah. "The pulse. That's it."

Just as Wyatt had promised him years ago, the worst things in the world were the easiest to find.

CHAPTER 34

Kinsella headed back to the ICE car with the coffee heating the palm of her hand. She passed a black Lincoln parked at the curb behind the ICE Dodge. She paused and read off the plates. *DPC 789.* "Well, look at that." She fumbled her notebook out of his pocket. Her handwriting was as perplexing as the rules of cricket, but when she found the right page in her notes, she confirmed that this was the Town Car Verrazzano spotted at the house of Doctor Weston's killer. She hurried to the Dodge. "Bill, it's the Lincoln. Right behind us."

Todd twisted in his seat. "That can't be coincidence."

"The driver's got to be in there, the Freedom Coin house." Kinsella grabbed the case file from Todd's lap. She paged through it for the photo of the limo driver that Haddad downloaded earlier from the Department of Defense. "The wife of the guy who killed Doctor Weston said the driver brought them money. Now we know where he got the cash."

She found the page she was looking for—a military photo of a man with a high forehead and mocking eyes. She held it up to Todd. "The limo driver. That's Jon Ivin."

"That's a *photo* of Jon Ivin." Todd pointed across the street. "*That's* Jon Ivin."

He came down the steps outside the Freedom Coin house. His hair was longer than it was in the military photo, and he had a bristly mustache. He carried a leather duffel.

Todd got out of the car. "Jon Ivin, hold it right there," he shouted. "Federal agents."

Ivin kept walking.

"Is *he* deaf too?" Kinsella muttered.

Todd crossed the street. He drew his Glock and called out again. Ivin looked around as though he couldn't imagine that the pale, balding man could be pointing his pistol at him.

Kinsella reached for her shoulder holster, but she realized she still had her coffee cup in her right hand. She was about to switch it to her left when Ivin wheeled the duffel at Todd. It caught the ICE agent off-balance. Todd went down hard. His pistol rattled across the sidewalk.

Ivin brought up a stubby Smith & Wesson Bodyguard. He kicked Todd as he tried to rise. He stood over him, the pistol directed at the agent's head, his upper body tensed to shoot. Todd's chest heaved. Ivin had only to pull the trigger and he was dead.

Kinsella didn't have time to draw her weapon. Her reaction was instant—she hurled the coffee cup. It struck Ivin in the head. The lid popped off on impact, and the scalding liquid spilled over his face and down his chest. Ivin roared and reeled away.

Kinsella leapt past the parked cars, drawing her Glock. She grabbed Ivin's wrist and hammered it against a brick gatepost. The Smith & Wesson dropped. She shoved the barrel of her pistol into Ivin's neck. "You have the right to remain silent." She leaned against him to hold him still. The hot coffee seeped into her linen jacket.

Ivin's face was the color of beetroot. He bellowed and snarled.

"What's the matter? You don't take milk and sugar?" Kinsella yanked Ivin's arms to cuff him. "Anything you say or do can and will be used against you in a court of law."

Todd rose slowly to his feet, shivering. Kinsella knew he was composing himself, letting go of the nearness of death. "Jesus Christ, that was close, Bill."

He retrieved his pistol. "My screw-up. Shouldn't have let him knock me down."

Kinsella admired the way Todd admitted a mistake and moved on.

Todd unzipped the holdall. Bundled twenties filled the bag. He reached down. The notes were six inches deep. "Jesus. How much is in here, Ivin?" His voice was loud, pitched to overcome the adrenaline of near-death.

"Fuck you." Ivin tried for rage, but the pain in his face made him sound tearful, like a teenager denied the keys to the car.

Kinsella hustled him into the back of the ICE car.

Todd climbed into the driver's seat. He started the engine.

"You okay?" Kinsella sat beside him. "You want me to drive?"

The outline of Ivin's size-ten ankle boots marked the shoulder of Todd's blue suit jacket. He dusted it off. "I'm good," he said.

"You know what you should've said, right?"

Todd frowned. Then he picked up on the humor around her eyes.

They both spoke at once. "D-d-d-don't sh-sh-sh-oot."

Kinsella punched his arm. Todd smiled and pulled out into the street fast.

CHAPTER 35

The sign above the sentry hut was in Arabic and English: "The Arab Board of Engineering Specializations and Research." The name was generic enough for the building to be anything from a clubhouse for university grads to a secret nuclear program. The guards wore loose leather jackets, hugged their machine-pistols close, and stood upright and vigilant. In the Arab world, that marked them as an independent militia—government troops always slouched. Each guard took a wary step forward as the red Mercedes Roadster drove down the drive.

The wires dangling from the steering column bounced against Quanah's knee where he had interlaced them to jump the engine. "You're sure the signal's in there?"

Verrazzano glanced at the screen of the phone. The blue dot that marked the location of the transponder showed just beyond the first building in the compound. "Yep. And it's not moving. I guess Doctor Weston didn't stitch this one inside somebody, the way she did with the Sufi."

The Mercedes rolled to a slow crawl before the steel barrier over the road. But Quanah didn't quite stop. The Syrian guards stretched their index fingers along the bodies of their AEK machine pistols, ready to reach for the trigger. The quality of the car surely unnerved them. Life in a dictatorship didn't encourage challenges to authority and wealth, even among men trusted to hold hardware that delivered nine hundred rounds per minute.

None of the guards wanted to be the one to question the driver of such an expensive vehicle.

Verrazzano called out in English, "Are my guys in there? The Molnir guys?"

The guards shifted nervously. One of them spoke up. "You mean Mister Lance?"

"I knew it." Verrazzano slapped Quanah's shoulder. "I told you Lance would be here. Is he alone? Is Joey up here?"

"Joey? Only Mister Lance. No one else."

At the entrance of the building beyond the parking lot, a lone American in desert camo came out and climbed into a blue truck. Perhaps that was "Mister Lance." Verrazzano didn't want to be at the gate surrounded by hostile weaponry when Lance came through.

"Okay, let's go," Verrazzano said.

Quanah edged the convertible forward.

The guard in the control hut hit the button to draw back the heavy electric gate. One of the others bitched at him, wanting the men in the Mercedes to show ID. He rushed into the hut and the gate squealed to a halt. The sentries argued briefly until Quanah yelled at them in Arabic, "Do you know who this man is?"

The guards froze. They hadn't expected the foreigner to understand their dispute. Now they would learn which powerful person they had affronted.

The engine of the truck roared up the slope toward them. Verrazzano tried to keep a commanding expression on his face, to play his Tom Frisch role. Inside he was a guy with a handgun against a guard detail armed with Czech assault rifles and a Special Forces veteran in a truck three times the size of his vehicle.

But he still had Quanah.

"This is Tom Frisch," Quanah shouted. "The head of Molnir Partners. He's a real son of a whore. You've got about fifteen seconds before he goes nuclear."

The guards all went for the gate release at once. The Mercedes accelerated down the drive toward the parking lot. The truck waited for them at the end of the approach road. The driver waved for them to pull up.

He climbed out and sauntered toward the Mercedes. He had muscular shoulders and a barrel chest. His ears were long and fleshy like a mastiff's jowls. He carried a Russian machine pistol at his side.

"You still Tom Frisch?" Quanah murmured to Verrazzano.

"This guy's Molnir. He must know Frisch."

"Then think fast. Because he's not going to believe that we're specialist engineering researchers looking to meet our Arab counterparts."

The man in the camo came to the driver's side front wheel and nodded. "Help you?"

Quanah ticked his fingernail against the steering wheel.

"You sure can, soldier." Verrazzano made his words orotund and deep.

The Tennessee drawl snapped Quanah around toward Verrazzano. He recognized the imitation.

"The first thing you can do is address me as 'sir.' The second is you can instruct those dumbfucks on the gate in how to question and verify a suspicious arrival. They're a bunch of zeroes, and their inadequacy endangers your mission."

The man drew himself up. His boys were being insulted, and he didn't like it. But he also worried who this irascible guy in the expensive car might be.

Verrazzano gestured for Quanah to drive on and called out to the soldier. "We'll talk over by the entrance, son."

They went across the parking lot toward the courtyard and came to a halt. The truck spun and followed them.

Quanah unwound the wires beneath the steering block and the engine cut out. In the passenger seat, Verrazzano checked the transponder reading on the cell phone. "Whatever Doctor Weston wanted us to find, it's right in there."

"But there's a Molnir guy out here, too."

"He's my guy now." Verrazzano climbed out and walked to the truck. He reached out his hand and took the soldier in a shake of iron like the one Verrazzano remembered the old man clamping on him years before. "Colonel Lawton Wyatt, son."

"Yes, sir. Sergeant Davis Baines."

"How long you been with Molnir, son?"

"Four months, sir. Captain Frisch brought me in directly from my last Rangers assignment."

Verrazzano glanced at Quanah. Frisch was pulling the same trick Wyatt had used on them—recruiting them to a secret unit right from their Special Forces regiments, then making them his personal army.

"How do you like it here, Baines?"

"I like it very well, sir."

"Show me where it's at, son."

"Sir?"

"I'm a nasty man, son. Take me to where the nasty shit is."

"Of course, sir. In through the gate at the side of the main building. Directly across the courtyard. It's right through there. All secure, sir."

"You have a guard on it twenty-four-seven?"

"Two men around the clock, sir. They're not Molnir. Just local subcontracted guys. But most of them are pretty good, for guard duty at least. I ride them as hard as I can, sir."

"Glad to hear it." Verrazzano walked toward the building. "You stay out here, Sergeant Baines. While I'm here, I don't want the doofus division on the gate letting anybody else in. There's a few guys maybe on my tail around this burg, and I prefer to ensure that someone's got my back who knows his ass from his elbow. That okay with you?" He smiled.

"Yes, sir, Colonel Wyatt, sir."

Even a man who despised Wyatt couldn't help but channel his charm and authority. Verrazzano smiled the way Wyatt did. It almost blew the top off his head. When Wyatt gave him that warm look, Verrazzano used to feel like a little boy who had his daddy's approval. Now he was grown up, and he was sickened by reminders of the father figure in his imitation of the man.

Quanah was already over by the gate beside the first building. Verrazzano led him into the courtyard. Lawn sprinklers sprayed dashes of gold through the floodlights in the courtyard. A Syrian guard loitered by a double door, smoking and scuffing the grass with his boot. He watched the two Americans approach, but when Verrazzano snapped a salute, he yanked his AK-47 to his shoulder and stamped a foot.

Beyond the doors, Verrazzano entered a big conference room. It was empty.

Except for the weapons crates.

The day's last light fell through the tall windows onto a dozen wooden boxes, each the size of a bathtub. The unfinished pine crates were smudged with oil and marked with dirty gouges—they had been on a long journey before they reached this room.

Verrazzano signaled for Quanah to watch the entrance. He jumped onto the small stage at one end of the conference room and laid the speaker's lectern on its side. He kicked off its angled top and hurried back to the crates with it. The top of the lectern had a heavy edge designed to stop papers from slipping to the floor. Verrazzano used it to batter the lid open on one of the crates. The wood splintered as the nails lifted. Packed inside were a dozen gray artillery shells, six inches in diameter and three feet long. Each was labeled with Arabic text and spray-painted with a stencil. Some also bore a freehand scribble in black marker. Stuck to the underside of the lid, a multicolored fire diamond delineated the flammability, instability, and toxicity of the contents:

$$1$$
$$4 \qquad 0$$

Sarin. Verrazzano's chest tightened as if the mere sight reactivated the traces of nerve agent in his lungs.

Quanah glanced inside the crate. "This shit's even more lethal than you."

"Brother, you know me better than that."

"Correction. *Almost* as lethal as you. What's the Arabic writing mean?"

Verrazzano shook his head. Like Quanah, the Green Berets taught him to speak good Arabic, but he had never bothered to learn the almost entirely different grammar used for writing. "Something about freedom." He jammed the lid of the box back into place.

"We could blow it up right here," Quanah said.

"To get the temperature high enough to burn off the nerve agent, we'd need a hell of a lot of explosives. There's a political dimension too. The UN inspectors should examine this. They have to figure out who's not keeping to the disarmament agreements."

"By the time we get back here with the inspectors, this stuff could be gone." Quanah surveyed the stack of crates. "We can't get it out of here in a dinky little Roadster."

"We have to take the chance on getting the UN here. The Molnir guy thinks I'm Wyatt. He's not in a rush to get this stuff out of here. Let's get back to the car."

The door opened. Sergeant Baines came in.

"I posted a couple of other guys in the parking lot, Colonel Wyatt. I wanted to come in and make sure you had found exactly what you needed."

"I sure did, son."

Quanah moved toward the exit. "We're out of here now, Lance."

Verrazzano tried to distract the soldier. "That's okay, son. We're—"

"Lance is sick," Baines said. "I'm filling in. Hey—"

"Aw shit, those assholes on the gate gave us the wrong name." Quanah drew his Glock.

"Quanah, no. This is Sergeant Baines. He's just—"

Verrazzano watched the Molnir man drop to his knee behind the sarin crates and raise his AEK.

Quanah took aim. Verrazzano grabbed his arm. "You might hit the sarin." They hurled themselves through the doors as the machine pistol opened up.

Verrazzano smashed the butt of his H&K across the jaw of the guard on the door. Another guard sprinted around the far corner of the courtyard. Quanah fired off a few rounds, and the guard ducked away.

Dust blew off the desert hillside and coated Verrazzano's throat as he fled across the courtyard. The Molnir man hurried outside, firing from the hip.

Verrazzano got off a couple of rounds and jumped into the Mercedes. "Let's go. We can't shoot it out with this guy. We've got to bring the UN inspectors back here."

Quanah dropped into the driver's seat.

Baines threw himself to the ground. He fired again. The bullets struck the side of the Mercedes with a sound like the lid peeling off a tin of sardines. Quanah twisted the wires under the steering column.

"Hurry," Verrazzano called.

The engine caught and roared. They raced for the gate. The guards had neglected to roll shut the big grille. At the sound of shots, one of them ran to the hut and pressed the button. The gate jerked across the road.

Verrazzano rose in his seat and waved. "Open that fucking gate, you assholes."

The grille went still. Quanah accelerated toward it.

The gate ground backward, opening once more. Quanah sped by the guards. He cut the Mercedes down the slope, in among the apartment buildings.

Baines swung up to the gate in a GMC truck. Two guards jumped into the rear bed. They braced their machine pistols on the roof of the cab as the truck pulled away in pursuit.

"Make for the hotel where the inspectors are staying," Verrazzano shouted. "So long as this guy is engaged in a pursuit, there's a chance Molnir won't get around to moving the sarin to another location. If we get the UN people back to that compound in time, maybe we can capture the nerve agent right here."

The Roadster should've left the GMC for dead. But five years of bombardment and disrepair had chewed up the roads. Quanah had to swerve around chunks of debris and shell holes. The truck stayed within range.

The gunmen clung to the rack behind the cab, blasting away at the Mercedes. Verrazzano let them have a few rounds from his H&K to keep their heads down.

The windshield of the GMC splintered. The Molnir man hammered it out of the frame. The guards ducked as the big rectangle of glass flipped over the cab and smashed into the road behind the speeding truck.

Quanah turned onto an empty four-lane at the foot of the hill. Big square blocks of concrete carved the roadway into a slalom to slow vehicles for a roadblock or an ambush. He made ground as best he could, but the bright-red car was a fine target in the ultra-power headlamps of the truck.

Verrazzano tried another shot. "Out of ammo."

Quanah handed over his Glock. "That's all we have. The spare mags are in my Jeep."

The situation was as clear to Verrazzano as if it were an equation on a whiteboard. He was in a car, which was only slightly more bulletproof than a ball of mozzarella, and he had a few rounds to defend against gunmen carrying assault rifles. Most people would've panicked. Then they would've died.

Verrazzano never panicked. Nor was he going to die.

"Better drive faster." He racked the slide on the Glock.

Quanah pumped the gas.

Verrazzano took aim. The speed of the car jostled him. He had Baines's head in his sights.

The Mercedes glanced off a concrete roadblock. Quanah wrenched at the wheel. The Roadster slid sideways. Verrazzano's shot went wide of the GMC.

The Mercedes struck the next block hard. Verrazzano's neck snapped back. His head seemed to empty out, as though his brain leaked all the blood and thought from inside it. He flew out of his seat and tumbled into the dirt and gravel at the roadside.

The crushed engine of the Mercedes hissed and groaned. *You and me both*, Verrazzano thought.

Quanah jumped from the wreck. He hauled Verrazzano toward the cover of the concrete roadblock. "Where's the pistol?" he said.

"Don't know."

The GMC halted ten yards away. The two gunmen in the back trained their weapons on Verrazzano and Quanah. Baines stepped out of his cab.

"Aw, fuck." Quanah lowered Verrazzano. The dirt was dry and fine under his fingers.

A sudden rush of air and light sawed through the descending night, loud as a locomotive. Panic flooded the Molnir man's features. He recognized the sound. Verrazzano knew it too. He had heard it often enough on his own shoulder—an antitank missile.

The front of the GMC truck bucked as the missile hit. It exploded in a dazzling flare of flame. The two gunmen jerked out of the rear bed like puppets tugged by a petulant child. The blast drove Baines off his feet. His face smashed on the pavement.

The shock wave passed over Verrazzano, teasing him with the proximity of death.

From out of the infernal rumbling of the flames came men's laughter. Six gunmen stepped into the light of the burning truck, their faces wrapped in red-and-white checkered kaffiyehs. One of them had the command-launch unit of a Javelin missile on his shoulder. He muttered lasciviously to it, as though it were a woman who had done something particularly dirty for him. The other men joined in his joking, until one of them ordered silence.

"Sorry, Abu Jihad," the missile man mumbled to the chief. It was the gunman who had watched Verrazzano leave the Sufi mosque.

Abu Jihad knelt to examine the prone Molnir operative. He grabbed the American's hair and lifted the head. Half the face stayed on the pavement. He ordered his gunmen to check the shooters who'd been thrown from the truck.

He waited, rolling a string of amber prayer beads through his fingers, ticking them against the magazine of his M16.

The guards from the Molnir truck groaned. Abu Jihad made a dismissive gesture. His gunmen drilled a dozen rounds into the injured men.

"I have a rule always to kill the people who're about to do the killing," Abu Jihad said. "It's like marrying an ugly woman.

It earns you gratitude and obedience, which is much better than love. Do I have your gratitude?"

"You do. And I can prove it." Verrazzano clutched at the concrete traffic block and dragged himself to his feet. "How would you like to win this civil war all by yourself?"

CHAPTER 36

Haddad stepped over the puddle on the Borough Park sidewalk where the coffee cup had struck the limo driver. She ought to wait for backup, because Todd and Kinsella were en route to the field office to interrogate Jon Ivin. But the sarin attack could hit the city any time, so she decided to go into Freedom Coin alone. A slurred growl challenged her buzz at the door. "Identify yourself." Either the intercom was defective or the staff had enjoyed a liquid lunch.

"Special Agent Roula Haddad. Immigration and Customs Enforcement."

A wheezing exhalation through the intercom. The lock snapped open.

The hallway was shabby and bare but for a spray of junk mail on the floorboards, as though the occupants had moved out weeks ago. Down the hall, two inches of Polish vodka were looking lonely at the bottom of a liter bottle on the kitchen table.

A clotted, rumbling voice from the front room told Haddad the intercom worked just fine. "I don't have any Mexicans here, Miss Immigration Agent."

Haddad followed the wet rattle of laughter to an office that was like the inside of a phone company terminal box. Gray wires snaked across the floor to a half-dozen hard drives flashing blue. A five-foot safe stood in the corner. The bookshelves in the niches either side of the fireplace were empty, except for a stack of cast-off modem routers and an open pizza box with one slice left.

The pizza balanced precariously so as to be within reach of the man at the desk. His thick, black beard was slick with grease from the slice he was finishing. His heavy belly competed with melon-sized man boobs for space in front of his slouching torso. He stared queasily at three computer screens, like a drunk watching a bartender pour him one too many. He moved his eyeballs just enough to give Haddad's body a slow, grasping glance. She detected the alertness that came over all men when they first saw her black ringlets, her blue-black eyes, her slim waist and wide hips.

"You want some pie?" he gasped. The accent—East European, with a bit of acquired Brooklyn.

"Thank you, no."

One bushy eyebrow went up, a low-energy alternative to a shrug. He took the pizza, folded it lengthways, and fed it through the hole in his beard.

"Take a load off." The man gestured to a low, white leather couch by the window. It was the only seat in the room, except for the one he sat in.

"I'll stand." She scanned the room for weapons and listened for other occupants in the house. The limo driver came out of here with a gun. Maybe this guy had one in his desk. She moved closer. A little rectangle of fresh business cards rested in a clear plastic stand on the desk. They bore the company's Star Wars–style logo. She picked one up and read it aloud: "Yuri Lifshitz. Chief executive officer and founder. Freedom Coin."

The man behind the desk twirled his hand as if he were taking a bow. "Call me Yuri."

"Mister Lifshitz, I have some significant—"

The phone rang. Lifshitz picked up a white cordless. Chewing the slice, he muttered in Russian. Orange pizza grease glimmered on the handset when he put it back in its cradle.

The corner of Haddad's mouth twitched with satisfaction. Now she knew how she'd get this guy. "Mister Lifshitz, a man left your office earlier today with fifty thousand dollars. Immediately outside on the street, he—"

"Once the money goes out the door, it's not my business."

"Mister Lifshitz, our agency has shut down several online currency systems similar to Freedom Coin. Do you want that kind of scrutiny?"

"Come look at the accounts any time you like. Next time, I'll dress up nice for you."

"Tell me about Molnir Partners."

"*Who* Partners?"

"We believe Molnir uses a Freedom Coin account to circumvent US tax codes."

Lifshitz shook his head. "That's on them. I'm registered in Costa Rica. The US tax code doesn't—"

"You're here in Brooklyn. You're subject to US law. The head of Molnir is a man named Tom Frisch. I want you to open his account for my preliminary examination. I'll get a warrant if you won't play along. But we have a very pressing deadline, and as soon as I'm done with Frisch, I'm going to be all over you."

Lifshitz dropped a thick finger on the return key. "It's done. I give you access. You got his password, right? Of course you do. Go ahead. I opened up the account just now."

She made for his side of the desk. "Let me see it."

He slipped the keyboard away. "You go back to your office, lady, and poke around from there."

Haddad put her business card on the desk. "Next time you're handing out a bag full of cash to someone from Molnir, you call me."

From the hallway, she heard him mutter, "Blow me."

She went out into the street. Lifshitz's insolence didn't faze her. She was too pleased with what she had seen. The guy used a cordless phone. The law protected cell phone networks and landlines from unwarranted snooping. But Congress had decided that sending a signal from a cordless handset across the room to its plugged-in base was no different from shouting your business in the street. Law enforcement could tap it without a warrant.

Haddad pulled out her cell phone and called a tech at the ICE field office to set up the trace. The tech had it working by the time she got to the subway station at the end of the street. "I can't believe the guy's on an insecure network," he said.

"Everybody's dumb about *one* thing. That's what keeps us in business."

A train hammered into the station.

CHAPTER 37

The antimicrobial ointment on Jon Ivin's scalded face glowed in the striplights. Bill Todd carried a paper cup into the interview room at the ICE field office. Ivin flinched.

"Don't worry. It's water." Todd smiled.

"Fuck you."

He paced across the bland room with its plain, white walls. He dragged the free chair to the corner of the empty desk so he could observe Ivin head to toe. He wanted to study his body language. To invade his space, to threaten him. "You've got a nice house out in Atlantic Beach, Jon."

"It's not mine. I rent the upper floor." The burned side of his mouth had lost sensation. He drooled onto his coffee-stained button-down. "Rent's not much. Every time there's a storm, the whole fucking street's under three feet of water."

"Our agent ran into a couple of nasty guys at your place. They opened fire on him."

Ivin shrugged. Then he winced. The coffee had stuck his shirt to the skin of his shoulder. He moved his fingers to his lips, forgetting there was no cigarette there.

Todd noticed the nervous tell. In the interview room, real bad guys kept their bodies inert and their faces so inexpressive that they appeared to be in an advanced stage of multiple sclerosis. By comparison, Ivin twitched like a sparrow in a dust bath.

"I want to see a doctor," Ivin said.

"You have second-degree burns from the coffee. The best thing to do is let them soothe themselves." He sipped his water. Kinsella and Haddad were watching through the two-way mirror, judging him. His first interrogation since he came back on the job. "Tell me about the fifty grand you were carrying when we picked you up."

"It's a delivery," Ivin said.

"To whom?"

"They were going to call and tell me who it was for when I was on the road."

"They?"

"The people who called me to make the delivery. They needed a car. That's what I do. I drive a fucking car."

Todd compressed his lips thoughtfully. His first interrogation back on the job, but maybe number ten thousand since he joined the Customs Service, before ICE even existed. This was the part he liked. He liked to hear the suspect curse. It meant he was on edge, ready to unravel. "You had dealings with these people before, Jon?"

"Never."

"How'd they find you?"

"Yellow pages. I just got a call from a guy named Yuri."

"He needed to send someone out the door with fifty K, so he picked the first guy he found in the phone book?"

"I guess."

"Sure, Jon. You've got such a trustworthy face. They should put you in a white coat so you can advertise aspirin."

Ivin touched his fingers to his mustache and watched Todd doubtfully.

"You want to know how we found you at Freedom Coin? Jeff Parry sent us."

Ivin's face turned a deeper purple. "Jeff's alive?"

"Why wouldn't he be?"

Ivin tried to correct himself. "He was sick. You know, breathing problems."

"Breathing's still his problem. I was shitting you. He's dead. Someone shot him in the head."

"Shit. Okay, see, I went over to check up on him today. That's all. Just to see him." Ivin's voice was tentative as a cold-sober karaoke singer. He worked his tongue and reached toward Todd's cup. "Can I get some of that water?"

"Later." Todd drank the water down and smacked his lips. "You went to see Jeff, and—?"

"We hung out a while. I left, and then later, like you said, someone must've come in and shot him in the heart."

"The heart? I just told you he got shot in the head. But in fact it *was* in the heart. How did *you* know it was in the heart?"

Ivin's hand went to his neck as though he were throttling himself, shutting off his voice. "All right, so I found him on the floor when I went over to hang out with him. He was already dead. There was nothing I could do for him, so I ran. I didn't want to be around when the cops came. I've been in trouble with the law a couple times."

Todd's stare said that he knew things Ivin didn't. "How long have you been driving a limo for Molnir Partners?"

"That job's like a favor. I can't say more than that. I don't want to get anyone into trouble over there at Molnir. I've got to think about client confidentiality."

Todd chuckled with genuine amusement. No comedian could ever crack him up the way he laughed at an outmaneuvered criminal forced to spin a line off the cuff. Ivin's desperation and dimness released some of his tension. "Let me tell you who can cite client confidentiality under interrogation: attorneys and psychiatrists— *not* limo drivers."

"One of the guys at Molnir was with me in Iraq. He put me on their records as an employee so I could get health care. But they don't pay me regular. I only get paid for when I drive their chief executive once in a while."

"Jeff Parry had a bundle of twenties in his pocket with a Freedom Coin paper band. He got it from you."

Ivin shook his head. "Jeff didn't have money. He was on food stamps."

Todd wished they'd found Ivin's prints on the cash in Parry's pocket. But the Freedom Coin band was clean. "Why'd you draw your weapon on me?"

"I had fifty grand in the bag. I figured you were going to take it off of me."

"I identified myself as a federal agent."

"And I could've asked to see some ID after you put a hole in my head."

Todd dropped his chin to his chest. There was one piece of leverage he had, and now was the time to use it. "Okay, get up. I'm through with you." He took him by the upper arm and hustled him out into the corridor. "I'm going to let you walk."

Kinsella and Haddad appeared in the door of the observation room. Haddad stepped toward Todd, but Kinsella caught her elbow and shook her head.

Ivin grinned. It didn't seem to hurt his seared face.

Todd ran him past the agents' cubicles toward the elevator. He felt the lightness and relief in Ivin's step.

"You guys should get me a new fucking shirt," he said. "I'll send you the fucking dry cleaning bill."

Todd stared ahead, his jaw stiff.

"You'll be hearing from my lawyer too." Ivin tried to shrug away from him, but he held on. "Remember the old lady that sued McDonald's? Tipped coffee in her lap? They paid her a million fucking bucks, and she wasn't even burned in the face like me."

The security guard buzzed them into the lobby. Todd thumped the down button. The elevator rang out its electronic tone. Ivin swaggered into the elevator.

"Hey, asshole," Todd said. "Have fun explaining to your boss what happened to the fifty grand you were supposed to deliver. The money stays here, and you don't get a receipt from me."

For a man who had suffered a second-degree burn only a couple of hours earlier, Ivin's face went quite pale.

The elevator chimed and the doors slid into motion. Ivin threw himself between them. He tumbled out at Todd's feet.

Todd grabbed Ivin's collar and tugged him back into the field office. Ivin stumbled at his side until he threw him into the chair in the interview room. Ivin slouched, panting and shivering. His eyes followed Todd, his head shaking side to side as if his desperation might persuade the agent to go easy on him.

Todd paced the room, reading a text on the screen of his phone, letting him sweat. Kinsella came in and grinned at him. She went to the table and sat down. She put a clipboard on the table and studied it, rapping the tabletop with her long fingernails but keeping her mouth shut. The silence of the two agents brought Ivin to the edge of his seat. Perspiration patched his shirt under his arms and across his stomach.

"You can't just keep that fifty grand," he said. "They'll fucking kill me."

Todd didn't look up from his phone. "Who are *they*?"

"That's what I'm telling you—I don't know. But no one loses fifty K and is just, like, 'Shoot, them's the breaks.'"

Todd put his phone on the table and brought his hands to his hips. "The money's gone. You don't want *them* to kill you? Then you'd better talk to *me*. Because I can put you on the street alone. Or I can keep you safe under surveillance. Do I make myself clear?"

"Yes, sir."

His fifty-thousand-dollar scare tactic had worked. The guy was ready to talk. "What's the money for?"

"Tom Frisch does business around the world. Freedom Coin is a way to bring the cash to the United States without declaring it."

"Why were you carrying such a large amount?"

"For Molnir guys who've been invalided out."

"Bundles of cash? That's how they're paid?"

"You want a pension direct to your bank account after health care and deductibles, you'd better go work for—I guess you'd better go work for ICE."

"What sort of injuries do these guys have?"

"Being a soldier is dangerous, right? They got all kinds of shit wrong with them."

"What about Jeff Parry?"

Ivin was weakened, but he wasn't beaten. Todd recognized pretense in his resigned sigh. The guy was still trying to work him. "He coughed a bunch, and he moved slow. He never told me why."

Todd rested his butt against the table, keeping himself high above Ivin and close. "You know Lee Hill?"

"Sure, I know Lee."

"Do you take him money?"

"I give it to his wife. The money, I mean." Ivin smirked. It smarted. He grimaced and lifted a hand to the raw skin on his cheek.

Ivin would be prepped to deny his crimes, to deflect Todd's questions. Todd decided to panic him, tagging him for something he knew the limo driver *hadn't* done. "Tell me why you killed Lee Hill."

"What the fuck?"

"Lee Hill's wife Jennifer says you promised the two of you would be together."

"I never promised her shit."

Todd shouted, "You killed Lee Hill, so you could have his wife. Then you killed Jeff Parry for the money."

Ivin tried to raise his volume to match Todd, but he was intimidated. The only thing that went up was the pitch of his voice. "I didn't kill Lee."

"But you *did* kill Jeff? I notice you're not denying that."

"Lee messed up. He got exposed to—" Ivin cut himself off. He put his fists on the table and glared at them.

"Exposed to what, Jon?" Todd leaned close. "The four-ten?"

Ivin's eyes snapped up at him. Kinsella was still, but Todd sensed her approval.

"We have an agent in Damascus right now. We know what Molnir is doing. It's sarin, right, Jon?"

Ivin's voice was a whisper. "Yeah, it's sarin."

"What's it for?"

"What's anything for? To kill people or make them do what you want. I do what I'm told. I'm a soldier."

"You're a limo driver on the hook for murder," Todd said. "So forget the hooey about following orders, Jon. I served in Iraq with the National Guard, and you don't see me running around wasting my old buddies."

The ointment on Ivin's face gleamed under the fluorescent light. His cheeks quivered. That was the bad feeling about what he had done, packed down for a long time, surfacing under interrogation.

"Your vehicle was seen outside the home of a man named Daryl Underwood," Todd said. "Just after the house was destroyed in an arson attack. I guess it's kind of ironic that a few hours later the arsonist got second-degree burns."

Ivin lifted his chin. "A couple of guys at Molnir were exposed to sarin in Iraq."

"Names?"

"Daryl Underwood, Lee Hill, Jeff Parry."

Kinsella flipped through the papers on her clipboard.

Ivin stared at her. "What you looking for?"

Kinsella ran her finger down a column of names.

"What?" Ivin leaned in, frowning, as though willing Kinsella to answer him.

Kinsella put her clipboard down. "You're lying."

"Hey, fuck you."

Kinsella turned the clipboard around and tapped at the top page. "This is a Department of Defense manifest of Molnir personnel admitted to Iraq under government contract. There's Jeff Parry on the fifth line, and there's you, Jon, halfway down. But no Daryl Underwood and no Lee Hill. They were never in Iraq."

Todd paced behind Ivin, making the driver twist to see him. "I'll put you back on the street minus the fifty grand if you lie to me again, Jon."

"I understand, sir."

"Where were these guys exposed to sarin?"

"Daryl got his dose in Damascus."

"How'd that happen?"

"Once it came out of Iraq, he was supposed to guard it until it was transferred on. There was some kind of accident when it was being stored in Damascus and Daryl got a low-level dose."

"Where did the sarin get transferred to after Damascus?"

Ivin shook his head, but his gaze was inward. It seemed to Todd the man was telling himself that the things he knew about should never have been allowed to happen.

"Jon, transferred to where?" Todd leaned down over Ivin's chair. "To the place where Lee Hill got exposed. Right?"

Ivin swallowed and grunted assent.

"Where was that, Jon?"

Hoarse and quiet, Ivin murmured, "In the city."

"New York City?"

"Someone fucked up. Lee got exposed."

"Where is the sarin?"

"That I do not know. For real."

Whoever was supposed to receive the fifty grand from Ivin's holdall was surely still active in the sarin plot. "The money—who were you supposed to take it to?"

"They didn't tell me yet."

Todd kept his eyes on Ivin. "Jon, are you going to have to be dead before you're done lying? Who was the money for?"

The gel on Ivin's burned face shone. "A guy named Chavez."

CHAPTER 38

The truck mounted the hill toward the compound where the sarin was stockpiled. The rebel commander pulled the kaffiyeh across his face, ready for action. In the backseat of the crew cab, a pair of gunmen sandwiched the two Americans.

"You're going to give sarin to these bastards?" Quanah growled through tight lips.

"To get it away from the Molnir guys?" Verrazzano said. "Sure."

"You always did have the wrong priorities."

"Here's my rule: the only plan worth following is the one that could easily go wrong. Maybe even cost you your life. Because it's the only one that'll ever really get you where you need. Anything else is too timid."

"That doesn't seem like a road map for a long life. So what's your secret? How come you're still alive?"

"Everybody who ever tried to kill me was an asshole, and assholes are too stupid to live by my rule. These guys are assholes too."

"That's the big insight? I thought you were going to quote from the philosophy of Colonel Wyatt again."

"'Pain is certain, suffering is optional.'"

"That sounds like him, the son of a bitch."

"No. That's a quote from the Buddha. Look, don't sweat it. We'll neutralize these goons when the time comes."

Abu Jihad hammered his palm against the ceiling. The gunmen in the back of the truck brought their Kalashnikovs to bear on the guard hut. The driver accelerated. The clamor of the engine in the quiet night drew a guard out of the hut. He reached for his machine pistol.

The gunmen on the truck opened up. The guard went down in the doorway, dead. The truck jerked to a halt. The surviving guard stood over the corpse with his hands up in surrender.

"Open the gate," the driver yelled.

The guard pantomimed his assent. The yellow grille slid back across the road. The gunmen mowed down the cowering sentry and shouted insults at his body. The truck entered the compound.

"Oh yeah, this is going just great," Quanah murmured.

The gunmen jumped out. Verrazzano led them across the courtyard to the conference room. To the sarin.

The gunmen's chief drove the stock of his M16 upward to snap open the lid of a crate. He pulled out a gray canister, wary and excited.

"Sarin," Verrazzano said.

Abu Jihad held the canister in two hands at arm's length, like a bachelor uncle with a newborn.

"Inside the shell, there are two chambers," Verrazzano said. "Each one contains a precursor chemical. When the shell is detonated, the precursors mix to form sarin."

"You weren't joking when you said I could win the civil war all by myself." Abu Jihad slapped Verrazzano on the shoulder. The canister slipped from his hand. He fumbled for it. It spun toward the floor.

Verrazzano caught the shell, inches off the ground. He puffed out his cheeks in relief. The squad of gunmen sniggered nervously.

"We have to get these crates out of here," Verrazzano said. "Before someone comes to reclaim them."

The rebel chief took a Motorola intercom phone from his jacket pocket. "Abu Latif, I need you. Bring your flatbed."

A deep voice rasped through the static on the radio network. "If Allah wills it, O Abu Jihad."

"Be here in fifteen minutes, if Allah wills it." Abu Jihad tossed the phone to one of his men. "Tell him how to find us. The rest of you, carry this stuff outside."

Verrazzano held the canister toward Abu Jihad. He tapped his fingertip beside the handwritten words scrawled in black marker across the shell. "What does this say?"

"*'Wahda, hurriya, istirakiya.'* Unity, freedom, socialism." Abu Jihad called out the slogan loud enough for his men to hear. One of them blew a raspberry. The others laughed bitterly. "This stuff must be old. Are you sure it's still usable?"

"Sarin decays quickly after the precursor chemicals are mixed. It can be stored a long time like this in its two separate component forms. How do you know it's old?"

"'Unity, freedom, socialism.' That's the motto of Saddam Hussein's regime. These canisters must be from before 2003, when you Americans overthrew that dog."

Verrazzano glanced at Quanah. His old partner nodded gravely. It took the Pentagon a decade to admit that US troops uncovered old, degraded nerve agent stockpiles in Iraq and that hundreds of soldiers were exposed during decommissioning. The sarin in these crates wasn't damaged or corrupted. He wondered what else the Pentagon had hushed up or who had concealed the existence of this deadly consignment.

"This quantity of sarin would be worth a lot of money," he said.

Abu Jihad shrugged, but Verrazzano registered that the gunman hadn't only been thinking of using the nerve agent to gain a military advantage.

"You could sell it to the Palestinian." Verrazzano needed the name. More precisely, he needed the *new* name and location of Marwan Touma, the arms dealer whose life he had spared years ago when Wyatt ordered him killed.

"Which Palestinian?" Abu Jihad said. "There's hardly one that *wouldn't* buy this."

"The diabetic. Injects insulin into his stomach."

"Fakri Kawasma. That bastard."

Verrazzano imprinted the name in his memory. "He'd give you a good price. Maybe we should take the sarin right to him?"

"So he can sell it to someone who'll use it to kill my people? The first thing I'll do with this sarin is go out to Jaramana and hit that son of a whore's compound. Screw him."

A heavy diesel engine sounded beyond the courtyard. One of the gunmen came in through the door. "Abu Latif is here."

"Let's load up." The rebel leader slapped Verrazzano's shoulder and went to the door laughing. "Unity, freedom, socialism."

Verrazzano watched the gunmen lug the first crates of sarin out to the truck. He doubled forward and groaned. "Bathroom," he muttered to the rebel commander. He shuffled to the corridor and followed his nose to a restroom done in flowery tile. He locked the door.

On his phone, he found the photo he had taken of the sarin shell and sent it to Haddad. He dialed her number.

"Thank God you called in, Dom," she said. "We've confirmed there's sarin in New York City."

"Is anyone exposed?"

"It's not a live incident. Not yet. Noelle and Bill confirmed it with the limo driver. Lee Hill was exposed to sarin while handling it here in the city."

"Did the limo guy give us any other leads?"

"He's supposed to deliver cash to a guy named Chavez in Queens. He's heading there now. Bill and Noelle are tailing him."

"Noelle mentioned a virtual bank called Freedom Coin. Anything more on that?"

"I got access to Tom Frisch's account at Freedom Coin. I'm checking it now. Looks like it was cleaned out a month ago. Maybe Frisch was tying up loose ends before something went down. I'll try to track the money further, but I've got to say, it could take more time than we have. The security protocols are pretty intensive."

"Okay, keep working on it. Do you see the photo I sent you?"

He heard the snapping of keys at Haddad's computer. "Oh man, this is sarin too?"

Sarin in New York and in Damascus. Which city was to be the site of the attack Doctor Weston warned about? "Confirm the text. The Arabic writing on the canisters."

"'Unity, freedom, socialism.' Saddam's official motto. Some-one brought the stuff to Damascus from Iraq?"

"Looks like it."

"What about those numbers?"

"The numbers on the fire diamond?"

"No, under the motto."

Verrazzano called up the image on his phone. Arabic numerals were the basis for the Western system, though only one and nine matched the Western characters. In the photo a row of Arabic numbers were scribbled in marker beneath the dead dictator's rallying cry. "I should've noticed. Read them off, will you? I forget which one is which."

"The one that looks like a backward seven is a two. This one that's like an uppercase *E*, that's four. This *V* is a seven and—"

"Roula, I don't need the lesson. Just tell me the number."

"Two-four-seven-eight-zero-zero-five-six. The numbers are followed by two letters. In Arabic they're called *ta* and *kaf*. Roughly they approximate to *T* and *K* in English. I'm running a check for that number." A few ripples of her fingers across the keyboard. "Nothing in our database."

"Check FBI and the Counterterrorism Division at State." Verrazzano heard footsteps in the corridor outside the restroom. He turned to the wall and cupped the phone close to his mouth. "Anything?"

"Wait a sec. Nothing."

"The canisters are marked with an Iraqi slogan," he said. "What about Defense Department records from the Iraq War?"

Verrazzano heard low voices in the corridor outside the restroom.

"Got it." Haddad was excited. "The numbers and letters are the identifier code for a weapons dump in Iraq."

The voices went quiet, but the footsteps reached the bathroom door. The handle turned. Verrazzano pressed the phone close to his ear so that no sound leaked out. He kept his breath soft and quiet.

"Where was the dump?" Verrazzano whispered.

Pressure on the door. The lock blocked it.

"The *TK* stands for Tikrit," Haddad said. "Saddam's hometown."

The handle moved again. Someone trying the lock.

"How come we didn't capture this sarin in Iraq?" Verrazzano said. "Didn't the Army check out the location?"

"Army doesn't have anyone in country to make the search."

The footsteps receded slowly.

"This is *recent* intelligence? Since the Army pulled out?"

"The intel came in less than a year ago. Some former Baathist chief was afraid the Islamic State jihadis were going to chop off his head, so he surrendered to Kurdish forces. The Kurds handed him over to CIA. He gave up the Tikrit weapons dump during his interrogation, and Langley arranged for it to be searched."

"What did they find?"

"No WMDs at the site. It was marked down as a bad lead."

The phone line vibrated with tension. Verrazzano sensed Haddad's stillness. She was putting it together too. Then it hit him. "CIA outsourced the search?"

"Yeah," she said.

"Who carried it out?"

"Molnir Partners."

CHAPTER 39

As she hung up with Verrazzano, the monitor on Haddad's desk flashed red to show an incoming call on Lifshitz's line at Freedom Coin. Anticipation pulsed through her so hard, she thought its reverberation must be audible all across the Homeland Security floor. She pulled on her headphones and listened.

"Agh, it's just his mother," she whispered to herself. "You don't call, you don't write. Blah, blah."

Right after his mother hung up, Lifshitz dialed a sex line. At three in the afternoon. He told the Jersey girl who answered to call him Daddy. "Analyze that," Haddad muttered.

After twenty seconds, Lifshitz hung up. "Speedy work, Daddy." Haddad logged the conversation.

Another call came in on Lifshitz's line. Haddad settled her headphones again.

"What's eating you, Yuri?" the caller asked.

"Why didn't you call me back until now?" Lifshitz said, wheezy and whiny.

"I don't have time for this, Yuri. What do you want?"

"Check the page."

"What? I didn't catch that."

"The Facebook page. Check it, Frisch. I won't say any more over the phone."

Frisch. Haddad glanced at her screen to be sure the surveillance program was recording the call.

"Okay, I'll take a look," Frisch said.

"Is it all okay? The plan's fine? I laid out a lot of cash for this."

"You'll be taken care of, Yuri."

"That makes it sound like you're going to kill me. You know, silence me."

The empty hiss down the line carried its own threat.

"Frisch, you there?"

"I'm not going to kill you, Yuri. You and I have a very fruitful future ahead of us."

"Good to hear."

"Unless you keep on with the needy bullshit. I hate neediness. So quit it, or maybe I'll cap you after all." Frisch chuckled and hung up.

Haddad flipped her headphones onto her shoulders. "Now that's a guy who knows how to motivate his team."

Tracking all but the most specific information through Facebook could take hours, days even. Which was why so many crooks set up a group page on Facebook for a specific operation. By keeping the language innocent, they evaded law enforcement algorithms and buried the page among the millions of groups on Facebook. Haddad needed to find the page Lifshitz mentioned, and she didn't have hours. But she had Ivin. He was back on the road, leading Todd and Kinsella to his next drop-off. She dialed his cell phone. He picked up.

"It's Special Agent Haddad. Where are you, Jon?"

"Heading crosstown to the Fifty-Ninth Street Bridge." Ivin sounded as though he had taken a cold shower. Jittery. Way too alive.

"I need the name of the Facebook page Frisch uses to communicate with his teams."

"The Scuba Club?"

"The what?"

"The Official Group of the Tough Gentlemen's Scuba Club of Pethel Sing Smashes."

She scribbled on her notepad. "Pethel Sing?"

He spelled it for her. "It's Javanese. Because, like, no one speaks Javanese."

"Yeah, I get that. What does it mean?"

"The hammer that smashes. Something like that."

Haddad ripped the sheet away from her notepad and hung up. No one would ever type the group's arcane name by chance. They'd have to know it was there to find it.

She opened Facebook on her monitor. She hoped she had the right page. Lifshitz may have referred to a different group, not the one Frisch used to send messages to operatives in the field like Ivin.

The page came up on the screen. She breathed hard. It *was* the one. The latest post bore an avatar with Freedom Coin's logo. Lifshitz must've been in a hurry. He hadn't disguised his identity. Haddad shrugged. *Everybody's dumb about something.* This was the same guy, after all, who made confidential calls on a cordless phone.

Lifshitz's post read: "Your driver flipped. Look for ice on his tail."

"Shit." Haddad reached for her phone and called Todd.

Todd's line bleeped. Call waiting. "Bill, pick up." Haddad slammed her handset down. "It's okay," she whispered, calming herself. She had flushed them out, Lifshitz and Frisch. "It's going to be okay." As long as she warned her agents.

She dialed Kinsella's number.

CHAPTER 40

Cardamom and nutmeg wafted out from the old limestone blocks as the gunmen stacked the sarin crates against the storehouse wall. Verrazzano remembered wandering the Casbahs of the Middle East and North Africa, delighting in these aromas and the bustling contact of passing pedestrians. Now his chest seized up, the aftereffects of the nerve agent stabbing at his lungs. Abu Jihad loitered beside the metal roll-up shutter at the entrance. He chivvied his men to work faster.

"When're we going to make our move, Dom?" Quanah said.

"Let them get the sarin off the truck first." Verrazzano approached the rebel chief. "Soon you'll be the most powerful guy in Damascus, Abu Jihad."

"Then your president will propose sanctions against *me* at the United Nations."

The gunmen joined the boss's laughter as they staggered into the storeroom with the final crate. The flatbed truck kicked into gear and rolled out of the Casbah. The gunmen's pickup reversed into the storeroom. Abu Jihad slammed down the shutter.

A naked bulb dangled at head height from a long, twisting wire. The storeroom was claustrophobic and shadowy. The Arabs closed in on the Americans.

"Thank you, my friend." Abu Jihad took Verrazzano and kissed him on each cheek. He repeated the procedure with Quanah. "Let's drink tea."

One of the men brought out a camping stove.

"I like my tea with lots of sugar." Abu Jihad held Verrazzano's hand. The dry sweat in his clothes overpowered the spices on the air.

"Not for me, thanks," Verrazzano said.

"You Americans like to look after your health. You have everything, so you must show that you can deny yourselves *something*."

"That's us, all right."

"When you live with nothing, as we do in Syria, deprivation teaches you cunning. But Americans never have to worry about shortage. So they are trusting souls." Abu Jihad laid the muzzle of his pistol against Verrazzano's neck. "Too trusting. Am I right?"

"You've proved your point."

"It's more than a theory."

The gunmen lifted their assault rifles and held them on the Americans.

"How's your plan working out, Dom?" Quanah said.

One of the rebels came through the dim light with an armful of gas masks. He passed them out.

"*Ya salaam.* Oh, dear." Abu Jihad made a clownish sad face for Verrazzano and Quanah. "We don't have enough for you."

The gunmen slipped their kaffiyehs down around their necks and pulled on the respirators. With a twitch of his finger, Abu Jihad ordered them to open a crate of sarin. He gave Verrazzano a gentle slap on the cheek. "I'd like to take you at your word about this stuff, but I think I should test it. Just to be sure, you know? Let's see how long it takes this sarin to kill you."

One of the rebel fighters puzzled over a sarin shell, trying to figure out how to activate it. Abu Jihad hectored him impatiently. The others bellowed advice through their gas masks.

"Time to make a move, Dom," Quanah said. "These guys are about to kill us."

"They're about to *try*," Verrazzano said. "The poor bastards."

He stepped forward. The gunman who had been set to guard the Americans jabbed with his assault rifle. Verrazzano ignored him. "Hey, Abu Jihad. One of these crates contains a signaling device. It lets my people know where the sarin is. They'll find you."

The rebel leader pushed his gas mask up from his face. "If you have 'people' nearby, why didn't you transport the sarin out of there yourself? Why did you need me?"

"The opportunity to work with you came along first. You and I are on the same side. My people want the regime changed. So do you."

"You don't have any idea what *I* want."

The gunman holding the sarin canister came to Abu Jihad's side. He gestured at the shell and barked through his breathing apparatus.

"You'll be pleased to know we figured out how to work this thing," Abu Jihad said.

Another gunman brought the camp stove over and set it on the floor. He unscrewed the frame and the burner cap to expose the small, brass propane valve. The man with the sarin raised the canister and jammed it down hard on the protruding valve.

"He's trying to hit the firing pin," Quanah said. "Dumb asshole's going to set off the charge."

The sarin canister slipped to the side on impact and pinched the gunman's finger painfully. He cursed and set himself to try again.

"It'll hurt a lot more than that when he blows his hand off," Quanah said.

"Not as much as it'll hurt us. When the charge goes off, it'll mix the precursors and cook the sarin." Verrazzano pushed aside the guard's Kalashnikov. "Abu Jihad, I'm serious. Our people are tracking the transponder. They'll be here soon. When they arrive, do you want to have a dead American agent and a dead United Nations official on your hands?"

"When your rescuers arrive, I'll be able to kill *them* with the sarin, too." Abu Jihad muttered to the man with the shell, "Do it right this time."

The gunman positioned the shell. He shoved down on it hard.

The rear of the canister exploded with the force of a grenade. The gunman dropped the sarin and screamed. His hand spurted blood. The gunmen huddled around their wounded comrade, reaching for him, shouting at each other in panic.

Propane hissed out of the camp stove. The sarin shell vibrated on the floor. The precursors were mixing. Behind the smudged lenses of his gas mask, Abu Jihad beamed with pleasure, as though the canister were a magic lantern granting his wish for power over men's lives.

Under the hubbub of the fussing gunmen and their bawling comrade, Verrazzano heard a new sound. Something rattled against the locked metal shutter, rolled, and settled on the stones outside. Someone was there, and they intended to come in. *They're blowing the shutter with a grenade*, Verrazzano figured. That gave him eight seconds to make himself secure.

Abu Jihad noticed the sound at the shutter too. His eyes flicked toward the entrance.

Verrazzano jumped at him. With all the weight of his body, he drove his forearm crosswise into Abu Jihad's throat. The gunman reeled into the wall, choking.

The human body can take a good deal of pain, but it can't sustain major injury. Verrazzano wasn't out to pummel his opponent—trading punches was for schoolboys. He had disabled Abu Jihad with the blow to the neck. He wanted only to finish him so he could take care of the man's stunned underlings before they reacted.

He speared his forearm under the rebel leader's groin and lifted him off his feet. He spun Abu Jihad's legs upward and hammered his head to the floor. He wrenched away Abu Jihad's gas mask and tossed it to Quanah. "Put it on."

The shocked gunmen gaped at their leader, splayed on the concrete with a broken neck and a shattered skull. Verrazzano reached for the man whose hand had been ripped apart by the detonating shell. He tugged off the startled man's gas mask and pulled it on. Backing away in confusion, the gunmen raised their weapons.

"Down," Verrazzano yelled.

Quanah threw himself under the pickup.

Verrazzano yanked a Makarov pistol from the belt of the dead rebel chief. He snatched the sarin shell from the floor and rolled under the truck.

The gunmen went onto their knees, aiming into the darkness beneath the pickup. But the man with the injured hand blocked their shots. He writhed in front of them, the sarin killing him. They shouted in vain for him to clear the way, their shrill voices muffled by the gas masks.

A crushing wave of pressure passed over Verrazzano. The shutter exploded behind the pickup. A burst of smoke billowed around the hysterical gunmen. Submachine guns opened up through the shattered doorway. The disoriented rebels convulsed in the gunfire.

Four sets of boots moved quickly past Verrazzano's hiding place. They were well balanced and set sideways. Their knees were braced, and they wore black boots and black combat pants.

The sarin drained from the punctured casing beside Verrazzano.

The newcomers put a bullet into the head of each of Abu Jihad's gunmen.

"You smell gas?" An American voice, slow and deep. Verrazzano guessed Texan. "Turn off that camp stove."

One of the men in black picked up the overturned burner. He twisted the tap shut.

The guy smelled the cooking gas, Verrazzano thought. *They're not wearing masks.*

"Check in back," the American said. "See if there's more of these assholes."

A response in English with an Arab accent: "Yes, Mister Lance."

Lance. The Molnir man who had been too sick to guard the sarin that day. The theft of the stockpile forced him into action. Just in time to save Verrazzano.

But that was bad news for Lance.

The Texan sniffled and coughed. "Shit."

"You are still feeling unwell, Mister Lance?"

"My chest is—Jesus Christ, the sarin's leaking. Get out of here." Lance stumbled past the pickup, his boots inches from Verrazzano's face.

"Leaking? No, I turned off the stove, Mister Lance." The Arab hacked out a cough. He dropped to his knees, spasming on the concrete floor. He puked and choked, reaching an arm toward Verrazzano. Then he was still. The others in black suffocated too, beside the crates of sarin.

Verrazzano tapped Quanah's shoulder. They crawled from under the truck. He picked up a machine pistol and went out into the Casbah.

The street was empty, the residents hidden away from the dangerous dark. Verrazzano blew a breath of relief. A single canister of sarin would disperse quickly in the air. By the time Damascus woke up, the gas would be at a harmless concentration.

Lance lay in a puddle of his own vomit, shuddering on his side, purple-faced and gasping. Sarin was odorless, but its effects were not. Lance had voided his bowels.

Verrazzano reached into his pocket. He took out the autoinjector of atropine the forensics tech had given him in the ICE field office. He pushed Lance onto his belly and yanked up the sleeve of his T-shirt.

He thrust the autoinjector into Lance's triceps. The orange syringe fed the antidote into the dying American.

CHAPTER 41

Kinsella trailed the Lincoln up the long rise of the on-ramp to the Queensboro Bridge. She had Ivin on speakerphone from the Town Car. "Did you get word on the address for your next drop-off?"

"I'll get a call when I'm closer. All I know is it's for this Chavez guy in Queens." Ivin's voice was reedy and nervous, almost girlish.

"Who's going to call you? Tom Frisch?"

"I'm not even sure Mister Frisch knows about this."

"You're saying it's a rogue op? It's nice that you think I look like an innocent young thing, Jon. But give me a break, okay? I'm not buying that."

"Mister Frisch goes for big government contracts. That's what *he* deals with. Shitheads like me sniff around for our own opportunities. If it works out, we cut him in."

Todd spoke up from the passenger seat. "Could Chavez be another case of sarin exposure?"

"I've never seen this Chavez guy. I don't know what he does, and I never drove him anywhere. I never took him money before."

"So maybe he just got exposed recently?"

They climbed above the speeding lanes of the FDR Drive and were over the East River. A silver Nissan Titan sped past the ICE agents. The truck seemed to brush the roof of the bridge's lower deck.

The Town Car crested the bridge's first span over Roosevelt Island. Todd's phone vibrated in his pocket. He picked up. "Yes?"

"It's Roula. The Freedom Coin guy warned Molnir about Ivin. They know we brought him in."

A crash and a screech of tires snapped Todd's attention back to the roadway. Ivin's Lincoln wavered across the deck of the bridge. Its wheels spat blue smoke as the driver struggled for control. The huge Nissan swung at the limo.

"What's that truck—?" Todd stared. "Jesus, it's ramming Ivin."

"What's going on?" Roula called down the line.

"I guess your information just got confirmed, Roula." Todd hung up.

The Nissan hit the Lincoln's hood just in front of the wheel. Ivin tried to accelerate past the truck, but he was caught by its high fender. His scream burst through the speakerphone in the ICE agents' Dodge.

"Ivin, brake and come to a complete halt," Kinsella yelled. "Ivin, do you read me? Jon?"

Ivin wasn't listening. His Town Car jerked ahead, trying to outrun the threat.

The Nissan shoved Ivin's car against the three-foot concrete barrier at the edge of the bridge. Sparks looped bright over the roof of the Lincoln.

Todd dropped his window and drew his pistol.

"Don't aim for the wheels. We don't have time," Kinsella said. "Take out the driver."

Todd stared at her. The shot came back to him, the one he hadn't been able to fire to subdue Pangiottis when the scumbag raised his gun toward him.

"Bill, shoot him now."

Ivin screamed over the phone line. Kinsella yelled, "Come on, Bill. Do it."

"Hold the car steady or I'll be lucky to hit Queens." Todd leaned his upper body out of the speeding car. His first shot pinged the rear gate of the truck.

A man leaned his torso out of the passenger window of the Nissan. He wore a stocking cap with holes cut for the eyes. He leveled a machine pistol at the ICE car.

Todd's second shot smashed the window in the back of the Nissan's cab. The truck swerved away from the Town Car. It veered back with even greater force. The front of the limo jumped.

The machine pistol kicked up the concrete beside the ICE car. The shooter's hand bucked. A dozen rounds streaked up into the roof of the lower deck. Todd heard the jangling ricochets and the screech and crush of cars swerving and colliding behind them.

The truck strained against the limo. The black car rose on the slight angle at the foot of the barrier.

"He's going over," Kinsella shouted.

The big Nissan poured smoke from its tires. The Town Car lifted. It ground along on the rims of its left wheels, its underside screeching against the barrier. The engine of the truck barked and growled. It surged against the limo.

Then the sedan was in the air and the bridge seemed to descend into silence.

The Lincoln pounded into the girders of the bridge and flipped sideways. It flew out over the pedestrian lane in the half-light, angled like a ski jumper leaning into his leap. The chain link fence beyond the bike path cradled it for an instant, then the car smashed through and dropped out of sight.

"Jesus Christ," Kinsella said.

The man in the stocking cap reached into the cab of the Nissan. He came out with a grenade. Todd took aim at him.

The grenade looped over the truck bed and bounced toward the ICE Dodge.

Todd squeezed down on the trigger. He had the bastard in his sights.

Kinsella swung the wheel to avoid the grenade. Todd's arm jerked upward. His shot streaked out over the river.

The grenade's asymmetrical shape kicked it to the right. The same way Kinsella had gone. She braked hard. The Dodge slewed across two lanes. It hit the barrier side-on. The engine cut out.

"Go." Kinsella threw herself from the car.

Todd's door jammed against the barrier. He wrenched at it, but it stuck. A flicker of panic shocked his brain. He was trapped.

"Bill, come on." Kinsella hammered the side of the car.

Todd forced himself out of the dead end of his alarm and dread. He crawled through the passenger window onto the concrete edge of the roadway.

He balanced on the barrier in the space between the road and the pedestrian lane. One hundred thirty feet below, Ivin's Town Car nosed into the water and sank. His head spun. His knees buckled.

A hand grabbed his upper arm and yanked him off the barrier onto the trunk of the car.

"Move it, for fuck's sake." Kinsella pulled Todd down to the roadway. He nodded dumbly. This was no place to be when the grenade went off. He scrambled away after Kinsella.

The Dodge's fuel tank went up in the explosion of the grenade. The heat of the flames breathed over Todd's back. Hot air fluttered in his ears like a raucous laugh.

The truck headed down toward Queens Boulevard. Kinsella stared after the Nissan. Then she turned toward Todd.

"I kind of froze," he said.

She glared at him, then her features softened. "You k-k-kind of f-f-f-froze. It happens, man. This isn't everyday shit we're going through."

She leaned over the shattered rail and scanned the surface of the gray river.

Todd shook his head. "Ivin's gone. The car sank."

Kinsella kicked the barrier. "So did our chance of getting to this Chavez guy."

CHAPTER 42

A Dutch doctor settled Lance on the top floor of the hotel where all the UN chemical weapons inspectors lived. The room was the way men who'd never been with a whore imagined a brothel—Napoleon chairs, velvet chaise longue, gilt rococo mirror. The Molnir guy glared at Verrazzano with vicious, glassy eyes. When he tried to speak, he squirmed on the bed. The doctor slipped an oxygen mask over Lance's mouth. "I'll watch him now."

"He's dangerous," Verrazzano said.

"I'm not a macho type, but I can hold my own against a man whose lungs just got filled with sarin. I'd prefer to transfer him down to the clinic."

"Soon enough. Right now it's easier to keep a watch on him up here. The clinic's too open, too insecure."

"You mean someone might come in and try to free him?"

"Or kill him. Just don't allow him any—" Verrazzano stifled a cough. He winced at the pain in his chest. "Don't allow him any communication."

"That cough—were you exposed?"

To the worst people in the world and the most horrible things. "Don't worry about me."

The doctor licked his lips nervously and returned to his patient.

Lance was alive, but Verrazzano needed to break him down. Perhaps he knew details of the attack Doctor Weston warned about. Maybe he could provide probable cause for ICE to bring in Tom Frisch, or at least give Verrazzano some new lead. He still didn't know how long he had before the attack. Or where it'd take place. His phone vibrated to signal an incoming call. He picked up.

"It's Roula. The limo driver's dead. Someone rammed his car off the Fifty-Ninth Street Bridge. They shot up Noelle and Bill's vehicle too."

"Are they hurt?"

"They're okay. Ivin was taking them to his next payoff, a guy named Chavez in Queens. But now we don't have any way to get to the guy."

"Where do things stand with the phone tap on Freedom Coin?"

"Yuri Lifshitz posted a Facebook update that connects him with the killing of the limo driver. It doesn't tie him to the sarin plot, though. We still don't know if this is a Molnir thing or just rogue operatives."

"No link to Tom Frisch?"

"The Freedom Coin guy made a call to Frisch. He mentioned that he put up a lot of money for some project. Do you think it was to buy the sarin?"

"No, Molnir picked up the sarin for free in Iraq, remember? Maybe there's another financial angle. Like a payment to someone in New York to facilitate the attack. Get Bill and Noelle to bring in the Freedom Coin guy. Sweat him on connections to a payoff or a bribe."

Quanah emerged from the elevator with a slim woman and two bulky Arab men.

"I have to go, Roula." Verrazzano hung up.

The doctor came out of Lance's room. He smiled at the woman. "Hello, Caroline. This is Special Agent Verrazzano."

"I'm with the UN chemical weapons inspection team." Caroline spoke with an Australian accent. She had as much vim as a kennel full of toy spaniels. "Verrazano, like the bridge, eh?"

Two days of pure tension had sucked his playfulness all away. So he said, "Yeah, like the bridge."

"We'll get this situation cleaned up as soon as we can." She glanced toward Lance's room. "How's our patient?"

"His symptoms are less severe than the expression on his face."

Quanah jerked his thumb at the two burly Arabs. "These guys will watch Lance while we're taking care of the sarin."

The guards wore wraparound shades and pistols stuffed into their belts. They nodded at Verrazzano with blank politeness.

"The man in this room appears to be very weak," he told them. "Don't let that fool you. He's extremely dangerous. Be alert for anyone who might come to break him out. I don't want you both in the corridor. One of you stays inside with Lance at all times. Okay?"

The men inclined their heads and set themselves in position.

"All right," the Australian woman said. "Let's go and see all this nerve agent you boys found."

Verrazzano walked with them to the elevators. "You handle this, Quanah. I've got something else to take care of."

Quanah followed him into the elevator with the Australian woman. "No way. I'm sticking with you."

"We can manage with just you, Quanah," the Australian woman said.

Quanah didn't look at her. "I'd prefer if Special Agent Verrazzano was with us."

They reached the lobby. UN chemical weapons experts gathered near the door, sweating in light-blue polypropylene bodysuits, their respirators swinging from their hands. Verrazzano took the Australian woman's arm.

"You're not taking any chances," he said.

"It's horrifying stuff, sarin. Outlawed since 1993, but so what, eh? If you're going to use it, you're probably not the type to give two hoots about international law and human rights."

"Did you think Syria was clean?"

"Officially, yes. The government was pretty quick to hand over its stockpile to us. By the middle of 2014, we'd decommissioned all of it, as far as we were aware."

"But?"

She waved to the other UN technicians and went out into the dark. "We figured there was still some out there. Frankly, the government wasn't the worst of our worries. The Islamic State crazies have used nerve agents in Iraq. We were waiting for the next shoe to drop here. Either stuff they bought somehow or a government dump they overran. The Syrians had a chemical weapons program since the seventies. VX and sarin, mostly. Blister agents like mustard gas, too. We're pretty sure they no longer have the capacity to produce more sarin."

"This load you're going to pick up came from Iraq."

Caroline was subdued and thoughtful. "I guess I'm not going home to my kids for a while. Quanah says you left it behind the Mausoleum of Saladin."

"He'll show you the way."

Quanah started to protest. The Australian woman gave him a stern frown. Verrazzano was impressed at the instant of command. Quanah gasped impatiently but kept quiet.

"Tell me about disposal," Verrazzano said.

"Based on Quanah's description," she said, "I think we can handle this amount on site."

"At the UN compound?"

"We have a facility in the desert outside Damascus under very tight security. There's a Field Deployable Hydrolysis System there. Ever see one of those?"

"Never did. They're new, right?"

She climbed into the cab of a white truck that had "UN" on its sides and hood. "No more than two years old. We're lucky to have one. The Pentagon developed it on the basis that chemical and biological weapons might be found in small amounts and in unexpected locations where a big operation to neutralize them may not be feasible."

"How long's it going to take?"

"Once we get the sarin to the hydrolysis site, no more than an hour. Want to come see it?" She shut the door of the truck and smiled through the open window. "It looks like a moonshine still designed by Rube Goldberg. A big, brass mixing tank about twenty feet high. Pipes running all over the place for blending the sarin with the neutralizing agent. We've got a crew of fifteen techs waiting for us to bring the sarin over."

Verrazzano stood by the window of her door while Quanah got into the crew cab. "How does the neutralization work?"

"We feed the sarin into the mixers along with the neutralizing agent."

"Which is?"

She leaned out of the window and whispered. "Tell you a little secret: science isn't always so complicated. It's water."

"Water? *That's* the neutralizing agent?"

One of the UN techs shuffled by. He pressed a respirator into Verrazzano's hands.

"Water breaks the bond between the phosphorus and fluorine in the sarin compound," Caroline said. "What you're left with is regular industrial waste. Don't get me wrong. It's not easy to do this without some leaks, unless you have good equipment like ours."

"And the best people for the job." Verrazzano grinned at Quanah. His old partner glared at him. He tossed the gas mask through the window into Quanah's lap. The trucks pulled away.

A Toyota Land Cruiser idled in the darkness outside a shuttered shoe shop. The driver flashed his lights. Verrazzano waited for the trucks to turn the corner. He crossed the street to the car.

Marwan Touma pushed open the back door of the Land Cruiser. Verrazzano settled into the seat beside him. A burly driver watched in the mirror, as inexpressive as a forty-year-old stripper.

Touma gestured to his reworked face. "I am beautiful, yes?" His nose was smaller than it had been when Colonel Wyatt sent Verrazzano to kill him. His eyes lifted in a permanent gape, and his cheekbones thrust out from the spare skin.

"Fakri Kawasma is quite a looker," Verrazzano said.

Touma laughed and slapped Verrazzano's thigh. "Inside, Fakri Kawasma is the same as Marwan Touma ever was."

"There's no cure for that shit."

The Palestinian wagged his finger, smiling. "Except that he learned American Army slang from some of his clients so that no one can trick him into ordering his own death again."

"I'm glad you wised up."

"When you failed to follow Wyatt's orders to kill me, I should have known that you would one day end up on the wrong side of the law. Which is to say the right side, as most people would see it."

"I need to get out of Damascus."

"You are on the wrong side of someone bad in a place where there is no law?"

"You could say that."

"You called me at a very good time, my dear one. I have a plane now at the airport. It arrived an hour ago with a cargo of small arms. It's leaving empty in forty-five minutes."

"Leaving empty? I don't get it."

"You don't trust me? Well, I don't trust me either. I gave in to my unnatural feelings of gratitude to you for sparing my life." Touma shivered comically, as though he experienced some unpleasant sensation. "I hope I am not becoming a reformed character."

"It'll pass."

The Palestinian's voice darkened. "Now Marwan Touma and Dominic Verrazzano are even. And Fakri Kawasma, of course, owes you nothing. Be at the airport at the top of the hour. There are no other flights. You will find my plane easily."

Verrazzano stepped out of the car. He felt suddenly how far he had come, even since he spared Touma's life.

The car pulled away. Verrazzano watched it round the corner and listened to its engine noise meld with the patter of gunfire from the suburbs. The heart of the city was fearful and empty around him. The moon glimmered on the surface of the Barada. Down in its culvert, the river twisted between banks of festering trash.

He jogged into the hotel lobby.

CHAPTER 43

Todd paced behind the Freedom Coin guy. Lifshitz sat in the middle of the interrogation room. He turned in his chair, following the agent. Kinsella leaned against the door, a signal there was no way out. Lifshitz cupped his hands over his groin as though covering his nakedness.

"You're in big trouble," Todd said. "If you don't talk, you're going to death row."

"Whatever you have on me, it ain't a capital crime. There's no death penalty in New York."

"No *state* death penalty. But we're federal officers."

"I know federal law. You get death for what? Treason? Espionage? You don't have that on me."

Todd trained his eyes on the center of Lifshitz's forehead, just far enough from a natural point of focus to be unnerving, but not so distant as to seem preoccupied with anything other than him. A disconcerted man was more likely to talk than one who felt secure, guilty or not. Telling Lifshitz he could get the chair was intended to ruffle him too. It also happened to be true.

"Yuri, you're not the dumb slob you appear to be," Todd said. "You're the first guy we've had in that seat who's got a PhD in system dynamics from MIT."

"That's just because you can't keep up with the technology. Once you people get your programming shit together, this room'll be like a gallery of Nobel Prize winners."

"You should've studied law too, because treason and espionage are *not* the only federal charges that carry the death sentence. There's genocide and war crimes. What else? Help me out, Agent Kinsella."

"Conspiracy to kill a member of Congress." Kinsella counted on her fingers. "Assassinating the president. Killing a member of the Supreme Court."

"How'd you know I was a highly paid hit man? Is it my suave good looks? Or my catlike agility?" Lifshitz's laugh was like the scrabbling of an animal trapped in a cage. His double chins shook.

"Large-scale drug trafficking." Kinsella went on. "Causing death by using an explosive. Causing death by using a chemical weapon. Authorizing the killing of a juror or witness in an ongoing case. It's a pretty long list."

"Now let me give *you* a civics lesson," Lifshitz said. "Get me my lawyer."

Haddad had passed along Verrazzano's idea that Freedom Coin may have funded a bribe. Todd would question Lifshitz on that, but he wanted him rattled first. "We know you've been in contact with Tom Frisch."

"He's a client. I already told you that. Your agent, the sexy Arab chick, I gave her access to Frisch's account."

"Do you warn all your clients that they're under federal investigation?"

"I want my lawyer."

"Why'd you post a message on this Facebook page?" Todd drew a sheet of paper from his jacket and shoved it into Lifshitz's hands.

"I don't got my reading glasses." He pulled the page so close, he seemed to be sniffing at it.

"The Official Group of the Tough Gentlemen's Scuba Club of Pethel Sing Smashes." Todd extended his finger at an avatar beside a post on the page. "That's the Freedom Coin logo, isn't it? 'Your driver flipped. Look for ice on his tail.' Explain that."

The Adam's apple crept down Lifshitz's gullet in slow motion, as if swallowing at a normal pace might incriminate him. "I post a load of different stuff every day. I'm online all the time. Looks like I was razzing the guy."

"What guy?"

"The guy—from the Scuba Club."

"The Scuba Club page is administered by a Facebook account tied to a Japanese e-mail address," Todd said. "We have an ICE agent stationed in Tokyo. He contacted the web-hosting service."

Lifshitz saw where this was going. His face froze.

"The hosting company gave us payment details for the e-mail's owner. Payment was through Freedom Coin. The account was in the name of Tom Frisch."

"Yeah?"

"'Look for ice'? I guess that'd be us," Todd said. "'Your driver flipped'? Frisch's chauffeur *was* helping us with our inquiries. Until he was murdered."

Lifshitz emitted a low choking sound.

"Let's go back to that list of federal capital crimes, Yuri. Do you remember Special Agent Kinsella mentioned 'authorizing the killing of a juror or witness in an ongoing case'? This is an ongoing case, and the chauffeur was a witness."

"My message didn't authorize a murder."

"I'm glad we agree it was your message." Todd glanced at Kinsella.

She smiled. "Noted."

"But the driver wouldn't have been murdered if you *hadn't* written the message, Yuri. Anyhow, we'll let the US attorney decide that. We've got quicker ways of getting you on death row." Todd thumped a chair down hard in front of Lifshitz and sat with his back long and tall before the slumping, sweating man. "Unless you talk now."

Lifshitz's eyes glowed. He spent so much time staring at a bank of monitors, their light-emitting diodes seemed to have migrated into his retinas.

"We're going to find the truth, Yuri," Todd said. "We've got forensics techs going through your hard drives right now. We'll get what we need eventually. But it may be too late by then. You want to be charged with causing death by using a chemical weapon?"

"A what?"

"Frisch has a quantity of sarin. You know what that is?"

"Holy fuck." Lifshitz shrank.

"It's here in New York. If you don't talk, by the end of today, you'll be party to the greatest act of terrorism and mass murder ever committed on American soil."

"This is fucking nuts."

It was time to bring in Verrazzano's hunch. "Tell me about the bribe, Yuri."

Lifshitz's head jerked. Kinsella shifted her weight. Verrazzano was right.

"That's why Frisch needed you," Todd said. "To put up some untraceable cash. To bribe someone who could help carry out this attack."

"There was a big security contract," Lifshitz said. "Frisch needed to bribe a guy to get the contract for his company."

"You put up the bribe?"

"You can't get me on that. The bribe never got paid. The guy didn't bite."

Todd took a look at Kinsella. He knew she was thinking the same thing as him. What if they were chasing the wrong angle? If Frisch hadn't paid the bribe, maybe that had been the end of it. Perhaps Molnir and Freedom Coin simply intended to pay off someone for a contract, but they failed and let the whole thing drop.

Kinsella shook her head. A barely discernible motion, but Todd read it. It meant, *Put that thought aside. Stay focused.*

"Who was the guy you tried to bribe?" he said.

"Head of security at some big operation," Lifshitz mumbled. "I don't know where. I'd tell you if I did. I don't know about no sarin. You think I want to go to the chair?"

Todd spoke quietly, but Lifshitz spooked as if he had yelled at him in a dark alley. "Will the sarin be released where this security guy works? Is Frisch telling him that if he doesn't give the contract to Molnir, he'll end up with the mother of all security breaches?"

"God help me, I don't know."

Todd walked over to Kinsella. "If we locate this security guy, we have a likely target for the sarin."

"Think, Yuri," Kinsella said. "Try to remember the security guy's name."

Lifshitz's black beard glistened with sweat. His breath was ragged and shallow like an amateur in the final stretch of a marathon. "Something fucking German."

"There are three million people in New York City with German family names."

"No, no. This guy isn't German American. He *is* a German."

CHAPTER 44

Outside the hotel room, there was no sign of the UN guards. Through the door, Verrazzano heard Lance's Texas accent. His tone was desperate, bargaining as though he were talking to a girlfriend who'd already given up on him. He certainly wasn't in conversation with the Dutch doctor.

Verrazzano moved to the next room and knocked quietly. He heard no movement inside. From his jacket pocket, he drew an Arduino microcontroller the size of his palm. Its circuits and chips were exposed like the motherboard inside a computer. He unraveled the red DC connector twined around it.

A second voice emanated from Lance's room, angry, disdainful, and American accented.

Verrazzano knelt and examined the bottom of the key-card lock protruding from the door. He found the power socket the hotel used to charge the mechanism and to feed in the thirty-two-bit security code. He connected his DC wire to the socket. His microcontroller read the security code and fed it back to the lock. The light on the lock switched to green. He eased the door open and unhooked his wire from the socket. He shut the door behind him.

Quanah's guards were dead in the bathtub, their legs splayed across the tiled floor. The thin, white shade billowed like a ghost over the open window. *Whoever killed them went along the ledge,* Verrazzano thought. *Into Lance's room.*

He drew his H&K and lifted himself onto the window ledge. Six floors below, the lights of the UN truck receded, heading to pick up the sarin and transport it to the Field Deployable Hydro-lysis System outside the city. Lance's window was open. Verraz-zano resisted the urge to swing across and dive inside. He recalled Wyatt telling him about Zaitsev, the great sniper of Stalingrad. His motto was "Impatience is death." The German snipers who stalked him died even before Nazism did. Zaitsev outlived the Soviet Union. Verrazzano pressed close to the wall, waited, and listened.

"I did *not* make a deal with the UN people." Lance's words came into the night, thick and weary. "You got it all wrong."

"What about the other guy?" The voice belonged unquestion-ably to a big body. It had a crushing power.

"Verrazzano? He's just an asshole."

"That's the last thing he is. Which makes you the asshole." There was a second American. "How we going to handle him, Brennan?"

Verrazzano knew that name. Wyatt used Brennan to send a message to his enemies when he wanted someone to feel as though they had died more than once.

"Verrazzano? He's going to wish he never walked out," Bren-nan said.

The desert breeze caught Verrazzano's sweat and chilled him. He drew himself up, confident and balanced on the ledge. It was time to ignore the lessons he had learned from Wyatt. He let his weight shift to the frame of the open window, leaning toward Lance's room, and he jumped inside.

A broad man with a shaven head spun toward him. His face was immobile and unsurprised, as though tall Americans with German pistols often came through windows at him. He drove the flat of his hand under Verrazzano's chin. The blow took the ICE agent off balance. His head struck the wall. His sight exploded into flashes of color. He felt a chop at his wrist and someone grap-pled his H&K from his hand.

The reactions were so quick and aggressive, Verrazzano knew this had to be Brennan, the deadliest man left on Wyatt's team. Verrazzano reached the moment that always came within seconds of the opening violence, when the untrained or the weak or the unlucky died. Special Forces sergeants took their recruits to this point again and again in hand-to-hand training to override the sluggishness in a battered brain when death seems a warm, welcoming refuge. That training propelled Verrazzano toward his assailant, blind as he was.

He threw out half a dozen quick punches to keep Brennan busy while his vision cleared. Brennan came back at him with short stabs at his kidneys.

Verrazzano pushed out his hips and shoulders. He exaggerated the motion so that it'd look like all he had. Brennan leaned in on him to counter the thrust. Verrazzano slipped to the side, and Brennan slammed face first into the wall.

With one step Verrazzano was behind him. He brought his knee up into Brennan's tailbone, took him by the neck, and smashed his teeth into the wall-mounted temperature control.

The second man charged at Verrazzano, swinging an extendable metal baton. Lance rolled across the bed and deflected the stroke. He tackled the man to the floor.

Brennan jerked his elbow and caught Verrazzano on the temple. The colors around him were vibrant and unreal again. He seemed to be fighting the man against a green screen. The room was a digital image projected behind them in a special effects suite. Brennan swung a right, his fist blurring toward Verrazzano out of a pulsing spectrum tunnel.

He blocked the punch with his left forearm and brought his elbow down on Brennan's clavicle. The vulnerable collarbone snapped. Verrazzano punched the break as hard as he could, driving the sheared edges of the bone back toward the lungs.

Brennan screamed and clutched his arm to his torso as though he feared it'd fall off. Drooling bright blood onto the dyed-nylon carpet, he dropped on his face.

Verrazzano opened his eyes wide, fighting his punch-drunk disorientation. Lance bit deep into the second man's neck, his face tawny with the effort of holding on. The man howled.

"Take your teeth out of him," Verrazzano shouted.

Lance let go, coughing the man's blood onto his shirt.

Verrazzano twisted the man's wrist high behind his shoulder blade and yanked the hair at the crown of his head. The man's nose was a slalom of bone spurs and mashed cartilage from old breaks. His neck was tattooed with a lizard curving from under his shirt.

The man panted hard. "We're not here to kill *you*."

"Mission accomplished." Verrazzano used his knee to overextend the man's shoulder. "Where is Wyatt? He's here, isn't he?"

"He just wants you to leave." The lizard gunman's tattoo seemed to recede under the collar of his T-shirt, as though the reptile were hiding.

"You understand who I am. I heard you say it."

Lizard Tattoo shivered and nodded.

"So talk. Before I do what you know I can do."

A deafening blast ripped through the hotel room. Lizard Tattoo flew out of Verrazzano's grip as though he were roped behind an accelerating truck. Across the room, Brennan held Verrazzano's H&K in his left hand, his right arm dangling from the wrecked collarbone, his eyes struggling to throw off the vacancy of recent unconsciousness.

Verrazzano dodged toward him. He grabbed Brennan's shaky wrist and flipped it to disarm him. "Your buddy was about to talk." He held the H&K at Brennan's neck and snarled. "Now it's your turn."

Brennan blew a gob of bloody spittle into Verrazzano's eye and punched the H&K out of his hand. It skittered across the room.

They stumbled into the bathroom, grappling to throw each other. Verrazzano hammered his shoulder into Brennan's broken collarbone. The thug bellowed. Verrazzano kicked his feet away and dropped him hard onto the bidet.

"Where's Wyatt?" he yelled. "What's his angle?"

Brennan shook his head. Blood sprayed on the spotless ceramic tiles.

"Where's the attack going to take place? The sarin attack? Tell me where and when."

"You worried some asshole's going to kill some people? The way you killed Maryam Ghattas?"

For an instant, Verrazzano recoiled at the name of his innocent victim.

Brennan sensed his indecision. He snatched the hair dryer from its wall mount and slammed it against Verrazzano's skull. He tugged the power line out of the dryer's handle and drove the live wire at Verrazzano's chest.

The alternating current fizzed through him. His heart hammered like a basketball bounced close to the ground.

Brennan snarled at him. "Back then in Beirut, Wyatt sent me to watch you. Make sure you got the job done. I followed you after you whacked that bitch. I saw you go down by the shore and cry like a little girl."

Another kind of electricity surged around Verrazzano too. Rage had a voltage all its own. But anger didn't help in a fight. He smothered it as he struggled against the arm that held the power line.

"I saw you fuck it up too," Brennan said. "The hit."

Verrazzano knew what he meant. The kid. Maryam Ghattas's son. Maybe six years old, holding his mother's hand as the American executed her.

"Wyatt sent me back there later to kill the only witness—the only person who could identify you. See how he took care of you? But you spat in his face and left the company."

Verrazzano shook his head. "Witness? You mean—"

"Her kid. You should've taken him out, and you know it."

The current incapacitated Verrazzano. Soon it would kill him. He had to finish this. He forced his body forward. He drove Brennan's shaven head hard against the tiled wall.

He had spared the little boy, but Wyatt had sent this thug to kill him too, to tidy up the operation. He growled and snarled with the effort of the fight.

Brennan jabbed with the wire. The current burned Verrazzano's neck. The surge of blood around his body seemed to shred his overloaded veins. He roared through his clenched jaw. He could barely move. He found enough control somewhere to tip his weight into his fist, crushing Brennan's throat. His heartbeat was the quaking thunder of dance-club bass. Brennan purpled and choked. Verrazzano held on.

The wire fell, sizzling in the blood on the floor. Brennan went still. Verrazzano stared into the man's empty features.

Lance shuffled into the bathroom. Verrazzano levered himself against the toilet and the bathtub to get to his feet. He shoved Lance toward the corridor.

"We've got a plane to catch," he said.

CHAPTER 45

Two UN workers in chemical suits strung red warning tape across the blown-in entrance to the Casbah storehouse. The flatbed crane they had used to load the sarin onto the truck stood in the narrow alley, its engine idling.

Verrazzano crept toward the crane. He checked the luminous dial of his watch. He had fifteen minutes to reach the airport. He figured drawing up at the curb in a taxi wouldn't cut it—someone might be expecting him. Most likely Brennan had been waiting for him at the hotel because Touma betrayed him. He'd have to force the pilots of the Palestinian's plane to take him out of Damascus anyway. But first he'd have to get around whoever Touma had sent to the airport to intercept him. It could be a team of local tough guys, or military intelligence, or some other institution with electrodes in the basement ready to snap onto his nuts. He didn't have time to go through the terminal anyhow. He had to get into the airport some other way.

That's why he was in the Casbah again. He climbed up to the driver's cab of the flatbed crane and took the wheel. Lance struggled in behind him.

Verrazzano put the flatbed in gear. He ignored the shouts of the UN workers and rumbled the truck out of the tiny streets.

In the dashboard light Lance was ghostly, coughing and shivering. Verrazzano wondered if the atropine was sufficient to counter the dose of sarin. "Are you going to live long enough to get to New York?"

Lance wiped his nose on his sleeve. "You bet. I'm running on the most powerful fuel there is. Know what I mean?"

"I used to have a tank full." Verrazzano knew Lance would make it. Rage could keep a man walking even after his body was destroyed.

"Used to? That's a fuel you don't ever run out of."

Verrazzano ground through the truck's gears. His jaw was tight. Lance was right. It was rage that kept him alive long enough to outfight Brennan. It would always be in him.

"You can't no more get rid of it than you can unkill someone you shot dead."

"Shut up," Verrazzano barked.

Lance smiled, then he winced and held his chest.

They reached the airport just before Touma's flight was due to take off. Beyond the high perimeter chain link fence, red runway markers lit a Sherpa, a freight version of an old British light airliner. "That's got to be the plane," Verrazzano said.

In front of the terminal, the headlights of an armored personnel carrier illuminated a squad of soldiers in the red berets of the Republican Guard, the nearest thing to an elite unit in the Syrian army.

Verrazzano had two minutes to get Lance onto the Sherpa. He cut the lights on the crane truck. He ran it off the road and bumped over the dirt to the perimeter. He aimed to break through it, but he spotted the tank trap between the two rows of fencing. He wouldn't get the crane across that ditch.

The Republican Guards walked slowly toward the truck, curious, suspicious. The plane's twin props started up.

Verrazzano pulled alongside the fence. He swung out the door and up behind the cab.

The guards went into a jog.

Verrazzano gripped the joystick of the hydraulic crane. He levered the boom out over the airport fence. Lance labored up to him.

The Sherpa taxied toward the perimeter. The main runway ran right along the fence.

Verrazzano hauled Lance onto the boom and shoved him forward. Lance edged ahead. He swung under the boom and struggled to haul himself back up.

Verrazzano remembered a rope strung over a gorge at Fort Bragg and a candidate for the green beret from New York dangling underneath just as Lance hung from the boom now. "Drop your fucking leg, Verrazzano," Colonel Wyatt had screamed at him. It felt like surrendering to the fall, but the only way to balance was to hook one leg over the rope and let the other hang straight down.

"Drop your fucking leg." Verrazzano heard the nastiness of his old boss in his voice.

Lance extended his leg. It balanced him. He shimmied along the boom and dropped over the fence. As he landed, he collapsed and cried out, "Ah shit, fuck."

Verrazzano crawled fast along the crane's arm. A gunshot passed close, splitting the air with a sharp crack. He crossed the fence. A second shot ricocheted off the boom with a sound like a cherry pit dropping into a bowl. Verrazzano added it to the thousands of rounds that had missed him. He jumped lightly to the dirt.

Lance hopped on one foot. "Fucking ankle. Twisted, real bad."

Verrazzano threw Lance's arm over his shoulder. They loped three-legged to the taxiway.

The Sherpa's lights caught them as it turned to the runway. The pilot's face appeared in the cockpit window. He noticed them. His mouth opened, calling to his copilot.

Verrazzano had to figure out how to get the pilot to let them onto the plane. But first he had to make it to the plane. He pushed harder. The 1,100 horsepower turboprops drowned the reports from the Republican Guards' guns. Still he sensed the disturbance the gunshots made in the air. Lance brayed with pain.

The plane slowed. The door opened and a short rack of steps unfurled. Verrazzano dodged behind the metal strut of the wheel for cover, but the man who leaned out of the door didn't aim a pistol at him. He wore a pilot's shirt and he beckoned urgently.

"I can't make it," Lance shouted.

If the Republican Guards executed Lance on the tarmac, it'd be the end of one bad man. It'd also crush the best chance of uncovering details of the sarin attack—and stopping it. The sand drifted at the edge of the tarmac, swept there by the force of the engines. Verrazzano tossed Lance over his shoulder in a fireman's lift and ran.

Dust filled the air in the draft of the turboprops. Each grain swept like a scythe over the interior of his lungs. He howled, expelling the dead air to make room in his chest for new oxygen. Lance beat his fists against Verrazzano's back. "Move it, motherfucker."

The copilot leaned from the doorway of the Sherpa. "Come on, man. You can do it."

A machine gun burst spat a track through the dust in front of Verrazzano. Once he stepped beyond it, he left pain and fatigue behind him, as if he had mainlined some miraculous drug that propelled him through time and space to an immortal wonderland. He charged along the runway.

The copilot extended his arm from the door of the plane. His lips moved, but Verrazzano heard nothing.

He caught up to the plane and tossed Lance into the doorway. The copilot yanked the injured man into the cabin. Verrazzano reached for the steps.

A bullet struck the boxy fuselage. The pilot must've heard it, because the whine of the engines ticked up an octave and the Sherpa drew away from Verrazzano.

His legs felt as though he still carried Lance's weight. If he didn't get on that plane, the Republican Guard would give him to the secret police. He imagined the cell where they'd torture him, the hose down his throat pumping fuel oil, the auto battery clips burning him, the cold and fatigue.

The lights of the plane dimmed, the noise of the engines receded. Into the darkness stepped Maryam Ghattas, beautiful and dark and dead. He ran to her. With each step, he counted off the horrors he had brought into the world and wondered if he might pay them back one day.

The copilot reached out from the doorway. "You're nearly there."

It was the Ghattas woman, rescuing him, her long fingers extended through the whirling dust.

The copilot howled over the noise of the engine. "Take my hand."

He pushed harder, caught hold of the hand and held onto it as though it were Maryam Ghattas who grabbed him. He threw himself onto the stairs.

Another shot hit the fuselage. The plane lifted off the tarmac. Verrazzano stumbled, his boots bounced against the runway, but the copilot kept his grip around his wrists. Then he was in the air.

He scrambled up the dangling steps and tumbled inside the plane. He rolled into the gangway, trembling with relief.

The copilot heaved the door shut. He went into the cockpit, shaking his head.

Verrazzano watched the cockpit door. He couldn't trust the pilots. He was certain Touma had sold him out, and these guys worked for the Palestinian arms dealer. He pushed himself to his knees. He had to make certain they were taking him where he wanted to go. He coughed hard. He took a pace toward the cockpit.

Lance snapped his fingers. Verrazzano turned toward him.

The Texan sat in the first row of seats. He trained his pistol on Verrazzano.

"The shit never stops, does it, Special Agent?" Lance smiled.

"Only one way to stop it, and I'm not going to die yet."

The Sherpa climbed to cruising altitude. Lance blinked his tearing, irritated eyes and elevated his sprained ankle on a seat. "Get me a deal. Or this plane doesn't go to New York."

"Nothing is more important to me than stopping this attack." Verrazzano took a step forward. "You'll have a deal. The federal government is going to need your testimony."

"Stop right there."

"We need to stay together on this, Lance. These pilots may be a threat."

"They'll go where I tell them to go. That's been my experience when I'm the guy holding the gun."

"Lance, tell me the target of the attack. The government will protect you. But please tell me the end game. What's the sarin for?"

Lance scratched his scalp, tense and deranged. "When we get to New York. You'll know it then."

"It's in New York. I know *that*. But how much sarin is there?"

"Enough."

"Enough for what?"

"You'll find out tomorrow."

Verrazzano stared. He knew the day of the attack at last.

Lance grinned. "See? I got what you want."

"It's in New York. But where?"

"Get me that deal, asshole."

The cockpit door opened. A second pilot stepped out. He wore unpolarized Ray-Bans and a ginger Fu Manchu mustache. He saw the gun. "My God," he said.

Lance twitched the pistol toward the pilot.

The instant the gun turned away from him, Verrazzano jumped at Lance. He slapped aside the weapon as Lance tried to swing it back toward him. He grabbed him and pulled him close, wrenching the gun from his grip.

He kicked Lance's broken ankle. "It'll take us ten hours to reach New York. We don't have time to waste. Tell me where the attack is going to take place." He smelled the corruption on Lance's breath, a hint of the death that almost had him in its hand and would close its grip around so many others if Verrazzano failed.

The Texan's watery eyes were helpless and desperate. Verrazzano made his voice quiet, but the urgency remained. "Who has the sarin?"

Lance turned toward the window, moaning.

The pilot came close. "What the hell is this?"

"Everything's under control," Verrazzano said.

"Who is this guy? What're you doing to him?"

Verrazzano turned the pistol on the pilot. "Just back off. I'll be right with you." He had ten hours to break Lance down. But first he should pass on his leads to the New York field office. He frisked Lance.

"I got no other weapons, asshole," Lance said.

Verrazzano headed for the cockpit.

The pilots wore polyester shirts with a charter company logo on the sleeve. The man with the mustache lit a French cigarette. "What's going on back there?" he said.

"Do you have a weapon in the cockpit?"

The pilots exchanged a nervous glance. The one with the mustache shook his head.

"Squawk sixty-one hundred," Verrazzano said.

The pilot glanced at the transponder in the overhead panel. "That's a defense code."

"Do it." Verrazzano patted down the mustachioed pilot.

"Listen, man, we're not going to call in to NORAD. How're we going to explain our point of origin and cargo? You think we were delivering Christmas cards to Damascus before we picked you up?"

Verrazzano reached for the manual dials. The pilot went to stop him. Verrazzano stabbed the heel of his hand onto the man's deltoid. The pilot cried out and his arm dropped limp. "Jesus," he whined. "What the fuck?"

Verrazzano turned the dials. The transponder signaled the identification code 6100. Most planes in the United States transmit a 1200 code to air traffic control systems. Some codes are restricted to defense agencies. One of those is 6100. He took the headset from the navigator station.

A stern, calm voice came over the headset. "This is US North-Com East. XPDR six-one-zero-zero, identify yourself. Over." It was the North American Aerospace Defense Command for the eastern region in Rome, New York, responding to Verrazzano's broadcast of one of its reserved transponder codes.

"This is Special Agent Dominic Verrazzano, Immigration and Customs Enforcement. I'm dealing with an urgent issue of national security. I need to be connected with Special Agent Roula Haddad at the ICE New York field office. Over."

The controller's voice burst through the headphones. "Roger. Please wait, Agent Verrazzano."

In the silence Verrazzano stood over the pilots. They chewed their lips and rolled their eyes like surly teenagers forced to ride in the back of the car heading to a family event. Perhaps Touma hadn't told them they'd be dealing with a federal agent. Now they knew, and Verrazzano hoped that would keep them in line.

Within a minute, Haddad came over the headphones. "Where are you, Dom?"

"En route from Syria. The sarin attack is set for tomorrow. In New York. I need to secure full legal immunity for a Molnir guy. Name, Lance Kirby, Kilo-India-Romeo-Bravo-Yankee. You have that?"

"Received."

He glanced into the cabin. Lance stared at him, his teeth set against the pain in his foot. "I have him in custody. I believe he knows the whereabouts of the sarin in New York. He'll only tell me where it is when we get there and he's sure of a deal."

"I'll get onto the US attorney's office."

"Tell them the stakes are too high to haggle about the terms of the deal."

"Can you get the guy to talk on the plane? You won't be in New York until midmorning, even with the time difference."

The pilot glanced up at Verrazzano and stepped out his cigarette. He touched the copilot's sleeve and mumbled to him.

"I'll keep trying," Verrazzano said. "What else on your end?"

"Freedom Coin was funding a bribe for Tom Frisch, as you suspected. We don't know who the target of the bribe was. Only that it was a German guy at a big institution. Noelle's calling around on that now."

"Thanks, Roula."

"Safe flight."

Verrazzano laid the headphones on the navigation shelf. He stepped into the cabin. Lance sneered at him. The details that could save thousands of lives were locked in his stubborn, furious, bruised head. Safe flight? Sure.

PART III

CHAPTER 46

The passenger cabin glowed with the sunrise chasing the plane across the Atlantic. Verrazzano rubbed his eyes. By the time the sun went down, this would all be done. Lance drowsed in his seat, exhausted by the persistent, fruitless interrogation. Verrazzano tried to figure out another way to come at him.

The pilot opened the cockpit door. The odor of cigarettes and brandy flushed through the cabin.

Verrazzano flipped the barrel of the pistol toward him. The pilot recoiled and lifted his hands. "Touch down in an hour." He went back into the cockpit.

Lance mumbled, "I need to take a whiz."

Verrazzano stepped down the aisle. He reached for Lance's elbow.

Lance pushed him away. "You want to hold my dick while I piss?"

Verrazzano shoved the Texan into the bathroom. Lance tried to shut the door. Verrazzano stopped it with his boot. "I won't blush," he said. "Do your business."

"Ain't you just friendly as a bramble bush." Lance stood a long time before he got any pee out. He cleaned up and stumbled back to his seat.

"Shit," he said. "I'm tired as a boomtown whore."

"You'll live."

"I'd have to get better to die."

"Guys like you are immune to death. You've got legal immunity too. Now tell me where the sarin is."

"When I step off this plane and I have my deal in writing from the US attorney, I'll give you what you want to know. Until then, you don't get squat from me."

Verrazzano clenched his fist. On an operation, it seemed every conversation was a zero-sum game, worming information out of assholes like Lance who'd just as soon kill him.

"Did you know Lee Hill?" Verrazzano said.

"I met Lee, sure."

"He killed himself thirty-six hours ago because he knew he was going to die of the effects of sarin on his body."

Lance's left eye fluttered.

"How about Jeff Parry and Jon Ivin? D'you know them? Both dead."

The Texan sucked at his teeth.

"When the sarin starts killing people in New York City, the federal government is going to hold you accountable. Unless you help me now." Verrazzano growled out his words. "Tell me where the sarin is."

Lance shook his head.

"What about your dead buddies?" Verrazzano said. "You'd been through some dangerous times with Hill, Parry, and Ivin. You owe them, Lance. What would *they* have sacrificed for *you*? In the field, they'd have given their lives for you. But now their buddy Lance won't open his mouth until he's got some bit of paper from a lawyer to cover his ass. I'm glad they're dead. I wouldn't want them to see what you've become."

"You must think I'm pretty fucking simple to fall for a goddamn guilt trip. If you've got nothing better than that, just shut your mouth and let me get some rest."

Verrazzano waited for Lance to make a big show of getting comfortable and shutting his eyes. Then he spoke quietly, "Yeah, they're dead. You don't have anything to worry about from them. They're not going to come after you."

Lance's relaxed posture overlaid a suddenly frozen core. Verrazzano detected it clearly. He waited some more. "Someone is though, aren't they? Someone's going to come track you down. Whether you talk to me or not."

The Texan shifted to his side, showing Verrazzano his back.

"He's going to find you and chop you into little pieces and send them to your mamma by the US mail."

"I ain't afraid of Tom Frisch."

"I'm not talking about Frisch. See, I know the guy who's going to come for you. I know him real well, and he's going to get you for sure."

Lance raised his middle finger and showed it to Verrazzano.

"Yeah, he'll probably start with your hands," Verrazzano said. "I saw him take a guy's fingers off with an acetylene torch, one by one. He sure does like to let you know how much he loves to hate you. That's his way. That's just how he is, old Colonel Wyatt."

Lance spun around in his chair, his face flushed. "The fuck you talking about?"

"The man who pays Tom Frisch, that's who I'm talking about."

"I don't know no Colonel Wyatt."

"Frisch worked for Wyatt in Special Ops. So did I. Then Wyatt started his own operations. Except he didn't tell anybody else. Only Frisch, maybe. By the time I found out what the asshole's game was, he'd sent me out to do stuff that I thought was US policy, which turned out to be nothing but mercenary deals for the benefit of Wyatt's secret bank accounts. I was ready to die for my country—I guess you might've noticed that I still am. But I wasn't going to check out for the enrichment of a crook just because he had a charming smile and a Johnny Cash baritone."

He grabbed Lance's collar and pulled him close. "Wyatt's still pulling the strings on this operation. I know it. Frisch as good as told me."

"As good as?"

"You need shit spelled out, go type up reports at the Pentagon. Special Ops is about filling in the blanks. You know that. Frisch and Wyatt are in this thing. Wherever you go with your plea bargain, you're going to need one of two things to happen. Best would be that we get hold of Colonel Wyatt. Maybe if we bury him in a secret prison in Wyoming, he won't be able to run you down. Next best, you have the full force of the federal government on your side in a witness protection program. But that's not going to happen if you wait too long and the sarin attack goes down. So give it up now."

Lance blew his nose with his fingers. He spoke slowly and quietly. "We got hold of the sarin a year ago in Iraq. We trucked it over the border."

"Why bring it to Syria?"

"Take the nasty shit to where the killing is. First rule of the arms trade."

Verrazzano understood that the Damascus regime was being set up. The sarin was never in the hands of the Syrian government. The missile he found in Atlantic Beach was a red herring, intended to convince law enforcement that Syrian agents were in New York, so that when the sarin attack went down, the Syrians would get the blame. *And get hit with the retaliation.*

"How did Doctor Weston become involved?"

"Our guy Daryl Underwood got exposed to the sarin by accident," Lance said. "I guess he didn't figure on dying just yet. Wanted to go home alive. See his little girl grow up."

"He went to Doctor Weston for treatment and told her everything?"

"Pretty much."

"The sarin in New York, what's it for?"

Lance closed his eyes and breathed deeply. Verrazzano waited. Lance licked his lips. "To set off a full-on regional conflict in the Mideast. It don't take much more than a gas grill to light up the place at the best of times. Right now you've got Islamic State chopping the heads off Christians and all them other sects in Iraq and Syria. So you do this sarin attack to piss off the West. You pin it on Syria, and the US Army brings down the Syrian regime."

"Then Islamic State takes over?"

"That's the idea. They're the most powerful on the ground right now. Syria's all fucked up because of the civil war, but it's still got oil and a lot of trade money, even with the sanctions. Them Islamic State assholes are all gung ho to use that cash for a fight with Israel and Saudi and Iran. They're going to need weapons."

Verrazzano's guts convulsed. "Wyatt's going to sell them the weapons?"

"You bet."

It was as though the colonel came into the cabin, genial and energetic and deadly. Verrazzano saw Wyatt's strategy. "He spreads the Syrian civil war beyond the country's borders?"

"Oh, brother. Way, way beyond those borders. And he sells arms to just about everyone involved."

The awful scope of the scheme stunned Verrazzano. "Lance, tell me where to find the sarin. You've got to talk. Now."

A sallow shadow passed over the Texan as if some horrible pain shuddered through him, a pain inflicted at some unexpected time in the future by a vengeful Colonel Wyatt. "I've got your word, don't I?"

"You'll get your deal."

The pilot stepped into the cabin. "There's somebody who's got a better deal for you, Lance." He raised a tiny Kel-Tec PF-9.

He gestured with the pistol as the Sherpa banked along the coastline of Long Island. "Come up here, Lance. You're going to wait this out in the can." He pushed the restroom door open.

Verrazzano cursed himself for failing to search the cockpit thoroughly. He'd known the pilots might be dirty. They were working for Marwan Touma, after all. He'd been so focused on getting the details of the sarin attack out of Lance, he'd neglected to check the second pilot for weapons.

Lance shuffled forward. Verrazzano stood.

"Not you," the pilot said. "Back in your seat."

"We're turning east. Where are we landing?" Verrazzano brushed against Lance as he sat down.

"We're not going to an airport. But you're still going to lose your luggage." The pilot shoved Lance into the restroom. He lifted the flap above the occupied sign and slid the lock into override. He leaned on the door.

"I'll take your gun," he said to Verrazzano. "Lay it in the aisle and slide it to me."

"I don't have a weapon."

"Don't bullshit me. I saw it earlier."

Verrazzano turned to show the empty holster in the back of his belt.

The pilot frowned. "You had a gun, God damn it."

A shot battered out through the restroom door. It struck the pilot in the ribs. He tumbled into the cockpit.

Verrazzano charged forward. He flipped the lock on the restroom. Lance reeled out with the H&K pistol Verrazzano had slipped him when he passed. Verrazzano grabbed the weapon back.

In the cockpit, the wounded pilot raised his gun. Verrazzano shot him in the head.

With its last impulse, the pilot's reflexive nervous system drew back his finger on the trigger. The shot blew away the copilot's jaw.

The plane's nose dipped. Verrazzano threw himself at the controls. He yanked the stick back. The copilot's weight dropped against him. He tumbled toward the cabin.

They headed for the water. The Atlantic was a desolate gray.

Verrazzano hauled the copilot out of his seat. He leapt into the chair and wrestled with the plane. The sand of the beach was the only thing visible when the Sherpa pulled out of its dive.

The long reeds of the wetlands stroked the fuselage. Verrazzano took his first conscious breath since the pilot entered the cabin with the Kel-Tec.

Then he held it again.

The tall cabin of a motor yacht splashed white across his vision as the plane skimmed the channel. Verrazzano saw the instant of horror in the face of the man at the helm.

Twisting the controls, Verrazzano knew he was done. The Sherpa's port propellers chopped into the yacht and rattled in pieces against the body of the plane.

The Sherpa kicked over and went down. The water came up in front of Verrazzano. He threw himself away from the cockpit window toward the cabin.

CHAPTER 47

Kinsella worked up a general alert for the field office's special agent in charge to send out about a possible chemical attack in the city. It went to the NYPD, to state and federal law enforcement, to major financial and political institutions that were thought likely terrorist targets. She felt as though she had typed up a death certificate for an entire city.

Then she followed up the lead from the Freedom Coin guy Yuri Lifshitz. Looking for a German head of security who was seeking a new subcontractor, she contacted the German banks and insurance companies in Midtown. She called Lufthansa and Air Berlin at JFK. She found the rep for the electronics company Siemens at a hotel breakfast and reached the director of the Bertelsmann publishing firm on his way out of Grand Central Station. In every case, either the security guy was American or there was no contract for tender. She was briefly excited to find the local branch of a Munich engineering firm with a security chief named Karl Bauman who was in the market for a new surveillance operator. But Bauman turned out to be from New Jersey—Lifshitz had specified that Molnir tried to bribe a German, not an American with a German name. Kinsella still didn't know the target of the bribe. Which meant she didn't know where the sarin attack would take place.

She shook her head. It *would* have to be a German company. She put off the call to Commerzbank until last. She still remembered the switchboard number a decade and a half later. The receptionist was a temp. She didn't know the nationality of the security chief. Kinsella left a message.

It was seven AM. She punched up a twenty-four-hour BBC news channel on her monitor and clicked to the live feed. The lead story highlighted the latest battle in the Syrian civil war. She sipped her coffee. It had gone cold while she made her calls. She spat it back into the cup.

It wasn't only the coffee that made her feel like spitting. Verrazzano should've landed with the Molnir informant by now, but he hadn't checked in. There was nerve gas in the city, in the hands of people who were as close to pure evil as it was possible to get. And Special Agent Noelle Kinsella couldn't even get some German guy on the line.

The screen of her desk phone flashed. She picked up. "Kinsella."

"This is Mark Giusti." There was a long blast on a horn in the background—he was calling from his car. "You were trying to reach me. I'm security manager at Commerzbank."

He had a New York accent and an Italian family name. He wasn't a German. One more dead end. Kinsella rolled her tongue, rebelling against the bitter taint of the coffee. "I guess it's not as important as I had hoped, sir. I appreciate that you called me back anyhow."

"The message says your first name's Noelle. Are you Ginnie Kinsella's daughter?"

She hadn't thought anyone would remember after so long—anyone except her. "Yes, I am."

"I was just starting at the bank when Ginnie was here. It's a hell of a thing."

A hell of a thing, yes. Kinsella listened to the traffic down the line, to the voice of a man who had known her mother—Virginia Dolores Kinsella, receptionist for the Frankfurt bank's operation on the fortieth floor of One World Trade Center. A floor that was low enough for people who went down to reach safety after the jet hit. Except that Ginnie went up the stairs, helping others evacuate. "I figured your call was something about Ginnie. Man, your voice sounds just like her. Did anyone ever tell you that?"

Her mother's friends told her she was like a voice from the grave. But the grave never spoke to Kinsella. "It's been said before."

"Ginnie was really great." The mention of the dead woman was loaded with whatever terror lingered from Giusti's own experiences on that day. His voice was taut and uneasy.

Kinsella sighed. *Ah, just get it done*, she thought. *Mom wouldn't have pussied around on this.* "Just for my information, do you have any security contracts out for tender right now?"

Someone leaned on the horn of a truck. "What's that? I didn't hear you," Giusti said. "Wait a second. Let me roll up my window. The traffic's really messed up today." The horn and the engine noise receded. "That's better. I wish to hell they'd hold the UN General Assembly on a weekend instead of tying up everyone's commute with their motorcades."

Cold coffee spilled over Kinsella's wrist. "Thank you, sir. You've been very helpful." She hung up the line.

The UN brings staff from all over the world, she thought. *Maybe the head of security is German.*

She called up the number of the UN security office on her screen and dialed. She muted the BBC feed on her computer. The UN would already know about the danger. Its headquarters on the East River was on the list of addresses to which the special agent in charge would've sent out Kinsella's alert. But that didn't mean the UN knew it was the target.

If it *was* the target.

The UN was doing construction work. Kinsella saw it from the bus every morning. Maybe Frisch and his people were after the security contract for the new building. That could've been why they offered a bribe to a German head of security.

An Indian-accented woman answered Kinsella's call. "Department of Safety and Security."

"Good morning. My name is Special Agent Noelle Kinsella. I'm with US Immigration and Customs Enforcement. Can you put me through to the head of security, please?"

"I'm afraid he's out of the office just at the moment."

"Is he on his cell phone?"

"It's off, I'm afraid. He's doing a television interview. May I take a message?"

"Perhaps you can help me. Is he German?"

"I beg your pardon?"

"The head of security. Is he a German national?"

"No, he's not German. And I'm not Indian, I'm Bangladeshi."

The woman's tone was strangely aggressive. Kinsella was puzzled. She wondered if she'd misheard her. "Beg pardon?"

"You Americans are always in such a rush to label people. Is there anything else?"

Kinsella shut her aching eyes and sighed. "No, that's all. Thank you."

On the BBC a blond man with a weak jaw, green spectacles, and a gray suit was responding to questions on a linkup with the studio in London. Through the window behind him, a long rank of national flags moved on the wind—the UN plaza. Kinsella figured there was a studio in the Secretariat tower that CNN and the BBC used for live broadcasts. A caption appeared along the bottom of the screen identifying the interviewee. "Andreas Holtz. Chief, UN Safety and Security Office."

Kinsella clicked on the volume tab. *Holtz. A German name. But not a German, apparently.* She caught the end of the anchor's question. "—any threats during this General Assembly?"

"The threats are always considerable during this very important period in the United Nations calendar," Holtz said. "It's also true that terrorism has changed greatly since the United Nations building was constructed in the 1950s. We have made significant ad hoc changes over the years. We believe security parameters have been reconfigured with measurable efficacy."

His accent sounded pretty damned German to Kinsella. She wondered if she'd had the right department when she spoke to the Indian. She corrected herself—the Bangladeshi. An idea crawled into her tired mind. *Where was Bangladesh? Right next to India.*

The anchor did her best to sound stimulated by Holtz and his careful, bureaucratic answers. "The UN has a very international staff, by definition. You're an Austrian, I understand. Don't you think you should recruit security staff from parts of the world like the Middle East where terrorism is more of a factor than it is in, say, Austria, because—"

Kinsella jumped from her chair and ran across the Homeland Security floor, her long hair streaming behind her.

Austria. Right next to Germany. But different. Just like India and Bangladesh. That was the connection that offended the woman on the phone at the UN. Thank God she was so touchy.

Kinsella wrenched open the door of the holding room. Yuri Lifshitz lay asleep on the bench with his face to the wall and his legs tucked into his belly.

She shook him hard by the shoulder. "Andreas Holtz. You know the name?"

Lifshitz rubbed his face. "I do. I don't know where from."

"The security chief Molnir tried to bribe?"

He was awake now. "That's the guy. Holtz, yeah. Holtz."

Kinsella burst out of the holding room and sprinted toward Todd's cubicle.

She yelled, "It's at the UN. The sarin's at the UN."

CHAPTER 48

Water rose cold over his chest. Color and detail rushed into his eyes. On the flooded ceiling of the overturned plane, Verrazzano came to. Lance flailed in the knee-high water, blinking hard and puffing like a drunk. Verrazzano forced open the cockpit door. A wave burst into the cabin. The nose was gone, sheared away when the aircraft flipped. The fuselage creaked and yawned. The tail lifted. Soon the plane would slip to the bottom.

"Let's go." Verrazzano went under. He groped out of the cabin.

The remains of the cockpit were a mass of sharp, twisted steel. It cut Verrazzano's back as he swam through it. The wound stung in the salt water. He let his pain drift away from him, rising to the surface with his air bubbles.

Something caught his foot. He wriggled his leg, but it held him.

He reached down. A bundle of wires from the smashed instrument panel tangled around his ankle. He wrestled with the cables to free himself. They didn't budge. Air rushed from his mouth.

Lance squirted toward the surface.

Verrazzano tugged at the wires. His foot stuck firm. He was out of oxygen. He felt his brain shutting down, synapse by synapse.

A jet of ice plunged through him and his blood clouded the water. The sheared metal was sharp as a razor. *Slice it free,* he told himself, reciting the phrase in his head again and again, each time slower as his brain choked out. He tugged the snare of wires toward the cutting edge. But the cables didn't reach the metal barbs. He couldn't cut them.

Freezing seawater sluiced through his nostrils. *Slice it free.* He heaved on the wires, locked his hands around his ankle and jerked.

He hauled at the wires. They shifted. An inch.

The last air in the fuselage broke free with a rumble. The wreckage of the plane slipped toward the darkness, dragging him down.

He had one last chance. A breathless effort. The wires gave as the mangled airplane shifted. He sawed them through, and he was free and rising, his head exploding.

Then he burst to the surface and the air tasted like a chilled beer in the desert. The sky seemed to lift him up so that he thought he had died after all and was ascending to the clouds before he realized it was the swell of the ocean and it was carrying him to the shore.

Lance grabbed him and kicked through the foam. Verrazzano sputtered brine from his mouth and nose. "You're okay, asshole," Lance said. "Hang in there."

Verrazzano saw that they were not in the sea itself. They splashed across the mouth of a wide tidal creek, edged with reeds on the fringe of the wetland flats.

Lance waded to the bank. Verrazzano vomited seawater. He rolled onto the mud, lifted his Suunto wristwatch, and checked their coordinates.

"Where we at?" Lance gasped.

"About fifteen miles east of Manhattan. My guess, the wetlands behind Jones Beach or Point Lookout. If we head inland a mile and a half, we'll hit a residential area."

"Hard going." Lance checked his own wristwatch. "We don't have time."

"We're lucky to be going at all. What do you mean, we don't have time?"

"It's nigh on zero eight hundred hours." The Molnir man studied the bank across the creek. He squinted and shivered.

"When is the sarin going to be released? Is it right now? Give me a deadline."

Lance shook his head, preoccupied. "Get us out of here."

Verrazzano took out his cell phone. He ought to contact Haddad to get agents out to search for him, to take him and Lance into the city. But the phone was drowned. He dropped it into his pocket.

"The pilots of our plane were supposed to land near here." Lance watched the flowing tips of the reeds.

Verrazzano followed the man's gaze—and his train of thought. There'd have been a squad to grab them on the beach. Working for Touma, like the pilots, or maybe Frisch's men, tipped off by the Palestinian. They'd have seen where the plane came down. "We'd better move. They'll be here soon."

"They're here already," Lance said.

Verrazzano scanned the wetlands again.

The Texan opened his mouth to speak. But no words came out. Instead bone and brain matter shot through it. His face exploded over the wide blades of manna grass, smashed by a heavy sniper bullet. He dropped dead in the mud.

Verrazzano strained to see beyond the wavering line of reeds on the far bank. No movement. It'd be tough enough if he just had to nail the shooter before the guy took *him* out. But now he needed to capture him. With Lance gone, the sniper was the only one who might lead him to the sarin.

He shrugged off his jacket and slung it over Lance's shoulders. He dropped onto his back and pulled the bloody body on top of him. Carefully he lifted the decoy.

A bullet ripped into the jacket just below the collar and tore through Lance. It hammered the dead body down on top of Verrazzano.

He wriggled out from underneath and traced the passage of the bullet through the jacket and out of the corpse. He followed the trajectory of the shot toward a patch of reeds that was a touch higher than the others around it. He waited. A sniper always moved after he made a shot. The change of position kept the target guessing.

A few fronds of water grass whispered. Most people would've ascribed it to a breeze wafting in with the tide. Verrazzano knew it was the sniper.

CHAPTER 49

The Janissary splashed across a shallow channel into a thick bed of sedge. Through the waving grass, he watched the spot where the two men struggled ashore after the plane ditched in the sea. He crossed his legs and rested his left arm on his knee just below the elbow to support the yard-long XM2010 rifle. It was the hardest sniping position to maintain. He felt the tension in the small of his back and in his shoulders, but it was the only way to keep the target in his sights through the tall reeds.

He peered into the Leupold scope and laid the second pad of his index finger on the trigger for a smoother pull. The first shot killed Lance. With his second bullet, he took out the ICE agent—the one he fought behind Doctor Weston's house. He was sure they were both dead, but he waited to be certain. In five minutes, he'd go over to confirm the kills.

The proximity of the two shots felt intimate. He liked that. Long kills were less fulfilling. He remembered his farthest take-down, on the edge of Aleppo in the north of Syria. A rebel chief, from a mile and a half. The Janissary fired seventeen feet wide of the target, and the wind bent his shot to strike the center of the man's torso. As sport shooting, it was perfect. But he missed being close enough to hear the 7.62 mm slug explode with a jet of blood and tissue.

A fish darted for a fly and sent a ripple across the water. The Janissary took his eye from the scope and watched the disturbance on the surface. He pictured himself as the insect, even though his business was to be the predator. That troubled him. He needed to relax for his next shot and to stay alert. He brought his eye back to the scope. Once the kills were certain, he would ride into the city in the boat he had moored nearby to support the sarin operation. He heard another plop as the fish carried on its hunt. His eyebrow twitched.

The high grass shook and staggered. The Janissary shrugged the tension from his shoulders. Had he made a mistake? His preference for the close hit had brought him in too tight. The little promontory where the two men lay was only a hundred yards away. If one of them were alive, he could be on the Janissary before he got off a shot or had a chance to escape in the boat.

He relaxed his jaw. He was judging himself, criticizing himself. That was a stupid thing to do. It created tension. Calling himself stupid made it worse.

A paddling sound in the creek behind him. His spine thrilled. Something was there. It had to be a bird. The targets were still over on the promontory. He twisted at the waist. An oystercatcher stuttered across the mud on its long, pink legs. The Janissary laid down his rifle. It raised its red, treacherous eyes, and the Janissary's smile faded. The oystercatcher fluttered into the air. The Janissary turned back toward his rifle.

A figure rose from the mud in front of him. Blue eyes glinted out of a face smeared in thick dirt. A Heckler & Koch jabbed into the Janissary's belly. Verrazzano's teeth were white in the mud camouflage. The Janissary took a sharp breath and aimed his punch just above them. The blow landed square on Verrazzano's nose.

The Janissary knew how much training it took for the ICE agent to jump forward at him rather than to sway back from the punch. Get in close, the first rule of real fighting. Don't give the other guy room to throw his weight into his swing.

Verrazzano hooked his foot behind the Janissary's knee to bend it and hammered him into the mud. The Janissary recognized the *kosoto gake* throw. But this wasn't a judo bout. He head-butted Verrazzano's cheekbone and locked his thumb on his trachea. The man's dammed blood pulsed against his finger pad. Verrazzano's eyes bulged and flickered up into his head. He was almost gone.

With a cry of surprise and rage, the Janissary shuddered as Verrazzano's knife entered his side. He jerked against the ICE agent's arm. Verrazzano was almost asphyxiated, but he refused to let go of the blade.

The Janissary released Verrazzano's throat and tumbled away, sliding into the creek. He touched the knife wound. It wasn't deep. Verrazzano staggered toward him, eyes flickering. The Janissary smiled thinly. The agent almost drowned in the plane ten minutes ago. He feared a fight in the water. The Janissary beckoned with both hands. "Come on."

Verrazzano took two shaky steps on the flattened reeds, but with the third, he launched himself. He reached the knife out ahead with his left hand. The Janissary brought his arms up to block. But Verrazzano made his real strike with his right fist, hammering the Janissary's neck where it was exposed by his stretch for the knife.

The Janissary went down as though his legs were vapor. Verrazzano's blade gashed his belly. He held onto the knife hand, but the ICE agent's other limbs came at him from every direction. He imagined it might be like this to fight a crocodile in a river—except that the crocodile would only want you for food.

"Wait. I know where the sarin is." He spluttered and coughed. "I'm supposed to go there now. I'll take you to it. My boat is near."

Verrazzano breathed through his nose, loud and deep. "Where is it?"

The Janissary pointed. "My boat? It's—"

"The fucking sarin. Tell me the exact location."

"Yes, okay. I'll tell you." The Janissary was almost on his feet. He let himself stumble. Verrazzano took his weight. "I'll take you there. I'll show you. You'll see it. With your own two eyes."

The phrase was like a warning. Verrazzano lifted his hand to stop the blow before it came. But the Janissary's fingers, braced in the shape of an arrowhead, lanced into his face. He felt the eyeball relent and heard the American scream.

The Janissary swung him into the stream, and set his knees on Verrazzano's shoulder blades. He held him in the mud. After the eye gouge, there was little fight left. He kept the agent's face under until he stopped struggling.

Exhausted and exultant, the Janissary rose to his feet. The current took Verrazzano's body away.

The Janissary went into the reeds to gather his rifle and gear, and he splashed through the shallows to his boat, a twenty-foot bow rider with a big outboard. A sky-blue wet tarp spread over the forward seatwell where the brochures always posed a girl in a bikini. He stowed his equipment aft, took the helm, and sped down the channel to the open sea.

He licked at the salt on his lips. The corner of the tarp was loose over the seatwell. It flapped in the wind. He shook his head. He should've pinned that down. He considered slowing and rehooking the tarpaulin taut over the seatwell, but the fight with Verrazzano had delayed him. He had to be in Manhattan for the attack. The timing would be tight, even without another stop. He bounced the bow rider into the waves.

CHAPTER 50

Martin Chavez rolled across the UN plaza. He passed the pacifist statue of a pistol knotted to prevent its firing. His guts felt like the barrel of the gun. He put a stick of Doublemint in his mouth. His tongue had no moisture. He worked the gum harshly and adjusted the extra cushion he used to keep himself from tipping forward. Underneath it, he had a thin computer bag with his laptop, a set of cables, and a USB drive with the software he figured he'd need. He toggled the chair into the security marquee.

Adela stood behind the first metal detector a few minutes into her shift. She chewed gum too. Her neck twitched. Chavez knew it was the adrenaline taking over her muscles. He tried to put on a reassuring face. He couldn't make it happen. He gave it up and went toward her.

An African woman with skin the color of sherry rushed past him. She checked the pockets of her Burberry jacket at the X-ray conveyor. When she noticed Chavez, she spoke with the back-throat *O* of a Maryland accent. "Oh, I'm sorry. You go ahead."

Adela passed through the metal detector. The apparatus made no sound. Chavez glanced at her belt. The electronic override pad usually dangled beside her pistol so that she wouldn't activate the machine. It wasn't there now. She was ready. The pad was detached, cupped in her hand.

"Ladies first," Chavez told the woman in the Burberry.

"Thanks." She laid her bag on the X-ray belt and unzipped it.

"Do you have a laptop, ma'am?" Adela stood at the woman's side.

"Sure. Been here a lot of times. I know the drill." She took out her laptop and laid it in a plastic tray.

"You from Baltimore?" Chavez said.

"You can tell? I can't lose that *O*."

Adela slid the tray into the X-ray. She slipped her hand under the conveyor.

"Man, I really love Cal Ripken," Chavez said.

"Everybody loves Cal Ripken," the woman said.

"He does great charity work," Chavez said.

The woman took in a breath. Chavez sensed her impatience. "For handicapped people and stuff," he said.

She glanced at his wheelchair. "Baltimore's very proud of him." She smiled.

Adela touched the woman's coat pocket lightly. Chavez held his breath. The lipstick plant. She was doing it.

"How do *you* get through the metal detector?" The woman took back her driver's license. "Sorry, I guess that's not my business."

"No problem." Chavez rapped his hand on the arm of his big chair. "This bad boy's all plastic. Every bit of it. Special so I don't have to go through extra searches."

"Yes, I suppose that would be—" The woman frowned awkwardly.

"Humiliating? Sure." He grinned.

Adela followed the woman into the metal detector, now without her override pad.

"Made in Sweden." Chavez drummed a beat on his wheelchair again.

The machine buzzed and flashed red. The guard seated at the X-ray screen glanced up. The Baltimore woman looked confused.

Chavez fumbled under the edge of the conveyor. He found Adela's override pad pressed firmly to her chewing gum. He peeled it away.

"Please go back and check if you have anything in your pockets, ma'am," Adela said.

Chavez rolled his eyes in sympathy as the woman hurried toward him.

"Really," she said. "Do I look dangerous?"

"Sure. Like one of them James Bond girls."

She laughed as she hunted through her pockets. She brought out a red metal tube. "It's lipstick."

Adela held out a small plastic basket. "Put it in here, ma'am."

"But it's not mine."

Adela shook the basket. The black woman dumped the lipstick and walked through. The metal detector was silent.

"I don't know how the lipstick got in there," she muttered.

Adela rolled the handbag and the laptop to the end of the table. She reached the plastic tray with the lipstick toward the woman.

"I told you, it's not mine."

Chavez went through the metal detector. The override pad neutralized the machine. The buzzer was silent. The light didn't flash, despite the computer equipment under the stumps of his thighs. He stopped as if waiting for Adela and the woman to move away.

He slipped the gum out of his mouth and stuck it under the table. He shoved the override pad into its soft surface. The gum held it. He took his hand away.

"Beep, beep," he said. "Move right along, ladies. The lipstick's a nice color. It'll look good on you."

"Men." The woman smiled at Adela. "As if anybody would ever use a stranger's lipstick."

Adela dropped the lipstick rattling into the trash. The seated guard gave another bored look in the direction of the noise. The black woman hurried away.

Adela slipped her hand surreptitiously beneath the table and felt around. She hissed at her husband, "It's not here. What'd you do with it, Marty?"

Chavez stiffened. "I put the fucking thing right there."

"Sir, you dropped something." A voice from the far end of the X-ray conveyor.

Chavez turned his wheelchair. A bony, middle-aged woman with long hair that was disheveled and dyed auburn and a muscular man with pale skin waited at the metal detector. The man's shoulders heaved, breathless, in a hurry.

The woman pointed to the floor. The override pad lay on the flagstones like a discarded coin.

Adela glared at Chavez. "Let me get that for you, sir." She bent and picked up the override pad, placing herself between the two people and the wheelchair. She laid her hand in Chavez's palm, but closed her fingers around the override disc. She dropped it into her pocket.

The redhead lifted her arm and flipped open her wallet. A gold shield glinted in the fluorescents of the security marquee. "We're US federal agents."

Chavez's belly chilled. He started to raise his hands in surrender.

"We're here to see Mister Holtz, your head of security," the woman said. "I'm Special Agent Kinsella. Agent Todd and I are from Immigration and Customs Enforcement. We're carrying weapons. I'm just going to walk through here, okay?"

Adela read the agent's identity card. "Uh, yeah. Go ahead."

The light flashed and the buzzer rang as Kinsella passed through the metal detector. She put her badge inside her jacket. Todd followed her. "Do you need to double-check our visit with Mister Holtz?" Kinsella asked.

Adela blinked as though she had been slapped. "No, ma'am."

Todd glanced at Chavez with a face that looked ready to curse in one hundred different languages. The agent was about to recognize the crime in his eyes, he knew it. His hands were on their way up again when Todd hurried off into the reception hall.

Adela moved away from her husband. "Next, please. Walk through."

Chavez entered the hall. The agents must be onto them. Maybe he left traces when he scouted the UN website from Massie's office. But why Immigration and Customs Enforcement? Had someone been in touch with the woman who interviewed him for a job at ICE? He still had her card in his jacket pocket. Special Agent Roula Haddad. Did he give something away when he spoke to her? *No, Martin, you dummy. That was before Kyle even told you about the UN deal.*

He crossed the polished tiles, feeling as though he'd been shot dead. "Got to get it together," he whispered. Still, he wondered how many times he'd have to die today.

CHAPTER 51

The gate guard poked a flashlight around inside the Airstoria Air Conditioning van. He checked the battered tool kits and riffled through the manifold pumps and vacuum-port adapters until he was satisfied they contained nothing suspicious. He directed the driver to the muddy parking lot at the edge of the construction site.

Three technicians left the van. Across the back of their white overalls, a snowflake logo topped a business address in Astoria, Queens. Stretching after their drive, they looked up at the new UN tower, as if imagining how it would be when it was complete. They hefted their kit between the dump trucks and went down a ramp wide enough for an earthmover. They entered a tunnel that connected the new site with the old UN facilities.

Kyle Massie toked hard on a Winston as he followed Clay and Slav along the plank path over the mud floor. A team of welders worked on a drainage pipe, shooting sparks up to the temporary lights strung along the bare concrete walls. A pair of electricians installed a transformer box in a deep alcove.

Two men came toward them. One was a squat security guard, rolling his muscular shoulders and heavy hips. The other, a thin man in a gray suit and a blue hard hat, walked bent forward from his great height. He wore a UN ID card on a loop around his neck. He was a dozen yards from Massie when he called out with a Central European accent, "There is no smoking anywhere on this site."

He nudged his light-green spectacles up to the bridge of his nose and peered closely at the air-conditioning techs. "Where are you going?"

"Main building, sir," Clay mumbled. "We're running the AC from that end all along this tunnel."

"Sir, we'd better hurry. We've got to finish the inspection," the security guard told the tall man. He moved around the technicians. "You want to make it around the perimeter before the session starts in the General Assembly."

The tall man held his hand up to silence the guard and addressed Clay. "You've made a mistake. The air-conditioning infrastructure was installed here last week. I saw you people working on it." He pointed toward the ceiling. Shiny steel brackets suspended a rectangular duct along the length of the tunnel.

Clay shuffled on the planks. "Well, I guess we—"

"Furthermore, there are only essential workers allowed on the site today, because of the General Assembly. Where are your clearances from my department?"

Behind the tall man, the security guard rolled his eyes and checked his watch.

"What department's that?" Clay said.

"I'm the chief of security. Show me your clearances."

Massie tossed away his cigarette. He squinted at the ID card around the man's neck. It said he was Andreas Holtz, director of the Safety and Security Department. *Just the guy we don't want to meet*, he thought. "The ducts are installed," he said, "but the dampers need to be centralized and hooked up to the existing system in the main building. That's down there at the far end." He moved off, hustling the other two men along.

"The clearances. Give them to me." Holtz put on what must've passed for a battle face among the office workers at the UN. To Massie it looked like the surface of a vanilla pudding that hadn't quite set.

Clay dropped his toolbox in the mud. Massie saw him crook his hand, ready to drive his palm at the UN man's throat.

Holtz's cell phone rang. He lifted a finger to indicate he wanted the air-conditioning men to stay where they were. "This is Holtz."

Clay nodded toward an alcove. Massie saw his intention. Bundle Holtz back in there and silence him. Take the security guard quickly too, and hope the workmen didn't notice. "Not yet," he murmured.

Holtz spoke into the phone. "The ICE agents are here?"

Massie hissed in annoyance. The Janissary was supposed to finish the ICE agent out on Long Island. As Holtz listened to his caller, Massie put two fingers to his eyebrow. *Plan B.* Slav acknowledged the signal with a nod.

Holtz ended his phone call and ran a hand through his thinning hair. Massie wondered what the ICE agents knew, what they'd told the UN.

Slav stepped before Holtz and spoke low and firm in Russian. "Do not continue to embarrass yourself. You hired us to track the NSA bugging program at the UN. We have reason to believe there is a surveillance conduit implanted in the air-conditioning system. Let us proceed with our task."

Massie hadn't been sure they'd use the Russian contractor angle, even after Frisch briefed them on it. The UN guy had told Frisch about it, but that could've been an empty boast. A hotshot like Frisch tended to bring out the braggart in other men. What if the Russian contract was already completed? But here they were with the chief of security of all people. Massie prayed the gamble paid off.

Holtz glanced down at his phone. It buzzed and flashed in his palm. The Austrian waved for the Airstoria men to carry on. He nodded to the security guard. "You can handle the perimeter check without me. As for these men, they are okay."

"Yes, sir," the guard said.

Holtz answered the call and jogged away from them with his phone to his ear.

The security guard muttered, "I could've handled the perimeter check just fine without you anyway, like I do every day, you micromanaging motherfucker." He grinned at the techs. "Because it's the General Assembly, asshole has to get involved in every little thing." He marched toward the far end of the tunnel.

"Well, that nearly sucked," Clay said.

Slav laughed and gave Clay a low five.

Massie's pulse stuttered. "Let's go."

He bent to pick up his toolbox. The security guard called out, "Hey, guys."

"What the fuck?" Massie muttered.

The guard pointed at the ceiling of the tunnel and beckoned with his other hand. "Check it out."

Slav and Clay hesitated. "What's he want?" Clay said.

"Wait here." Massie walked quickly toward the guard. As he approached, he followed the man's gesture. A section of the air-conditioning pipe had come away from the ceiling and the sharp ends had cut into the soft duct within.

"That's dangerous," the guard said. "We can't have something like that just swinging around up there."

"We'll come back and fix it," Massie said.

"No way, man. I've got to have this tunnel open for emergency work. I've got to keep it ready in case there's an emergency evacuation of the main building. You got to fix this now."

Massie stared at the duct. The electricians along the tunnel shut off their drills. He could hear the creaking of the air-conditioning brackets above him. They could fall any moment. *What're the chances?* he thought. *Of all the shitty luck.* "It's good. It'll hold."

He started to walk away.

The security guard jumped and yanked at the duct. He slapped his hand against it and the blow echoed in the pipes. The duct swung and screeched. "I told you this thing could come down any minute. Look at it, man."

Massie touched a finger to his cheek and scratched. "Okay, we'll take a look." He jerked his head, signaling for Clay and Slav to join him.

"You should've done it right in the first place. You wouldn't have this thing dangling down from here anyhow."

"Okay, sir. We'll take care of it. You just go on and—"

"I'm going to stay here until you fix it." The security guard reached out his walkie-talkie. "We've got to get a sign down here, make sure no one walks right underneath it."

Massie gestured for Clay and Slav to start work on the duct. "No one's going to walk under it. We'll be working on it."

"Regulations say you need a warning sign at ground level." He spoke into the walkie-talkie. "Janie, I need a wet triangle in the north tunnel. Bring one down here ASAP."

Now there'll be two of them, Massie thought. "We've just got to fix the damn thing up and get moving," he muttered to Clay.

Slav reached up into the duct. As soon as the weight of his arm rested on the lip, the bracket in the ceiling gave way. The end of the duct dropped down, swinging at hip height.

"Shit." The security guard jumped back. "Didn't I tell you? If you guys had done your job . . ."

"Sure, you were right."

Massie glanced down. The top of the duct was visible now. It bore a long, white plastic label that read, "Ace Air Conditioning, Bensonhurst, Brooklyn, NY." He moved his hand over the Airstoria decal on his left chest. If the security guard saw the real air-conditioning company's name, he'd start asking more questions about these guys with a different logo emblazoned on their overalls.

Clay leaned across the duct to lift it. The big logo across his back lined up beside the Ace Air Conditioning sticker. The security guard was too busy yammering into his walkie-talkie to notice. Massie edged in front of Clay. He bent down and picked at the edge of the sticker.

Clay noticed the words on the sticker and laid his hand across it swiftly with a tense glance at Massie.

"Get it off there," Massie said. He moved toward the security guard, blocking his view of Clay. Clay yanked at the sticker. He coughed loudly as he ripped it off the metal.

Massie relaxed a little when he heard the sticker come away. He turned around.

Clay stared at him with the sticker balled in his hand. He shook his head.

Massie looked down at the vent. Massie looked down at the vent. The sticker had left an imprint, long and rectangular, its area filled in with tiny specs of white plastic except for the outline of the name of the real air-conditioning company and its logo, which were spattered with red. It was completely legible.

He turned back to the security guard. The man was a couple of steps closer than he had been. He read off the name of the company on the duct. Then he looked up at Massie's overall and the Airstoria logo. The man's brain was going to take a while getting there, but Massie saw it grinding toward the conclusion that the men before him weren't who they claimed to be.

As he opened his mouth to divert the guard, to explain, a splash of clear liquid streamed through the air beside him. It hit the security guard in the eye.

The guard blinked once, then he slapped his hand across his face and bellowed.

Massie twisted toward Slav. He was screwing the cap back onto a pint bottle of cyanide.

It was done. No more talking. Massie kicked the guard on the knee. When the man dropped, Massie stamped on his throat. The cyanide would kill him within a minute, but Massie needed him dead before he opened his mouth one more time. He stamped again and felt the guard's neck break. He looked accusingly at Slav, who shrugged and put the bottle away in his toolbox.

Massie wrenched a long length of soft concertina duct from inside the metal air-conditioning casing. He ripped into it with his fingers and used the edge of his hand to carve across it. "Watch that way."

Clay looked toward the electricians. They were focused on the switch box on the wall. "We're cool."

Massie slipped one end of the soft duct over the dead guard's head and shoulders, careful not to touch the cyanide. He slipped it down to the man's shoes with a couple of feet spare on each end. "Duct tape."

Slav tossed him a roll of silver tape. Massie wrapped each end of the duct with the tape, sealing the guard inside. "Lift that end."

Massie and Slav took the guard into an alcove and wedged him upright. Massie lifted a plank from the gangway on the mud floor and laid it in front of the guard to hide him. He stood back.

Unless someone looked hard, they'd see a piece of duct and a random length of wood—the kind of detritus that littered any construction site.

The three men hustled along the tunnel. As they reached the end, a female security officer came to the door.

"Motherfucker," Clay muttered.

The security officer put a hand on her gun belt and set her cap. The electricians wandered up behind Massie's team. There was no way to silence the woman without taking out the other workers, and at this end of the tunnel, they stood a good chance of being observed by someone inside the UN building.

"Let's go, guys." The electricians halted on the gangway behind Massie.

The security guard reached down to her right. Massie twitched. She was going for her gun. He stepped off the planks into the mud, ready to turn and run.

Her hand got to her pistol and kept going. She gripped the top end of a reflective warning sign. "Danger: Work in Progress," it read. She lifted it and slung it across her belly, holding the leg in her other hand.

"Guys, the lady's waiting for us to go through," one of the electricians said.

Clay went by the guard with a tip of his cap. Slav passed her. Massie stepped out of the mud and entered the UN building with the electricians behind him.

He watched the security guard waddle down the planks. She shook her head at the dangling AC duct and set up her warning sign. She leaned over the duct and shook her head again.

Massie cursed the logo on his overall again. What if she had made the connection?

The guard hitched up her pants and came back along the tunnel.

He could get clear now. But if the guard had noticed the Airstoria logo, she might raise the alarm and send out a team to track them down. He turned about him, wondering how to get rid of her.

The first thing he saw was a closed-circuit television camera. They were inside the UN. There was nowhere in the public areas that they couldn't be seen.

"What's up, Randy? Let's go." Clay touched Massie's arm.

Massie took a step toward the tunnel.

The guard came toward him. Her hands were on her belt, her right close to her pistol. She watched Massie as she labored up the final steep section of planks out of the tunnel.

He could bundle her back down into the tunnel. There was no one there now. Or was there? Maybe someone had come in at the other end while the security guard slouched back to Massie. He bent to look along the tunnel.

A group of workers carried lengths of metal scaffolding slowly down the planks from the far entrance. Massie couldn't take the security guard down there.

His mouth was dry. His heart sped. Worst of all, he doubted himself. Maybe this was it. This was where his ingenuity ran out. Where it all ran out.

The security guard stopped a couple of yards in front of him. She straightened and looked him up and down. "We got some big trouble."

Massie stared at her. He dared not move his mouth to reply. His jaw would shake.

"Lucky for you Airstoria guys, it's some outfit named Ace Air Conditioning that fucked up. We're going to have to call them in here right away." She moved past Massie. "Lucky for you, right?"

"Right, baby." Clay gave Massie a little punch on the elbow. "Randy?"

"I'm okay. I'm okay." Massie went into the works area that connected the tunnel to the UN basement. But he knew he wasn't okay. If he had been, he would've been somewhere else entirely.

CHAPTER 52

Over his Bluetooth earpiece, Frisch heard Holtz mumble to himself, panicky and irritable, about the ICE agents waiting in his office. He wondered what information they had. A text came through from the Janissary. Frisch read it as he climbed the maintenance stairs of his building. "Verrazzano eliminated." Maybe not before he passed on what he knew, Frisch figured. That's why the other ICE agents were at the UN. He came out onto the roof and hid in the shadow of the elevator winch house. Holtz muttered in German, "Damn you, Frisch." Frisch grinned and unpacked his Russian sniper rifle. When he visited the UN, he had made a play of examining the ID card around the Austrian's neck, waiting for a group of schoolchildren to distract the guy so he could attach a wire-thin UHF transmitter to the edge of the plastic wallet with transparent tape. This morning he listened in as Slav spoke to Holtz in Russian and the call came in about the ICE agents. He set the Vintorez on its tripod and tilted the sniper rifle toward the UN tower.

"Where are the agents, Aisha?" The Austrian was back in the security department.

"Waiting in your office, Andreas," said the Bangladeshi secretary.

Frisch trained the sniper scope twelve floors up, six blue-tinted windows from the corner. Holtz's office. The figures inside were shadowy but clear enough for him to take them down if he had to. The Austrian entered.

257

"I'm Andreas Holtz, chief of security." He shook hands. Two ICE agents, three targets total. Frisch would take Holtz last. The ICE agents would be primed to move, but the Austrian was a wimp. He'd never make it out of the room. He'd freeze, staring at the dead agents until the next bullet struck him.

"I'm Special Agent Kinsella. This is Special Agent Todd. Immigration and Customs Enforcement."

"Is this about the nerve agent?"

Frisch twitched at the Austrian's mention of nerve gas. He shifted the cross hairs on his scope to the Austrian. He settled his breath, ready to kill the man before he spilled everything.

The ICE agents paused too, wondering perhaps at Holtz's manner. He was nervous, but not in the way you'd expect from the head of security at a major public building on a day when the federal government issued a warning about a terror attack. More like a man with a guilty secret.

"Why do you ask, sir?" The female agent's voice was so New York that the politeness of adding *sir* seemed at the very least mocking, perhaps even contemptuous.

"You sent out an alert." Holtz gathered himself. "Did you not?"

The ICE agent didn't hurry to respond. She waited, to see if Holtz would run his mouth as the guilty often do. He was quiet, so she said, "We have reason to believe there's a quantity of sarin nerve agent here in the UN building. You need to shut the place down."

"Good God. But on what basis do you say this?"

"What action did you take this morning when you received our alert?"

"All the actions that are mandated in our procedures."

"I didn't see anything special when we entered the building just now."

"We don't call in the Marines every time someone in the US authorities gets nervous." Holtz snorted a laugh. The ICE agents were quiet. "I don't understand your questions."

"Maybe you figured you were safe, that the threat to carry out an attack had been made, but you could stop it."

"I don't understand at all. What on earth can you mean? How could I stop an attack?"

"By complying with a request someone had previously made to you, maybe."

"I am sorry, but I do not follow your reasoning."

A pause. "Did someone recently try to bribe you, Mister Holtz?"

"Bribe me? Are you mad?"

"Someone named Tom Frisch?"

For the moment, Holtz was in charge. ICE had no jurisdiction. They couldn't force him to evacuate the UN building. That little chunk of Manhattan wasn't officially part of America. Frisch had to bank on Holtz guarding his bureaucratic turf—and covering his ass.

"Why would anyone bribe me?" Holtz said. "Who is this person Frisch?"

Frisch smirked. Holtz wasn't about to admit anything. Not on the biggest day in the UN calendar. He hadn't accepted the bribe, but he ought to have barred Frisch from bidding anyway. He wondered if Holtz had been holding out for a bigger payoff.

"Why would someone bribe you? How about to secure a contract? Maybe on that new tower you're building?" It was the woman's voice again, stepping her tone up to full no-bullshit New Yorker.

"The UN has very specific procedures for contract tenders, Agent Kinsella, just as we have clear procedures for security measures in case of a terror alert. I can assure you, I have had no such offers to be bribed. What other basis do you have for suspecting sarin is present in this building?"

He was deflecting them. Holtz wasn't a complete wuss, after all.

"We arrested another suspect in the plot who says the sarin is here at the UN."

"Can the suspect give a location? When will this attack take place?"

The ICE agents were quiet. One of them coughed awkwardly. Frisch willed them to talk. He wanted to know what they had on him. No, it was what they had on Wyatt that worried him. He could look after himself, go to ground if he had to. But if he'd slipped up and exposed the colonel, he was a dead man. He was as tough as he had ever been, but he noticed that the thought of dying chilled the back of his brain and burned in his throat like cheap grain alcohol. Because he knew Wyatt would make it painful.

"The suspect is presently unavailable," the male agent said.

"What on earth—? Do you mean that you don't know where he is? Well, I really can't evacuate the building on such flimsy—"

"Are you not hearing us?" The woman again.

"Don't just send them away," Frisch whispered. "Draw them out. Get them to tell you—" *Tell him what? Something comforting?* Wyatt used to say, "You want reassurance? Your mamma has the soft titties. I'm the one with the hard ass." The ICE agent certainly wasn't motherly.

"I hear you loud and clear. I hope you are hearing me. Now, if you'll excuse me," Holtz said, "this is a very busy time."

He showed the ICE agents out. The woman turned in the door. "We're not done here, Holtz. We're going to find that sarin."

"I'm sure you will keep me informed. Aisha, I am not to be disturbed." Holtz locked the door and reached for his phone.

Frisch's cell phone vibrated. He picked it up. "Andy Holtz, what's the good word?"

"I know what you are doing." Holtz's voice was a whisper. "There is sarin in my building."

"No shit?"

"Frisch, it is you who brought the sarin here. I know it is. Everything you said when you came to talk to me makes sense now."

"Only now?"

"Don't play with me, Frisch. I cannot close down the building. Not today. I would look like an idiot."

"You'd look like a *corrupt* idiot."

"*Ich will einen*—I make with you a deal. *Der Vertrag*, the contract." His English was breaking down under pressure. "It's yours. The security contract, you can have it. Fifty million dollars a year. That is what you want. Am I right?"

If the day passed off as he intended, Frisch would make that much in the next month. He settled the butt of the Vintorez against his shoulder. "That *was* my plan. Things have changed."

"What do you mean by that? Look, I don't want the bribe. You can keep the five million dollars. I know you are trying to show me how much I need your company. You aren't seriously going to attack the United Nations. *Komm schon*, come on. You won't do that, Frisch. Remember what you said about me needing you like a banana republic needs Kalashnikovs and Swiss banks? I agree, yes, I need you, Frisch." Holtz leaned his hand against the window, bent almost double with the stress. He dropped his head.

"You know what happens in banana republics?" Frisch sighted on the crown of the Austrian's balding scalp. "The yellow bastard gets skinned." He pulled the trigger.

"Frisch?"

The bullet went through Holtz's head and lodged in his lower spine.

CHAPTER 53

Chavez left the freight elevator. New fiber-optic cables in bright-blue plastic sheaths weaved among the aging copper pipes on the cinder block walls. Kyle Massie gave a sickly grin and led him at a fast walk through the basement toward the air-conditioning room. He shouted over the noise of the massive air compressor, "Doesn't that wheelchair have a turbocharger or something?"

"Going as fast as I can, Kyle."

The onset of the operation seemed to have rattled Massie. He twisted toward Chavez without breaking his stride. "Haul ass, for Christ's sake."

"Kyle, watch out."

Massie walked shoulder first into a tall stack of newspapers bundled for recycling. He grabbed at the falling bales. Dust dropped in sheets onto his head and chest. The floating dirt filled his mouth. "Shit, damn it." He coughed gray sputum onto the forearm of his overalls.

Chavez's nerves ticked up a notch. He knew why Massie caught the spit on his sleeve. A gob of saliva on the floor would leave a DNA record. The mission was illegal, but such extreme precautions surprised Chavez as much as Massie's edginess.

Down a narrow spur, they entered the air-conditioning control room. Massie shut the door and the noise of the corridor subsided. The room was unpainted brick and bare pipes. A rectangular length of air-conditioning duct ran along the wall at head height. A hard drive whirred on a gray metal desk beside a dusty monitor. Two men in white wrenched out a section of the wall duct. One of them was black. The other had a deep, fresh scratch on his face. The men who attacked Chavez and Massie outside the billiard club.

"Jesus," Chavez said. "These guys are—Kyle, what's going on?"

Massie pulled a knife from his pocket. He slashed through the tape and glue of the repairs he had made on the wheelchair backrest.

"Kyle?" Chavez twisted his neck to see Massie dig the blade into his chair.

Massie held up the gray knife. "You like it? Superstrong composite nylon. Don't show up on metal detectors."

Chavez didn't understand. Massie had flipped out. The guy was overexcited and nervous. Now he pulled this stunt with the wheelchair.

Slav reached inside the cushion of the wheelchair and pulled out a dull, gray canister. It was tapered at one end. At the other it had fins, like an artillery shell. Slav tossed the canister to the black man. "Yo, Clay. Suck it like a big dick, you faggot."

The black man caught the canister and laughed. "You trying to kill us, Slav?"

"These guys *pretended* to attack us?" Chavez's voice was slow, disbelieving. "You put that shit inside my chair? Kyle, tell me this ain't happening."

Massie knelt before Chavez, his face troubled. He shook his head regretfully. Chavez felt relief at the touch of his old friend's hand. He'd see it was all okay soon enough.

Slav unscrewed the battery cover under the wheelchair. He yanked out another canister and a gray box, six inches across and an inch high, a spray of red and blue wires extending from the rear.

"That's a timing device," Chavez said.

"Tick tick tick," Massie said. "Kaboom."

Everything flashed and cut out, as though all signals to Chavez's brain were interrupted. The shock was too much to register. He tried to find a way out for his buddy Kyle, for himself. For Adela. The soldier who saved his life in Iraq had tricked him.

But Chavez had betrayed the woman who loved him like an angel. "You're making a bomb?"

Clay cut a hole in the exposed, soft duct inside the wall-mounted metal casing. The room heated up as the forced air billowed into the confined space.

"That'll blow the shit right on through," Massie murmured in satisfaction.

Slav took a plastic bottle from his toolbox. He shook a half-pint of clear liquid in front of Chavez's face. "You thirsty, man? This here's cyanide. It'll knock your boots off."

"Oh shit." Clay laughed. "He don't got no boots. He don't got no legs."

Slav tipped the tools out of his plastic case. He laid the canisters inside the case and put the timer on top. He bent over the device, rigging the charge to the canisters.

"You're going to blow up the AC?" Chavez said.

Massie's cell phone rang. "Yeah, boss. Is the ICE agent dead? Okay, we'll find the Janissary." He hung up. "Clay, come with me. Slav, set it up."

"What's happening?" Slav said.

"We got to clean up. We'll be back." Massie headed for the door.

"Kyle," Chavez called, "I won't do the computer stuff. You can't *make* me do it. I'm going to stop this."

Massie bent low over the wheelchair. "Let me catch you up, Specialist Chavez. There *is* no computer stuff."

"You just needed me to get you in here?"

"We needed your wife and your fucking wheelchair," Slav called out. "We didn't need *you* at all."

Numbness spread around Chavez's body as the realization hit. For a moment Massie's face twisted as though unexpected regret needled him. Then he glared with hard, mean eyes, like something Chavez might see through the bars of the zoo on a day trip with his son. He headed for the door. "Clay, bring the cyanide."

Clay gestured at Chavez with the poison bottle. "I thought this was for him?"

"Half a bottle's enough to kill him," Slav said. "He's half a man."

"Shut up. Do your job." Massie went out to the corridor with Clay.

Slav followed the others out of the room. "You want me to set it for the same time?"

Chavez heard them shouting over the noise of the air-conditioning blower. He ran the wheelchair forward and looked into the box that held the bomb. The two canisters were inscribed with a scrawling script that appeared to him to be Arabic. They each bore a multicolored diamond about four inches wide that showed a series of numbers.

1

4   0

Chavez had to find help before Slav set up the timing device.

He remembered the ICE agents who came through the metal detector behind him. If he got a message to them, they might arrive in minutes, provided they were still in the building. He reached into his breast pocket for the business card of the ICE agent who interviewed him for the job.

He lifted himself and reached under the cushion for the thin laptop case he smuggled through the security check. He unzipped the case and powered up the laptop.

The drive spun through its boot-up. "Come on." Chavez flicked the ICE agent's card between his fingers.

Slav's voice came closer. "You want it with the trembler?"

Massie responded from along the corridor, his words indistinct.

"Shit." Chavez stared at the door. He didn't have time. Slav was coming back.

"I'm going to rig both canisters, right?" Slav moved away from the door again. "Kyle, I can't hear you."

The laptop completed its boot-up. Chavez clicked on Skype and typed in the address from Roula Haddad's business card. He sent a request to call.

Haddad's avatar appeared in the left column of the screen. Request accepted.

Chavez clicked on her name. The six-note dial tone boomed out of the computer. He punched the volume down, cursing, expecting Slav to dash through the door.

Haddad answered the call. "Yes?"

Chavez spoke fast, as loud as he dared. "Agent Haddad, you interviewed me for a job. I'm Martin Chavez."

"I'm sorry, Mister Chavez, the decision—"

"I'm not calling about the job."

"I really can't speak just now."

"I'm at the UN. Somebody's going to blow it up."

The distraction left her voice. "How do you know that?"

"I'm right beside the bomb. There are two canisters and a timing device."

"Can you describe the canisters?"

"Gray. They look like artillery shells. There's Arabic on them and a fire diamond."

"Where are you?"

"What's in the canisters? Is it nuclear stuff?"

"No, Mister Chavez. It's a nerve agent. It's sarin."

"Oh, shit."

"Mister Chavez, I need you to give me an exact—"

"My wife is in the building. If this goes up, she's going to— Shit, what've I done?"

"Just tell me your exact location."

"I'm down in—"

A strong hand grabbed the laptop. Chavez jerked backward in shock. Slav threw the computer against the wall, smashing the lightweight plastic and cutting the connection.

"You've got balls after all," Slav said. "Except you're using them for brains."

He drew his fist back. Chavez watched it come straight at his jaw.

CHAPTER 54

The air carried the lentil-soup scent of light harbor fog as the Janissary's bow rider ran up the East River. Under the tarpaulin, Verrazzano lay in the seatwell, feeling the dramatic lift and fall of the hull as though he were scudding over his own rushing pulse. Everything around him was fast and noisy, the agitated river and the traffic thrumming overhead on the bridges.

He peered out from the loose corner of the tarp. The boat came around the crook in the river under the Williamsburg Bridge, hugging the shore. The fishermen in East River Park lifted their rods clear and bellowed insults in Spanish. The Janissary shuffled behind the helm. Verrazzano recalled the few details Haddad had found in the file on the guy, tried to make connections to Lance, to Frisch and Molnir. But he came up with nothing.

He heard a zipper go down and legs slipping into a pair of pants. The sniper was changing into clothes that weren't muddy from the fight in the wetlands.

When the Janissary stabbed at his eyes and wrestled him into the water, Verrazzano had instantly made his calculations. He was certain the man was beyond pain and coercion. He could've won their fight and threatened him at gunpoint but the Arab's lips would've stayed shut. So Verrazzano let the guy beat him, let him think he was dead. By the time he drifted away into the wetlands on the current, he almost was. He scrambled through the mud to the boat while the Janissary gathered his sniper gear, and as he hid in the seatwell, he brought his focus slowly to each section of his body until every part of him agreed that though this had been a very rough day, he was indeed alive. Or at least not dead. He gambled that the Janissary would head for the sarin to be part of the attack, leading Verrazzano to the nerve agent. It was the only way left to trace it.

His bet was on track. They seemed to be headed toward the UN. But his phone was dead. He couldn't contact Haddad at the ICE office.

The bow rider glided up beneath the gray stanchions of the Queensboro Bridge and thumped gently against the concrete pontoons of the FDR Drive. Verrazzano listened to the Janissary climbing out of the boat and the outraged blasts of the car horns that marked his crossing of the highway.

He waited. Even if the sarin was at the UN, he needed the Janissary to lead him to its precise location. He slipped the hooks to release a bigger section of the tarp and came out from his hiding place in the seatwell. He clambered onto the prow.

The Janissary hurried beneath the rusted pylons of the FDR off-ramp and up the slope to Forty-Second Street. Verrazzano leaped the barrier onto the street and darted through the traffic.

At the light on First Avenue, police sawhorses blocked access to the UN. The Janissary pulled out a laminated ID card and flashed it at a city patrolman. The cop read the card and stepped aside. The Janissary jogged along the sidewalk in front of the UN compound.

Verrazzano reached the cop. He pulled out his ICE shield. "What ID did that guy show you?"

"Syrian mission to the UN." The cop hooked his thumbs in his belt, looking up and down at Verrazzano's muddy clothing and face. "What the fuck happened to you?"

Verrazzano grinned darkly. "Rough commute."

On the plaza in front of the UN Secretariat, the cops briefly examined the Janissary's pass and waved him through. Verrazzano ran along the black railings. A fountain splashed like the reports of a machine gun beyond the gate. The Janissary rounded the water and glanced behind him. His eyes locked on Verrazzano. The ICE agent saw admiration in the Arab's smile. It was a dangerous emotion. It made people work harder and better, and the Janissary was already good.

Verrazzano rushed through the crowd around the fountain. Pantsuited entourages of hard-faced, skinny women trailed gray powerbrokers into the Secretariat. Construction workers lumbered toward the scaffold elevators of the new tower. At a fast jog the Janissary entered the Secretariat.

Verrazzano followed. Inside he briefly lost the man in the crowd heading for the General Assembly Hall. He spotted him at the rear door, exiting to a courtyard that was built around a massive temple bell. The Japanese Peace Bell dangled from a cypress-wood Shinto shrine.

Only one other person was in the courtyard—a burly black man who wore white overalls with the logo of an air-conditioning company. He tossed aside a cigarette as though he'd stepped out for a quick smoke and walked toward the doors, holding a cup of coffee in his hand. He collided with the Janissary. The coffee spilled over the Janissary, soaking him from chest to navel.

"Whoa, sorry, buddy," the air-conditioning man said. "You okay?"

The Janissary ignored him. The air-conditioning man went into the hallway and through the crowd as Verrazzano rushed into the courtyard.

Verrazzano drew his gun. The Janissary stared about him, looking for a way out. He backed toward the two-hundred-fifty-pound bell. The shrine and the sculpted cloud trees hid him from the diplomats in the hallway.

"Get on your knees. Hands behind your head," Verrazzano shouted.

The Janissary went onto one knee, alert, not finished yet.

Verrazzano reached for the cuffs in his pocket. Fluid dripped from the Janissary's jacket. "The coffee that guy spilled," Verrazzano said, "it didn't burn you?"

"It wasn't hot." The Janissary's eyes widened with realization just as the pain hit. He grabbed his stomach. He vomited, choked, and spasmed as the cyanide seeped through his clothing.

Verrazzano was pitiless. For him, the consequence of failure would be a massacre. The Janissary was only going to die. "Where is it?" he shouted. "Where's the sarin?"

The Janissary fumbled for Verrazzano's wrist. He gripped tight. "You couldn't kill me, ICE man," he whispered.

The Janissary would rather die than be defeated. Verrazzano knew he shared this fatal tenacity. It had been the hidden bond between them as they stalked each other.

The man murmured the phrase by which a Muslim hopes to guarantee a home in Paradise. *"Inna lillahi wa inna ilayhi raji'un." We belong to Allah, and to Him we shall return.*

"No. You belong to *me*," Verrazzano yelled. "Where is the sarin?"

The Janissary had no breath left.

Beyond the neat cedar bushes, the last few UN bureaucrats bustled down the corridor to hear the US president's speech. Verrazzano looked for the killer, for a dash of the white overalls among the dark suits. Nothing.

He burst through the glass doors and ran toward the assembly hall.

CHAPTER 55

Motorcade sirens howled outside on First Avenue. Adela wiped sweat from her lip. The hot air was on full in the security tent. That was fine for people coming in from the October chill, removing their overcoats for the metal detectors. But for Adela, working a shift on her feet, it was stuffy and dehydrating. She reached for the plastic water bottle she kept behind the X-ray machine. It was empty. She waved it at the guard manning the screen. "I'm going to get something to drink. Leonie, you all set?"

The X-ray guard gave a sleepy nod.

Adela turned to the second screener. It was almost nine AM, and the full shift was on duty. "Kenton, you want water?"

"Get me a rum and coke." The screener patted down a heavy tourist who wore a Rangers shirt the size of a parachute.

Adela crossed the visitors' lobby to the vending machines.

A tall man with short, blond hair and blue-tinted sunglasses dodged purposefully between the diplomats ahead of her. He wore white overalls with a blue snowflake on the back.

Adela looked down at her hands. She had crushed her empty bottle in her fist. She tossed it into a trashcan and moved quickly through the crowd.

After Kyle Massie.

She followed him into the fire stairs. He was one flight down when he saw her. "Adela, how you doing, girl?"

"Where's Marty?"

"He's at work, sweetheart. Like you're supposed to be."

"Take me to him."

"What're you talking about, hon?"

Adela wondered if she was embarrassing her husband. She imagined him telling her that he could handle himself, angry and resentful at her intrusion. But she had seen his nervousness when he came through the security check. He needed her reassurance. Otherwise, he might get distracted and make a mistake in his computer work. That'd be a disaster for the whole family. "You heard. Take me to him."

"You've got to let your man roll on his own four wheels, Adela."

The ugliness of the joke shocked her. In that instant, she understood. Her husband had been used. The guy Kyle pretended to be would never have spoken about his buddy's injury with such contempt. She trained her pistol on Massie. "Take me to my Marty."

Someone called for Massie down the maintenance corridor. He took a step toward the voice. Adela set herself to shoot. "Don't move," she said.

"You want to see Marty? Let's go. Come on, Adela. I don't got time for this."

She advanced carefully down the fire stairs.

"He's not doing this because of me, Adela. He's doing it because it makes him a man again."

"Marty's a better man than you'll ever be."

"You're telling me shit I already know. I held Marty's hand when the jihadis blew him up. I told him he wasn't going to die. He heard me, and he didn't fucking die. That's a real man, Adela. Losing his legs don't make him any less of a hero in my eyes."

The perspiration showed black on Adela's blue uniform shirt.

"But in *his* eyes, he's weak. He's half a man." Massie moved slowly toward her. "You've done your best to show him it isn't true. But he's stubborn. He's doing this op to prove to *himself* he's got what it takes. That's why I recruited him for the agency."

"The what?"

"He works for the government, Adela. So do I. We're ICE agents."

"But he got turned down for the job. I saw the letter."

"Boy, he's good. He even had you fooled."

"He's an agent?" Her eyes puddled with tears.

"Marty's undercover." Massie pointed over her shoulder. "So's that guy there."

She turned. "Who?"

He flew at her and slapped her face hard. Shrieking, she slipped on the step and tumbled forward. The gun went off. Their bodies muted the noise of the blast, but the percussion rippled through them like thunder.

Massie reeled away from her. Blood spread over the sleeve of his white overalls. "God damn it, Adela. What the fuck?"

"Where's Marty?"

"Ah, Christ. Just follow me." He prodded at his wound. "Fuck's sake, Adela."

She looked down to descend the steps. She didn't want to fall again.

He sprang, shoving her head up as he took her throat in his hand, choking her. She went limp and dropped to the floor.

CHAPTER 56

Martin Chavez floated back into consciousness. A laptop lay smashed beside his wheelchair. He remembered that the computer was his, and then he remembered the punch to his head. He tried to move, but his hands were bound behind his back with plastic restraints. The sarin device was on the floor in a toolbox with a pair of pliers discarded at its side. In the corridor Slav shouted for Massie. "Kyle, where you at?" His footsteps went farther away, with a rustling sound like crepe paper in a gift box. *He's wearing a chemical suit*, Chavez thought.

He hooked his elbow over the armrest of his chair and swung down to the floor. He picked up the pliers behind his back and levered himself around, lying across the chair's rear panel. The lid of the battery housing was free where Slav had unscrewed it to remove the smuggled timer. Chavez reached his hands toward the battery. If he could connect the pincers of the pliers to the farthest battery post and lower the metal handle to the other post, cradled against his wrist restraints, the battery would release a massive charge and burn through the plastic cuffs.

His shoulders strained back, reaching over into the battery case. He slipped the pincers around the short post and squeezed. He got it.

He laid the handle of the pliers against his cuffs. At best he was about to run an electrical charge through himself and give his wrists a nasty burn. The battery might explode, too, showering him in sulfuric acid. He swallowed hard and eased the handle toward the battery post.

"Kyle?" Slav shouted, still in the corridor.

Chavez rushed to short the circuit before Slav came back. The pliers dropped from the cuffs. The handle touched the battery post and a white heat seared Chavez's hands. He grimaced and held back the bellow of pain that rose through his body.

He tried again. He lifted himself, reaching over the rim of the battery casing for the pliers. Sweat bit at his eyes. He fumbled the pliers into his damp hands.

He snapped at the battery post once, twice, until he had it in the pincers again. He pressed his wrists against the handles. The burn would be worse, but he wouldn't drop the pliers this way.

His breath shivered as he lowered himself toward the battery post. A tiny click of metal against metal, then a shudder and a blast as the electricity and the heat scorched his forearms and hands. His mouth opened wide and silent, his lungs robbed of all air by the pain.

Then the cuffs melted through, his wrists whipped apart, and he dropped onto his face. His heart raged. But he would not die until the bomb was defused. He rose up on quaking arms. Inside the toolbox, the timer showed it was on standby. Slav hadn't activated it. Chavez had to stop him from getting at the bomb.

He ripped one of the sarin containers away from the detonator. He shoved it under his arm and dragged himself to his wheelchair. He hauled his weight up into the seat. Panting hard, he unscrewed the direction toggle on the control panel in the armrest.

"Kyle?" Slav shuffled a few steps toward the room. The chemical suit rustled again, but his voice was clear. He wasn't wearing the respirator over his face.

Another distant door hammered shut. Slav waited, listening. "Kyle? What the fuck?"

The control toggle came away. Chavez laid the sarin canister in front of his crotch. Reaching under his shirt, he peeled off the tape on the catheter that drained his bladder. The bag was half full. He stuffed it under his arm and held it against his ribs.

The other end of the catheter ran into his penis and up into his bladder. He took a long breath and tugged. It felt as though the tube brought his entire abdomen with it. He cursed and groaned. Blood and piss spilled over him and onto the wheelchair. But the tube came out.

He gripped the firing mechanism of the sarin canister and twisted it, straining against the years of ingrained dirt in the rusty bevels. The cap moved. He spun it out, working the detonator away from the explosive. He didn't want the canister to blow up in his hands when he hit the firing pin. He laid the charge on the seat beside him.

Slav came closer. A loud sneezing fit took him. "Fucking dust in here."

Chavez closed the canister. He shook the projectile hard, mixing the precursors. Making the sarin.

He braced the canister against his belly and picked up the detached toggle of his wheelchair control. He took the end of the catheter tube in his other hand and checked the set of the bag under his arm.

He imagined his wife and son rushing through the door, hugging him. He didn't want them to come. He whispered their names and told them he loved them. What he was about to do was for them.

Slav came in, fumbling with the hood of his chemical suit. He glanced at Chavez. He noticed the sarin canister and the thin plastic tube poised above it. "What the fuck?"

A chill flow of sarin sighed against Chavez's finger. He squeezed the drainage bag between his upper arm and his ribs. The fluid gushed along the tube. It squirted out, through the leaking sarin, and arced across the room.

The stream hit Slav in the face. He lifted his hands and ducked away.

Chavez adjusted the tube, keeping Slav in the jet of sarin.

Slav lunged forward and seized Chavez around the neck. Chavez choked. Then he felt the pressure of Slav's grip recede. *He's dying*, he thought. *The sarin got him*. His eyes teared. The nerve agent was working on him too. He determined not to expire first.

Slav let go of Chavez. He groped for his gas mask. He pulled it on, cursing and coughing. He slouched over the toolbox that held the timer and the other sarin canister.

"Don't," Chavez gasped. "Don't activate it."

Slav glared through the thick lenses of the gas mask. Shakily, he came to his feet and brought the toolbox to chest height. He slid it into the air-conditioning duct.

"You can't want people to die the way you're dying right now."

The air from the main duct would circulate around the entire UN building. Into the General Assembly Hall. Into the lungs of the world's envoys. Stopping their breath. And Adela's breath.

The pulse in his neck rocked and thundered like an express subway train. Mucus streamed from his nose. His arms spasmed. Chavez knew the symptoms of sarin exposure—any soldier assigned to the Iraq theater was drilled in them. He had failed. All he did was poison himself.

You gave up on yourself before. But Adela never did. Chavez smiled. *She's right more often than you are.* "You'll be on surveillance footage. They'll catch you."

Behind his respirator, Slav's eyes were hunted and confused. "Anything goes wrong, the boss'll take care of my little boy. Army sure as shit don't care about him."

"A guy who sent you to carry out a terror attack is going to look after your son? You're fucking nuts. What's your boy going to think of his daddy when he hears what you did?"

Slav glanced at Chavez hesitantly. Then he stepped away from the bomb. "I fucked up when we was bringing the sarin into New York, man. I exposed them to it. Lee Hill and Parry. So we covered our tracks. Rubbed out Parry. As good as killed Lee." He slumped against the wall. "To keep this whole shitty thing alive."

Chavez toggled his chair to the duct. His chest heaved and his hands trembled. The sarin was taking hold. "We have to deal with this bomb." He stretched up to pull the plastic container out of the airflow.

"Don't. Motion switch."

Chavez stared, horrified. A sharp movement and the bomb would be instantly activated. Probably with a short delay of fifteen seconds before it exploded. "You've got to defuse it. I've got a son too. Don't give up on your boy."

Slav drew himself to his knees.

Chavez's heart thrashed. His vision went black and burst back as bright geometric shapes and colorful wafts. "Take that fucking thing apart. That's it."

Slav leaned inside the air duct.

"Thank God," Chavez said.

Slav reached for the timer.

Chavez knew the sarin was killing him. But it was only his life that was coming to an end. This thing, this threat to the entire world, was over.

He heard a footfall behind him.

Kyle Massie crossed the room. A sound like a bowling ball rolling down its lane built in his chest. When he spoke to Slav, the words clattered out of his throat like the pins falling in a strike. "Don't you fucking move. Frisch ain't paying you enough? You and your fucking family are going to be set for life. And me. No more going to the VA with a begging bowl. You want to take that away from me, asshole?"

Slav shook his head. "It's not right, Kyle."

Massie grabbed him by the collar. He rammed the barrel of his gun to Slav's temple and pulled the trigger.

CHAPTER 57

The lobby outside the General Assembly Hall was empty except for the security guards by the visitors' entrance. Everyone else was inside, waiting for the president's address. Verrazzano turned a circle, focusing, trying not to miss any sign, any clue.

Two people in chemical suits jogged out of the corridor. They ran at Verrazzano. Who the hell were *they*? Verrazzano's lungs labored for every atom of oxygen. Maybe the sarin exposure at Doctor Weston's house was killing him after all.

The figures in the chemical gear halted. The smaller one pushed the respirator up to reveal her face. "Jesus, Dom," Kinsella said. "Where the hell have you been?"

Verrazzano gasped, "Did you find the sarin?"

Kinsella shook her head. Beside her, Todd's eyes showed deep concern through his respirator. "Are you okay, Dom?"

"I'm having a great day." Verrazzano reached for Todd's sleeve. He checked the pockets. Inside were two atropine autoinjectors, in case the protective gear wasn't pulled on in time.

The double doors of the auditorium opened. A heavy, despondent man in a gray suit came out. His shoulders sloped, and the knot of his tie hid beneath his black goatee. Two men and a woman, all smartly dressed, scuttled from the hall behind him.

"Abu Hafiz, why are we walking out?" the woman called in Arabic. "We received no directive from the Ministry."

Verrazzano recognized the Syrian dialect. He rushed toward them. "What's happening? What're you doing?"

"A protest," the man mumbled. "I am the ambassador of the government of the Syrian Arab Republic. Our nation insists that—"

"This has nothing to do with the government of Syria." Verrazzano saw the surprise in the ambassador's eyes at his aggression. "Someone planted weapons in New York to make it look like Syria was planning an attack. The same people got to you. Who are they?"

"I don't know what you—"

He grabbed the ambassador and jammed his pistol into his fleshy neck. "There is a major terrorist attack about to take place. Thousands of people could die. So talk."

Todd stepped forward. Kinsella held his arm and shook her head. The Syrian diplomats backed away.

"Please. I don't know who they are," the ambassador whimpered. "They threatened my daughter. They'll kill her."

"What did they tell you to do?"

"They ordered me to walk out before the American president speaks."

So that it would look like the Syrian government knew about the sarin attack in advance. Like Damascus was behind it. It was happening right now, and *it* was the killing of the US president and diplomats from every country of the world.

Applause filtered from the auditorium. The president was coming to the podium. Verrazzano let go of the ambassador. The sarin would be released during the speech. He had minutes to neutralize it.

But where? He glanced about him. His sweat chilled in the cool air.

The air.

The man who killed the Janissary wore the overalls of an air-conditioning company. The sarin was going to be pumped through the air vents into the General Assembly Hall. Verrazzano called to Todd, "Bill, give me your phone."

Todd reached inside the chemical suit and brought out his Blackberry. Verrazzano dialed Haddad at the ICE field office. "Roula, call up the emergency service engineering plans for the UN building. I need to know where someone could access the main air-conditioning ducts nearest to the General Assembly Hall."

"Checking now," Haddad said.

A gunshot resounded nearby. In the fire stairs.

Verrazzano sprinted over the blue carpet. Kinsella and Todd went after him. The lobby was the size of a football field. The door was fifty yards away.

"It's in the basement, Dom," Haddad said.

"I'm near the fire stairs. Southeast corner of the lobby."

"Okay. Go that way. At the bottom, go left."

He charged through the fire doors.

A UN security guard lay in the stairwell. Blood smeared the floor. Verrazzano lifted her head and examined her for a wound. The blood didn't appear to be hers.

She opened her eyes. Her pupils were wide and dilated. The name tag above her breast pocket read, "Adela Chavez."

"Adela, I'm a federal agent. What happened?"

She pointed toward the maintenance corridor in the basement. "Tall guy. White overalls. Kyle Massie."

"Is this Kyle Massie's blood? Is he wounded?"

"In the arm."

Verrazzano ran down the steps. Kinsella knelt beside Adela. Todd took her respirator as he passed.

"Don't hurt my Marty," Adela said.

In the maintenance corridor, the big air-conditioning blower growled. The material of Todd's chemical suit crackled like a pack of chips with each movement. Verrazzano stared into the eyepieces of his gas mask. He saw a hard readiness there. Todd handed Kinsella's respirator to Verrazzano and tapped at his earpiece. "The president's speaking now."

A trail of blood spattered along the corridor to a closed room. Verrazzano pulled on Kinsella's gas mask and gestured for Todd to break down the door. He lifted his boot and shattered the lock with a sharp kick. The door flew open. Todd ducked to the side. Verrazzano jumped into the room.

Two men. One in white Airstoria overalls, on the floor, head shot. A respirator lay beside him. Much of his face was still inside it.

The other man was in a wheelchair. His pants were soaked and bunched underneath him. His eyes and nose ran. He clutched his chest. "Sarin," he wheezed.

Verrazzano snatched the respirator from the floor. He wiped out the blood and bone and brain matter onto the dead man's overalls. He yanked the mask over the head of the man in the chair. Verrazzano pulled an atropine injector from the pocket on Todd's sleeve and peeled away the man's shirt. "What's your name?"

"Martin Chavez." He was barely breathing.

"Martin, this is the antidote for exposure to a nerve agent." Verrazzano drove the orange syringe into Chavez's pectoral. It fed atropine into the muscle.

"Did you shoot this man?" Verrazzano gestured to Slav's corpse.

A stuttering breath, but an easier one. "Kyle did it."

"Where's Kyle now?"

"Don't know. I passed out. But—" Chavez choked. "There's a sarin bomb."

"Where?"

"In the AC."

Verrazzano went to the big duct bracketed along the wall. He peered over the top of the toolbox. A red light flashed. The thing was primed. It'd be set to go off while the president spoke. He scanned the wires, the charge, the canister marked with the "4-1-0" fire diamond. He set himself to lift the toolbox out of the duct.

"Don't," Chavez said. "Trembler."

A motion sensor, most likely a U-shaped tube filled with mercury. If he moved it, the mercury would slop around the tube, completing the circuit and sparking the detonator. Verrazzano touched the opposite section of duct behind him as he removed his hand. He felt fluid against his palm. He brought his hand into the light and examined it. Blood, still warm. Someone was hiding in the duct across from the bomb, guarding the device, and bleeding.

Todd called through his respirator, "Dom, there's another canister of sarin here." He knelt beside the shell Chavez had used to spray Slav.

Chavez swallowed hard. "I hit the firing pin a while back. That thing's empty."

Todd checked the weight of the canister. "It's more than half full. You disconnected the explosive charge, right?"

"Yeah."

"You siphoned off some of the sarin. But the charge didn't detonate, so the pin closed back up and resealed the canister. Lucky for you, or you'd have been dead by now."

"If the sarin in this device goes through the AC duct," Verrazzano said, "it'll circulate around the building and kill everyone."

He picked up the empty autoinjector from the floor. He eased down on the firing pin of the sarin canister and slipped the needle of the orange syringe into the end. He slid back the plunger on the syringe, filling it.

He returned to the duct. The main artery for the entire building's air conditioning, it was wider than a man's shoulders. He hid the syringe inside his closed hand and faced toward the bomb. But he focused his awareness on the duct behind him, listening for a creak in the metal or a whisper of clothing that would tell him the hidden man was moving.

He lifted his hands into the toolbox, showing that he didn't hold a gun, and reached toward the bomb in front of him. "I see how to defuse this."

The barrel of a pistol nudged him hard between his shoulder blades.

"Don't move." Kyle Massie lay flat in the duct, just beyond the traces of blood from the wound Adela gave him.

"Why're you doing this, Kyle?" Verrazzano said.

"Because veterans like me get the shaft when they come home."

"This won't change that, Kyle."

"I'm past making things right, asshole. Those shitheads are going to feel a little piece of the hell I've been through. I'm going to—"

Verrazzano wheeled quickly and batted the pistol aside. He thrust out the orange syringe.

Massie jerked away, but even the building's main air-conditioning duct gave him little room to maneuver his big frame. Verrazzano pinned him. The needle of the syringe bit into Massie's neck. He sank his thumb down on the plunger, injecting the lethal dose of sarin into Massie's trachea, directly into his respiratory system.

Verrazzano strained against the big, roaring man thrashing in the air-conditioning tube. Massie's spasms shook the duct on its wall brackets. The timer on the sarin bomb emitted an electronic beep.

"The motion sensor went off," Todd shouted. "It'll go to a short count."

Verrazzano dragged Massie flailing from the duct and threw him to the floor.

He lifted the toolbox out. No need to be gentle now. The fifteen-second countdown was rolling. He put the box on the ground and swung around toward Todd. "I'm going to have to defuse—"

"Dom," Todd called out.

Massie's fist struck Verrazzano in the teeth. His head whipped back against the sharp edge of the duct.

Massie dropped on the toolbox. Verrazzano tried to wrestle him away, to get at the device and defuse it. Massie gripped the leg of the desk and crooked his other arm tight around the bomb. If Verrazzano didn't shift him, the blast would disembowel Massie. But the explosion would mix the sarin. The gas would filter up into the air duct—and on into the General Assembly chamber.

"Shoot him, Bill." He heaved at Massie's heavy body.

Todd drew his Glock. He pulled Kyle Massie's head up. The dying man's skin was purple and his ears leaked blood as the sarin Verrazzano had pumped into his throat asphyxiated him. He'd be gone in a minute. But they didn't even have seconds.

Behind the Perspex of the respirator, Todd's eyes were desolate, as though *he* would be the one to die. They were not the eyes of a killer. They were without malice.

The bomb mechanism beeped out a half second. Todd put a bullet into the back of Massie's head.

Verrazzano braced to haul the body off the device.

Too late. The timer went silent.

"Aw, Christ," Todd said.

Verrazzano shoved Todd's shoulder and sent him rolling away. He dropped onto Massie's corpse, bearing down on the bomb.

The explosion tore up from the toolbox. Massie jerked beneath him. The percussion rippled through Verrazzano's torso. His breath shivered out of him. His throat was dry. But he was alive when the blast subsided. That much of his gamble had paid off.

Straddling Massie, he hauled the dead man off the toolbox and threw him on his back. Massie's stomach was ripped open. Chavez moaned at the gruesome display.

Todd moved forward. "Dom, the sarin."

Verrazzano leaned over the toolbox, the remnants of the timing device, and the shredded sarin canister. Invisibly, fatally, the sarin rose toward the air-conditioning vent.

He sat astride Massie's legs. He laid the sarin shell in the dead man's gutted stomach and grasped it at its base.

"What're you doing?" Todd said.

Verrazzano shoved the canister up inside Massie's chest cavity. It slashed through the lungs. He thrust it out of sight beyond the heart. He slammed his forearms down crossways, closing the ribcage over the sarin, straining against the resistance of bone and tissue. Blood seeped through his sleeves and around his elbows.

"Dom?" Todd said.

"Hydrolysis."

"I don't get it."

"Sarin's neutralized by water. Blood's mostly water."

Todd stared at Massie's face, as though the nerve agent might leach out of his dead eyes. Verrazzano knew better. Todd would have to see the man's soul to catch the true traces of poison.

CHAPTER 58

After he killed Holtz, Tom Frisch stayed on the roof in case he needed to shoot again. His cell phone relayed video of the president's speech from the UN: "I have laid out for you, the international community, my plan to bring an end to the scourge of civil war in the ancient land of Syria. It is our fight, just as much as it is the fight of the people of Syria. Because it is a battle for democracy, freedom, and life itself. It is a battle for all the noble ideals we in the United States hold in our hearts. I call on this Assembly to endorse it. I implore the warring sides to grasp this opportunity. Thank you all." The president stepped down from the podium. The delegates rose and applauded—a surprising sight, because many of them detested the United States. The speech contained such humanity and compassion that they were as close to being genuinely moved as an international diplomat ever comes.

"What the fuck?" Frisch murmured.

The president and the delegates in the hall didn't clutch their throats or their chests. They didn't die. Frisch shut off the video. He ticked his fingernail against the barrel of his Vintorez.

The phone rang on the Silent Circle app. He picked up. "I don't know what happened, sir."

"I did some infiltrations during the Balkan ethnic cleansings. Supposed to be creating pro-American Serb militias to take control from the bad guys." Wyatt's voice was strained. "One of my Serbs used to say, *'Planiranje Bogu radovanje.'* You were in Sarajevo for a while, Tom. You know what that phrase means?"

"We make plans to give God the joy of destroying them."

Wyatt laughed, low and thoughtful. "You're a talented guy, Tom, a real linguist. But on today's evidence, I would say that you are not talented enough." He hung up.

Frisch broke down the sniper rifle and packed it into its case. He hurried down the stairwell to Molnir's suite. He headed straight for the security door, but when he shoved it, it held steady. He turned to his receptionist. "Zissel, will you just buzz me in? I'm in a big hurry, for Christ's sake."

She looked at him like a mother wondering how to give her rambunctious teenager the rope he needed and yet prevent him going too far. "I sit here all day. I pay attention to the guys coming and going. I don't like the look of some of them lately, Tom."

"I can handle them."

"Like those two guys who've been with Kyle lately."

"That's the business we're in. It'll work out."

"One of them's waiting for you in your office."

Which one? It didn't matter. The solution was the same for all of them.

"You need tough guys, Tom. I know that. But you've got to keep your sickos from going psycho. I'm worried some of them have crossed that line. You should call that nice ICE agent and ask for his help."

"I never asked for help in my life. Let me deal with this my way."

"You ask for *my* help every day."

"Just open up."

She buzzed the door, and he went into the corridor. She reached for her phone. Frisch caught the door and leaned back through it. "Zissel?"

"Yes, Tom?" There was fright in her voice this time.

He was sorry for that. "If anything happens, Zissel, you'll be taken care of." He ran along the corridor to his office.

Clay turned when Frisch came in. He must've seen something pitiless in his boss's face because he brought his hands up to protect himself. "It ain't my fault."

"What the fuck are you doing here? Why aren't you with Kyle?"

"I did my job. I want my money and I'm out of here."

"You abandoned your post."

"My post? This ain't the fucking US Army, man."

Frisch raised his pistol. "Then I guess we can skip the court martial." He shot Clay in the forehead and twice in the chest.

He yanked open the cabinet door in his desk. He took out a titanium briefcase as big as a pair of gallon cans.

The traffic caterwauled on Second Avenue. Frisch found himself tuning into each honk and rev. The drivers thought their day had turned to shit because the motorcades tied up the avenues and cross streets during the UN General Assembly.

They didn't know what shit was.

Inside the briefcase was a small transponder. Frisch transferred it to the breast pocket of his suit jacket. He designed it so that if the case was more than a hundred yards from the transponder, the alarm was triggered. The handle delivered a six-hundred-volt shock to whoever held it. Enough electricity to leave the thief twitching like a hillbilly with fleas. That was Kyle Massie's joke.

What the fuck went wrong, Kyle?

Frisch lifted the mat under his desk and twirled the lock on his floor safe.

He was the commander. He was responsible. He didn't know yet *why* it had happened, but soon he'd figure it out and wonder how he failed to foresee whatever went wrong.

He kept two million dollars in the floor safe. He stacked the bundles into the briefcase with urgent, angry jabs from the heel of his hand.

He knew it already. Him. That's what went wrong. *Tom fucking Frisch went wrong.*

He snapped the locks on the briefcase, dropped his pistol into his hip pocket, and dashed to the elevator.

Zissel was on the phone. "Yes, right now," she whispered. She put the receiver softly in the cradle and blew her nose. She looked at Frisch with love and disappointment. "Good-bye, Tom."

The elevator opened. Frisch stared at Zissel. He prized loyalty, and she was devoted to him. But he had forfeited her obedience.

He made a fatal mistake when he took on one final operation with Wyatt. *Can't call it fatal*, he thought. *Not until I'm dead.*

He glanced about the lobby. He'd fight back, but he wouldn't see this place again. He felt the heft of the briefcase. *Here's two million bucks says, "Fuck everyone."*

The elevator dropped fast.

CHAPTER 59

The shells fell closer than ever to military intelligence head-quarters. Nabil Allaf watched them detonate in the night. On his TV, a Gulf cable station ran constant discussion and analysis of the US president's plan for Syria, taunting him with clips from the speech. He lit a cigarette. He had been so close to his dream, so close to watching the destruction of his native land from a bar in Cannes with a European blonde on his arm, a bank vault full of Euros, and an Audi R8 parked out on the Promenade de la Croisette. The Holy Koran said that if God punished every person as they truly deserved, no one would be left alive. It was the only statement in all of Prophet Muhammad's recitation with which Allaf agreed. Syria was entirely culpable in the sufferings of his own twisted soul. *So let the place burn*, he thought, *the way I've burned through all these years as a slave to a dictator.*

He would burn with it, and he felt cold.

His Blackphone rang. The encrypted Silent Circle app. He stared out the window at the artillery detonations. He had been so close. He picked up the line. "Yes, Colonel Wyatt," he murmured.

His skin crawled with stifling heat as he listened to the Tennessee accent, at once precise and drawling. He slid the window open. The cigarette smoke gusted out into the warm night. He put a finger in his ear to block the shattering percussions. Desperation threaded down to each of his ragged nerve endings.

"It isn't fair. I did my part." Allaf sounded like a child denied a new toy. Well, so he was. He had dreamed of a French blonde and a German car on the Riviera. But he had only this savage city. "If this whole thing didn't cause a war, that's your problem. You're the one who'd have profited from it. I want my fee in full. No, I insist."

The line went dead.

A shell landed two buildings away. The artillery battery was walking its shots along the valley, finding its range. Allaf watched the people in the next building, the Institute of Business Administration. They stayed late at the office because the government kept the electricity going in its own buildings, while the residential neighborhoods were blacked out. Now they were rushing to escape. Allaf shook his head. There was nowhere to go.

Wyatt would find other ways to make a war happen. To provoke an attack on Syria that would bring the Islamic State nutcases to power. To sell the Islamists the weapons they needed for their conflict with the Western-backed regimes of the Middle East. Allaf stared at the Blackphone. With the line cut, the screen reverted to a photo of his wife and children. He put it face down on the desk. He picked up the remote and flicked off the television. "I'm sick of it," he mumbled.

He hauled himself out of his chair and tossed the cigarette butt into the night. It scattered sparks on the concrete five floors below.

Another shell smashed down, this time a direct hit on the Institute of Business Administration. Walking a step closer. When the jolt of the impact and the racket of the falling rubble receded, Allaf heard people scream. Finally, he felt at home in his city. He sat on his desk and watched the sky. The next shell would find him. He opened his arms wide in welcome and laughed.

CHAPTER 60

The sirens of the president's motorcade echoed down East Forty-Third Street. Verrazzano took the call from Tom Frisch's receptionist. He thanked her and hung up. He pulled on a Yankees cap and tugged the brim low over his shades. The signal. *Target on the move.*

He walked briskly along the sidewalk. Kinsella matched his pace on the opposite side of the street. They headed away from the UN toward the headquarters of Molnir Partners. From Second Avenue, Haddad watched them come. She read a copy of the *Daily News.*

A man in a dark suit carrying a deep-based briefcase came sharply out of the ziggurat tower of 820 Second Avenue and turned toward the river. Haddad folded the newspaper. She had identified Frisch.

The Molnir chief strode along the block. Verrazzano felt like a lone safety watching a massive running back speed toward him, anticipating the collision, knowing the stakes if he didn't stop him. He wore a raincoat borrowed from one of the president's Secret Service agents to cover his muddy clothing and the cap and sunglasses to disguise his face.

Kinsella crossed the street, angling in front of him. She headed for the door of the bakery beyond the sidewalk. Frisch pulled up, but he still bumped her with his shoulder.

She spun on her heel, shrieking. She grabbed Frisch's lapel and dragged him down. He bent forward under her weight, his lips contracted in fury, white and bloodless.

Verrazzano leaned over her too. "You all right, ma'am?" His shoulder jolted Frisch's chest. "Sorry, man."

Frisch tugged his jacket away from Kinsella. His magnolia cologne sweetened the metallic scent of traffic on the air. Verrazzano touched Frisch's chest. "Looks like you got this covered, man."

Kinsella flexed her foot and rearranged her hair across her shoulders. "I think I'm okay. I'm sorry. It was my fault."

Frisch glanced back at Verrazzano as he walked away. He checked his pocket holster, a little tap against the side of his thigh. Verrazzano smiled grimly. *I didn't take your gun, asshole.*

He counted the man's paces. *Twenty-five.*

Fifty.

Todd leaned against a Toyota at the other end of the block, drumming a beat on the roof of the car.

Seventy-five.

Kinsella brushed down her pants. Haddad came to Verrazzano's side.

One hundred.

Frisch stiffened. His step stuttered. He bellowed in pain, staggering into a parked truck as the current from his briefcase alarm streamed through him. He shook the case, tried to drop it. But six hundred volts welded it to his hand.

Todd moved toward the stumbling, spasming man.

Verrazzano juggled Frisch's transponder.

"Nice lift, Dom," Kinsella said. "It looked like you just gave him a friendly pat."

"Do you think he's had enough?" Verrazzano stepped forward and the electric current shut off in the handgrip of the briefcase.

Frisch lay on his back, twitching. Todd knelt to check his pulse.

Verrazzano displayed the transponder between his thumb and forefinger. "Cool invention, Frisch. You're a clever guy. Shouldn't tell the people you work for about gadgets like this. Eventually they go and tell us. Particularly the ones who're nearly dead from sarin exposure and want us to go easy on them."

He recognized the expression that lit up Frisch's eyes. The man thought he'd been caught by Wyatt's people. He expected to be executed now for the botched sarin attack. In the interrogation room, Verrazzano would use that. Frisch would give up the whereabouts of Wyatt. Talk or die. It was that simple. And men like Frisch never chose death.

"I guess your guy Randy must've told Martin Chavez. Now Chavez told me, and you're twitching like a hillbilly with fleas."

He rolled Frisch onto his belly and yanked his arms behind him. He cuffed him with a contented smile. The meditation lesson came to him—*The world is what you are.*

"I'm Special Agent Dominic Verrazzano, Immigration and Customs Enforcement," he said, "and you're under arrest."

Todd shoved Frisch into the backseat of the ICE car. Haddad and Kinsella climbed in the front. Verrazzano waved for them to go ahead. He wanted oxygen for his scarred lungs, and he certainly didn't want to breathe the same air as Frisch.

He walked toward First Avenue and took out the cell phone he had borrowed from Haddad. He dialed Quanah.

When the line connected, he said, "The situation's neutralized at this end."

Quanah blew a heavy breath of relief. "Jesus, you cut that fine, Dom."

"I like to keep things spontaneous. Where do things stand with you?"

"I'm at the decommissioning facility right now. The Field Deployable Hydrolysis procedure was completed about a quarter hour ago. You did it, man."

Verrazzano closed his eyes.

"I've been hard on you," Quanah whispered. "About what happened years ago. I was unfair. I did shit at least as bad as what you did. I guess laying everything on you let me off the hook. I'm sorry. You hate me for it?"

"Like I hate peanut butter. Not like I hate Hitler."

It was the kind of dark banter that first brought them together as friends. Quanah laughed quietly. "Later, brother."

Verrazzano hung up. The phone buzzed in his palm to signal an incoming text from an unidentified number. He thumbed it open.

"The thing about the past," the text read, "is that it's all ahead of you."

"Ain't that the truth, Wyatt," he whispered to himself.

The sun dazzled off the East River. Narrowing his eyes, Verrazzano walked on into his past.